THE
BLACKTHORN
KEY

THE
BLACKTHORN
KEY

KEVIN SANDS

ALADDIN

NEW YORK   LONDON   TORONTO   SYDNEY   NEW DELHI

ALADDIN

An imprint of Simon & Schuster Children's Publishing Division

1230 Avenue of the Americas, New York, NY 10020

This Aladdin paperback edition January 2016

Text copyright © 2015 by Kevin Sands

Front cover illustration copyright © 2015 by Antonio Javier Caparo

Back cover and spine icon illustration

designed by James Fraser copyright © 2015 by Puffin Books

Cover photographs (used in icon illustrations) copyright © 2015 by Hermann Mock/cultura/Corbis

Also available in an Aladdin hardcover edition.

All rights reserved, including the right of reproduction in whole or in part in any form.

ALADDIN is a trademark of Simon & Schuster, Inc., and related logo is a registered trademark of Simon & Schuster, Inc.

For information about special discounts for bulk purchases, please contact Simon & Schuster Special Sales at 1-866-506-1949 or business@simonandschuster.com.

The Simon & Schuster Speakers Bureau can bring authors to your live event. For more information or to book an event contact the Simon & Schuster Speakers Bureau at 1-866-248-3049 or visit our website at www.simonspeakers.com.

Interior design by Karin Paprocki

The text of this book was set in Adobe Garamond Pro.

Manufactured in the United States of America 1215 OFF

2 4 6 8 10 9 7 5 3 1

The Library of Congress has cataloged the hardcover edition as follows:

Sands, Kevin.

The blackthorn key / by Kevin Sands.

p. cm.

Summary: In 1665 London, fourteen-year-old Christopher Rowe, apprentice to an apothecary, and his best friend, Tom, try to uncover the truth behind a mysterious cult, following a trail of puzzles, codes, pranks, and danger toward an unearthly secret with the power to tear the world apart.

[1. Apprentices—Fiction. 2. Supernatural—Fiction. 3. Pharmacists—Fiction. 4. Friendship—Fiction. 5. Secret societies—Fiction. 6. London—History—17th century—Fiction. 7. Great Britain—History—Charles II, 1660–1685—Fiction.] I. Title.

PZ7.1.S26Bl 2015   [Fic]—dc23   2014048032

ISBN 978-1-4814-4651-8 (hc)

ISBN 978-1-4814-4653-2 (eBook)

ISBN 978-1-4814-6930-2 (Scholastic pbk)

A WARNING:

The recipes and remedies in this book were used by real apothecaries. There's a reason we don't see them anymore. Some are devious, some are dangerous, and a few are just plain deadly. So, as they say: Don't try this at home. Seriously.

THURSDAY, MAY 28, 1665

Ascension Day

I FOUND IT.

Master Benedict said he wasn't the least bit surprised. According to him, there were several times over the past three years when he was sure I'd finally discovered it. Yet it wasn't until the day before my fourteenth birthday that it came to me so clearly, I thought God Himself had whispered in my ear.

My master believes occasions like this should be remembered. So, as he ordered, I've written down my formula. My master suggested the title.

The Stupidest Idea in the Universe

By Christopher Rowe,

Apprentice to Master Benedict Blackthorn, Apothecary

Method of manufacture:

Snoop through your master's private notes. Find a recipe, its words locked behind a secret code, and decipher it. Next, steal the needed ingredients from your master's stores. Finally— and this is the most important step—go to your best friend, a boy of stout character and poor judgment equal to your own, and speak these words: Let's build a cannon.

CHAPTER
1

"LET'S BUILD A CANNON," I SAID.

Tom wasn't listening. He was deep in concentration, tongue pinched between his teeth, as he steeled himself for combat with the stuffed black bear that ruled the front corner of my master's shop. Tom stripped off his linen shirt and flung it heroically across the antimony cups gleaming on the display table near the fire. From the oak shelf nearest to him, he snatched the glazed lid of an apothecary jar—Blackthorn's Wart-Be-Gone, according to the scrawl on the label—and held it on guard, a miniature ceramic shield. In his right hand, the rolling pin wobbled threateningly.

Tom Bailey, son of William the Baker, was the finest fake soldier I'd ever seen. Though only two months older than me, he was already a foot taller, and built like a blacksmith, albeit a slightly pudgy one, due to a steady pilfering of his father's pies. And in the safety of my master's shop, away from the horrors of battle like death, pain, or even a mild scolding, Tom's courage held no equal.

He glared at the inanimate bear. The floorboards creaked as he stepped within range of its wickedly curved claws. Tom shoved the curio cabinet aside, making the brass balances jingle. Then he hoisted his flour-dusted club in salute. The frozen beast roared back silently, inch-long teeth promising death. Or several minutes of tedious polishing, at least.

I sat on the counter at the back, legs dangling, and clicked leather heels against the carved cedar. I could be patient. You had to be, sometimes, with Tom, whose mind worked as it pleased.

"Think you can steal my sheep, Mr. Bear?" he said. "I'll give you no quarter this day." Suddenly, he stopped, rolling pin held outward in midlunge. I could almost see the clockwork cranking between his ears. "Wait. What?" He looked back at me, puzzled. "What did you say?"

"Let's build a cannon," I said.

"What does that mean?"

"Just what you think it means. You and me. Build a cannon. You know." I spread my hands. "Boom?"

Tom frowned. "We can't do that."

"Why not?"

"Because people can't just build cannons, Christopher." He said it like he was explaining why you shouldn't eat fire to a small, dull child.

"But that's where cannons come from," I said. "People build them. You think God sends cannons down from heaven for Lent?"

"You know what I mean."

I folded my arms. "I don't understand why you're not more excited about this."

"Maybe that's because you're never the one on the pointy end of your schemes."

"What schemes? I don't have any schemes."

"I spent *all night* throwing up that 'strength potion' you invented," he said.

He did look a little dark under the eyes today. "Ah. Yes. Sorry." I winced. "I think I put in too much black snail. It needed less snail."

"What it needed was less Tom."

"Don't be such a baby," I said. "Vomiting is good for you, anyway. It balances the humors."

"I like my humors the way they are," he said.

"But I have a recipe this time." I grabbed the parchment I'd leaned against the coin scales on the countertop and waved it at him. "A real one. From Master Benedict."

"How can a cannon have a recipe?"

"Not the whole cannon. Just the gunpowder."

Tom got very still. He scanned the jars around him, as if among the hundreds of potions, herbs, and powders that ringed the shop was a remedy that would somehow get him out of this. "That's illegal."

"Knowing a recipe isn't illegal," I said.

"Making it is."

That was true. Only masters, and only those with a royal charter, were allowed to mix gunpowder. I was a long way from either.

"And Lord Ashcombe is on the streets today," Tom said.

Now *that* made me pause. "You saw him?"

Tom nodded. "On Cheapside, after church. He had two of the King's Men with him."

"What'd he look like?"

"Mean."

"Mean" was exactly what I'd imagined. Lord Richard Ashcombe, Baron of Chillingham, was King Charles's loyal general, and His Majesty's Warden here in London. He was in the city hunting for a pack of killers. In the past four months, five men had been butchered in their homes. Each of them had been tied up, tortured, then slit open at the stomach and left to bleed to death.

Three of the victims had been apothecaries, a fact that had me seeing assassins in the shadows every night. No one was sure what the killers wanted, but sending in Lord Ashcombe meant the king was serious about stopping them. Lord Ashcombe had a reputation for getting rid of men hostile to the Crown—usually by sticking their heads on pikes in the public square.

Still, we didn't need to be *that* cautious. "Lord Ashcombe's not coming here," I said, as much to myself as to Tom. "We haven't killed anyone. And the King's Warden isn't likely to stop by for a suppository, is he?"

"What about your master?" Tom said.

"He doesn't need a suppository."

Tom made a face. "I mean, isn't *he* coming back? It's

getting close to dinnertime." He said "dinnertime" with a certain wistfulness.

"Master Benedict just bought the new edition of Culpeper's herbal," I said. "He's at the coffeehouse with Hugh. They'll be gone for ages."

Tom pressed his ceramic shield to his chest. "This is a bad idea."

I hopped down from the counter and grinned.

To be an apothecary, you must understand this: The recipe is everything.

It isn't like baking a cake. The potions, creams, jellies, and powders Master Benedict made—with my help—required an incredibly delicate touch. A spoonful too little niter, a pinch too much aniseed, and your brilliant new remedy for dropsy would congeal instead into worthless green goo.

But new recipes didn't fall from the sky. You had to discover them. This took weeks, months, even years of hard work. It cost a fortune, too: ingredients, apparatus, coal to stoke the fire, ice to chill the bath. Most of all, it was dangerous. Blazing fires. Molten metals. Elixirs that smelled sweet but ate away your insides. Tinctures that looked as harmless as water but threw off deadly, invisible fumes. With each new experiment, you gambled with your life. So a working formula was better than gold.

If you could read it.

↓Mo8→

0216091110182526131009261122131524032213241022071009261 1221315141607011613010417261122131514142207151126152613o 213040925142611221322152607200809419

Tom scratched his cheek. "I thought there'd be more words and things."

"It's in code," I said.

He sighed. "Why is it always in code?"

"Because other apothecaries will do anything to steal your secrets. When I have my own shop," I said proudly, "I'm putting everything in code. No one's going to swipe *my* recipes."

"No one will want your recipes. Except poisoners, I suppose."

"I said I was sorry."

"Maybe this is in code," Tom said, "because Master Benedict doesn't want anyone to read it. And by 'anyone,' I mean you."

"He teaches me new ciphers every week."

"Did he teach you this one?"

"I'm sure he'd planned to."

"Christopher."

"But I figured it out. Look." I pointed at the notation ↓M08→. "It's a substitution cipher. Every two numbers stand for one letter. This tells you how to swap them. Start with '08,' and replace it with *M*. Then count forward. So 08 is *M*, 09 is *N*, and so on. Like this."

I showed him the table I'd worked out.

A	*B*	*C*	*D*	*E*	*F*	*G*	*H*	*I*	*J*	*K*	*L*	*M*
22	23	24	25	26	01	02	03	04	05	06	07	08

N	*O*	*P*	*Q*	*R*	*S*	*T*	*U*	*V*	*W*	*X*	*Y*	*Z*
09	10	11	12	13	14	15	16	17	18	19	20	21

Tom looked between the cipher and the block of numbers at the top of the page. "So if you replace the numbers with the right letters . . ."

". . . You get your message." I flipped the parchment over to show the translation I'd inked on the back.

Gunpowder

One part charcoal. One part sulfur. Five parts saltpeter.

Grind separately. Mix.

Which is what we did. We set up on the larger display table, farther from the fireplace, based on Tom's reasonable suggestion that gunpowder and flames weren't friends. Tom moved the bleeding spoons from the table and got the mortars and pestles from the window near the bear while I pulled the ingredient jars from the shelves.

I ground the charcoal. Sooty clouds puffed into the air, mixing with the earthy scent of the dried roots and herbs hanging from the rafters. Tom, glancing uneasily at the front door for any sign of my master, took care of the saltpeter, crushing the crystals that looked just like ordinary table salt. The sulfur was already a fine yellow powder, so while Tom swirled the ingredients together, I got a length of brass pipe sealed at one end from the workshop in the back. I used a nail to widen a hole near the sealed end. Into that, I slipped a loop of woven, ash-colored cord.

Tom raised his eyebrows. "Master Benedict keeps cannon fuse?"

"We use it to light things from far away," I said.

"You know," Tom said, "things you have to light from far away probably shouldn't be lit at all."

The mixture we ended up with looked harmless, just a fine black powder. Tom poured it into the open end while I propped up the pipe. A narrow stream spilled over the side, scattering charcoal grains onto the floor. I stamped the powder in the tube down with cotton wadding.

"What are we going to use for a cannonball?" Tom said.

Master Benedict didn't keep anything in the store that would fit snugly in the pipe. The best I could come up with was a handful of lead shot we used for shavings to put in our remedies. They scraped down the brass and landed with a hollow *thump* on the cotton at the bottom.

Now we needed a target, and soon. It had taken a lot longer to put everything together than I thought it would, and though I'd assured Tom that my master wouldn't return, his comings and goings weren't exactly predictable.

"We're *not* firing this thing outside," Tom said.

He was right about that. The neighbors would not look kindly on lead shot flying through their parlors. And as tempting a target as the stuffed beaver on the mantel was,

Master Benedict was even less likely to appreciate us going to war with the animals that decorated his shop.

"What about that?" I said. Hanging from the ceiling near the fireplace was a small iron cauldron. "We can shoot at the bottom of it."

Tom pushed aside the antimony cups on the other table, leaving enough space to put down the cauldron. I picked up our cannon and pressed it against my abdomen to hold it steady. Tom tore a scrap of parchment from our deciphered recipe and held it in the fire until it caught. Then he lit the cannon's wick. Sparks fizzed, racing toward the pipe like a flaming hornet. Tom dived behind the counter and peeked over the top.

"Watch this," I said.

The blast nearly blew my ears off. I saw a burst of flame, and a mound of smoke, then the pipe kicked back like an angry ox and nailed me right between the legs.

CHAPTER

2

I HIT THE FLOORBOARDS LIKE A
sack of wheat. The cannon bonged off the wood next to
me and rolled away, smoke pouring from the end. From far
away, I heard a voice.

"Are you all right?" it said.

I curled into a ball, hands cradling my groin, and tried
not to throw up.

Smoke billowed everywhere, as if the air itself had
turned gray. Tom appeared through the haze, waving his
hands and coughing. "Christopher? Are you all right?"

"Mmmunnnggguhh," I said.

Tom scanned the shop for some remedy that could help

me, but sadly there was no Blackthorn's Private-Parts Pain Poultice. Suddenly, he spoke, his voice strangled. "Christopher?"

I squinted up through the smoke. There I saw the problem. I wasn't the only one who'd taken it where it counts. The cauldron I'd so carefully aimed at didn't have a mark on it. The bear in the corner, however, now had a real reason to be angry. The lead shot from our cannon had shredded the fur between his legs. He roared in silent outrage as his straw guts spilled into a pile between his paws.

Tom held his hands to the sides of his face. "Your master will kill us," he said.

"Wait," I said, the pain slowly being replaced by the pit of horror growing in my gut. "Wait. We can fix this."

"How? Do you have a spare bear's crotch in the back?" Tom clutched his cheeks and moaned.

"Just . . . give me a moment to think," I said, and naturally that was when Master Benedict came home.

He didn't even take one full step inside before he jerked to a halt. So tall that he had to duck to pass through the door, my master just stood there, hunched over, the long, dark curls of his wig swinging in the evening breeze. He was hugging a large leather-bound book to his chest with his lanky arms; Culpeper's new herbal. Peeking from under his dark velvet coat was his burgundy canvas sash, one foot wide, wrapped around his waist. It was covered with pockets, each one not much larger than a man's thumb. Tucked into each pocket was a glass vial, stopped with cork or wax. There were other pouches, too, with all kinds of useful things: flint and tinder, tweezers, a long-handled silver spoon. My master had designed the sash himself to carry ingredients and remedies—at least the ones I didn't have to lug around behind him when we went out on a house call.

Master Benedict stared at the brass cannon, which had rolled away and come to a stop at his feet, still trailing a wisp of smoke. His eyes narrowed as they tracked from the pipe to the two of us, still on the floor.

"Let's get inside, Benedict," a voice boomed from behind him. "It's cold out here."

A burly man shouldered past my master and shook the dust from his fur-trimmed cloak. This was Hugh Coggshall, who fifteen years ago had graduated from his own apprenticeship with Master Benedict. Now a master himself, Hugh owned a private workshop in a bordering parish.

His nose crinkled. "Smells like—" He broke off when he spotted me and Tom. He covered his mouth, glancing sidelong at my master.

Moving as gingerly as I could, I pushed myself off the floor to stand in front of him. Tom stood beside me, as rigid as a statue.

A deep, dark vein pulsed in Master Benedict's forehead. When he spoke, his voice was like ice. "Christopher?"

I swallowed, hard. "Y-yes, Master?"

"Did I miss a war while I was out?"

"No, Master."

"An argument, then? A discussion of court politics?" His words dripped with sarcasm. "Have the Puritans once again seized Parliament and overthrown our returned king?"

My face was burning. "No, Master."

"Then perhaps," he said through grinding teeth, "you could explain why in God's holy name you shot my bear."

"I didn't mean to," I said. Tom, beside me, nodded vigorously. "It was an accident."

This seemed to make him even angrier. "You were aiming for the beaver and missed?"

I didn't trust myself to speak. I pointed at the cauldron, still tipped on its side on the display table near the fire. For a moment Master Benedict was silent. Then he said, "You fired lead slugs . . . at an iron cauldron . . . from six feet away?"

I glanced at Tom. "I . . . we . . . yes?"

My master closed his eyes and held his hand to his fore-head. Then he leaned in close. "Thomas," he said.

Tom trembled. I thought he might faint. "Yes, sir?"

"Go home."

"Yes, sir." Tom sidled away, bowing awkwardly over and over again. He grabbed his shirt from the display table and fled into the street, the door slamming behind him.

"Master—" I began.

"Be silent," he snapped.

I was.

This would normally be when the apprentice—in this case, me—would receive a solid, heartfelt beating. But in the three years I'd lived with Master Benedict, he'd never struck me, not once. This was so unusual that I'd passed a whole year under his care before I realized he really was never going to hit me. Tom, who felt the sting of his father's hand every day, thought this was unfair. I felt it was more than fair, considering I'd spent my first eleven years in the Cripplegate orphanage, where the masters doled out beat-ings like sweeties at an egg hunt.

Sometimes, though, I kind of wished Master Benedict *would* hit me. Instead, he had this way of looking at me when I'd done something wrong. His disappointment burrowed into me, sinking to my heart and staying there.

Like now.

"I put my trust in you, Christopher," he said. "Every day. Our shop. Our *home*. This is how you treat it?"

I bowed my head. "I—I wasn't trying to—"

"A cannon." Master Benedict fumed. "You could have burned your eyes out. The pipe could have exploded. And if you'd actually hit the cauldron—and the Lord must love a fool, because I can't see how you missed the thing—I'd be scraping pieces of you off the walls from now until Christmas. Have you no sense at all?"

"I'm sorry," I mumbled.

"And you shot my bloody bear."

Hugh snorted.

"Don't you encourage him," Master Benedict said. "You've already given me a lifetime of grief." Hugh raised his hands in appeasement. Master Benedict turned back to me. "Where did you even get the gunpowder?" he said.

"I made it," I said.

"You *made* it?" He finally seemed to notice the jars on the table. Then he saw the parchment with the code Tom and I had left beside them. My master peered at it, turned it over. I couldn't read his expression.

"You deciphered this?" he said.

I nodded.

Hugh took the page from my master's hands and examined it. He glanced up at Master Benedict. Something seemed to pass between them, but I couldn't tell what they were thinking. I felt a sudden swell of hope. My master was always pleased when I surprised him with something new. Maybe he'd appreciate that I'd solved this puzzle on my own.

Or maybe not. Master Benedict jabbed a bony finger into my ribs. "Since you're feeling so creative, I'd like you to write out your recipe for today's little adventure—thirty times. Then write it another thirty times—in Latin. But first you will tidy this room. You will put everything back where it belongs. And then you will scrub the floor. The store, the workshop, and every step in this house. Tonight. All the way up to the roof."

The *roof*? Now I really wanted to cry. I knew I hadn't exactly been on the side of the angels this evening, but apprentices were already worked to exhaustion. Master Benedict may have been kinder than any master I knew, but my duties didn't change. My days started before the cry of six. I had to wake first and get the shop ready, help customers, assist my master in the workshop, practice on my own, study, and so on, until well after the sun had fallen. Then I had to put everything away, prepare the day's last meal, and clean the shop for tomorrow before I finally got to sleep on my palliasse, the straw mattress that served as my bed. The only rest I got came on Sundays and the rare holidays. And we were right in the middle of a once-in-a-decade *double* holiday: today, Ascension Day, and tomorrow, Oak Apple Day. I'd been dreaming of this break all year.

According to the papers of apprenticeship, Master Benedict wasn't allowed to make me work on a holiday. Then again, according to the papers of apprenticeship, I wasn't allowed to steal his goods, make gunpowder, or shoot stuffed bears. Any bears, really. So I just slumped my shoulders and said, "Yes, Master."

I returned the pots and ingredients to the shelves. My master took our cannon and hid it somewhere in the workshop in the back. I then spent the next several minutes gathering soot-stained lead pellets, which had rolled to every corner of the store. That left me wondering what to do about the poor bear.

Master Benedict had hung up his apothecary's sash with the vials of ingredients and remedies behind the counter before he'd disappeared into the back. I looked from the sash to the bear in the corner. If we stitched some pockets into a blanket and wrapped it around the beast's hips—

"I wouldn't do that if I were you."

Hugh was slouched in the chair beside the fire, flipping through pages in my master's new herbal. He hadn't even looked up to speak.

"I wasn't going to use *that* sash," I said. "But I can't just leave him like this." I thought about it. "What if we gave him some breeches?"

Hugh shook his head. "You're an odd sort of boy."

Before I could respond, the front door creaked open. I smelled the man before I saw him, a nose-curling stink of rose-water perfume and body odor.

It was Nathaniel Stubb. An apothecary who owned a shop two streets over, Stubb waddled in to foul our air once a week. He came to spy on his closest competition, if "competition" was the right word. *We* sold actual remedies. He made his money selling Stubb's Oriental Cure-All Pills, which, according to the handbills he slapped on every street corner, fixed every ailment from pox to plague. As far as I could tell, the only real effect Stubb's Pills had was to reduce weight in the coin purse.

Still, his customers bought them by the handful. Stubb

wore his profit for all to see: heavy, jeweled rings squeezing his fat fingers, a silver snake-head walking cane in his hand, a brocade doublet strained over a shiny silk shirt. The bottom of the shirt was puffed ridiculously through his open fly, supposedly the new fashion. I thought it made him look like he'd stuffed his drawers with meringue.

Stubb waved his cane curtly at Hugh. "Coggshall."

Hugh nodded back.

"Where is he?" Stubb said.

Hugh answered before I could. "Benedict's busy."

Stubb straightened his doublet and eyed our shop. His gaze lingered, as usual, on the shelves behind the counter, where we kept our most valuable ingredients, like diamond dust and powdered gold. Finally, he seemed to notice me standing beside him. "Are you the apprentice?"

It being a holiday, I wasn't wearing the blue apron that every apprentice was required to wear. I could see how that had confused him, since I'd only lived here for three years.

I nodded. "Yes, Master Stubb."

"Then go get him," Stubb said.

Stubb's command put me in a bind. Officially, I was only required to follow my master's orders. On the other hand, showing anything but the utmost respect to another master could get you in big trouble with the Apothecaries' Guild, and Stubb wasn't the kind of man you wanted to cross. Still, something in Hugh's manner made me think it would be better if Stubb didn't speak to Master Benedict tonight. So I made a second mistake that evening: I hesitated.

Stubb hit me.

He thwacked me on the side of my head with the end of his cane. I felt a sharp spike of pain as the snake's silver fangs bit into the top of my earlobe. I fell against the curio cabinet and clasped my hand to my ear, crying out in surprise as much as hurt.

Stubb brushed his cane on the sleeve of his doublet, as if touching me had fouled it. "Go get him, I said."

Hugh's expression darkened. "I told you, Benedict is busy. And the boy isn't yours. So keep your hands to yourself."

Stubb just looked bored. "The boy isn't yours, either, Coggshall. So keep your words to yourself."

Master Benedict appeared in the doorway behind the counter, wiping his hands on a rag. He took in the scene, frowning. "What do you want, Nathaniel?" he said.

"Did you hear?" Stubb said. "There's been another murder." He smiled. "But perhaps you already knew that."

CHAPTER
3

HUGH CLOSED THE BOOK HE'D BEEN
reading, his fingers still between the pages. Master Benedict
laid the rag carefully on the counter and slowly straightened
its corners.

"Who was it?" he said.

Another apothecary, I thought, and my heart began to
thump. But it was someone else this time.

"A lecturer, from Cambridge." Stubb poked each word at
Master Benedict like a needle. "Rented a house in Riverdale
for the summer. Pembroke, his name was."

Hugh's eyes flicked to my master.

"The laundry girl found him," Stubb said. "Guts sliced

open, just like the others. You knew the man, didn't you?"

Stubb looked like a cat who'd cornered a mouse. I thought he might start purring.

Master Benedict regarded him calmly. "Christopher."

Me?

"Go clean the pigeon coop," he said.

Of course. Why would I want to stay? It's not as if I *cared* that a man who knew my master had just been murdered. But an apprentice wasn't allowed to argue. So I just left, grumbling under my breath.

The ground floor of our house had two rooms, both set aside for my master's business. The store was in the front. The back held our workshop. It was here, three years ago, that I'd first learned what it meant to be an apprentice.

I hadn't known what to expect that day. In Cripplegate, the older boys loved to taunt the younger ones with stories of the cruelties masters inflicted on their apprentices. *It's like being a prisoner in the Tower dungeon. They only let you sleep two hours a night. All you get to eat is half a slice of moldy bread. They beat you if you dare to look them in the eye.*

Seeing Master Benedict for the first time didn't ease my mind in the slightest. When he plucked me from the huddle of boys in the back of the Apothecaries' Guild Great Hall, I wondered if I'd drawn the worst master of all. His face didn't seem unkind, but he was so absurdly *tall*. The way he towered over eleven-year-old me made me feel like I'd just met a talking birch tree.

The orphan boys' tales replayed in my mind as I followed Master Benedict to my new home, making my stomach flutter. *My new home.* My whole life, I'd wanted nothing more than to leave the orphanage. Now that my wish was coming true, I was more scared than ever.

It was swelteringly hot in the noonday sun, and the piles of animal dung clogging the drains let off the worst stench London had smelled in years. I barely paid attention to it, lost as I was in my head. Master Benedict, seemingly lost in his own world, barely paid attention to anything at all. What had to be at least three pints of urine, dumped from a chamber pot out of a second-floor window, splashed inches from his feet, yet he didn't even flinch. A hackney coach nearly ran him over, the iron-shod wheels clattering over the cobbles, the horses passing so close, I could smell their musk. Master Benedict just paused for a moment, then continued on toward the shop like he was strolling through Clerkenwell Green. Maybe he really *was* a tree. Nothing seemed to faze him.

I couldn't say the same. My guts twisted as Master Benedict unlocked the front door to the shop. Above the entryway hung a weathered oaken sign, swinging on a pair of silver chains.

BLACKTHORN

RELIEFS FOR ALL MANNER OF MALIGNANT HUMORS

Carved leaves of ivy, filled in with a deep mossy green, ringed the bright red letters. Underneath, painted in broad gold brushstrokes, was a unicorn horn, the universal symbol for apothecaries.

Master Benedict ushered me through the front door and toward the workshop in the back. I craned my neck to see the store: the stuffed animals, the curios, the neatly stocked shelves. But it was the workshop that really made me stop dead and stare. Covering every inch of the workbenches, jammed on the shelves, and tucked underneath rickety stools were hundreds of apothecary jars, filled with leaves and powders, waters and creams. Around them were endless tools and equipment: molded glassware, heated by oil-fueled flames; liquids bubbling with alien smells; pots and cauldrons, large and small, iron and copper and tin. In the corner, the furnace huffed skin-scalding waves of heat from its gaping mouth, twelve feet wide and four feet high. Dozens of experiments cooked on its three racks, glowing coals at one end and a blazing fire at the other. Shaped like a flattened onion, the smooth black curves of the furnace rose to the flue, where a pipe bent away, pumping fumes out the back wall to mix with the stink of garbage, waste, and manure that wafted over from the London streets.

I'd stood there, open mouthed, until Master Benedict dropped a cast-iron pot in my hands. "Set the water to boil," he said. Then he waved me onto a stool at the end of the center workbench, near the back door, which led to a small herb patch in the alley behind the house. In front of me sat three empty pewter mugs and a small glass jar filled with hundreds of tiny, black, kidney-shaped seeds. Each one was about half the size of a ladybug.

"This is madapple," he said. "Examine it and tell me what you discover."

Nervously, I plucked one of the seeds from the jar and rolled it between my fingers. It smelled faintly of rotten tomatoes. I touched it to the tip of my tongue. It didn't taste any better than it smelled: bitter and oily, with a hint of spice. My mouth dried almost instantly.

I told Master Benedict what I'd experienced. He nodded. "Good. Now take three of those seeds, crush them, and place them in the first mug. Place six in the second, and ten in the third. Then pour the boiling water over them and let them steep."

I did as he ordered. While the infusion brewed, he asked, "Do you know what asthma is?"

"Yes, Master," I said. Several children in the orphanage had had it. One summer, when the air had been soaked in smoke and stink, two boys had died of it on a single day, their own lungs choking the life out of them as the masters stood by helplessly, unable to assist.

"In small doses," Master Benedict said, "madapple is effective for treating asthma." He pushed the first cup toward me. The three crushed seeds swirled at the bottom of the darkening water. It smelled rank. "This is the correct dose for a man of ordinary size."

He pushed the second cup toward me. "This amount of madapple will cause terrible hallucinations, true waking nightmares. Once those are gone, the patient's body will be racked with pain for days."

Finally, he handed me the last cup. "This will kill you. Drink it, and in five minutes you'll be dead."

I stared at the mug. I'd just made *poison*. Stunned, I looked up at Master Benedict to find him watching me intently.

"Tell me," he said. "What have you just learned?"

I shook off my surprise and tried to think. The obvious answer was the properties of the madapple, and the recipes I could make from the seeds. But the way Master Benedict was watching me made me feel like he was looking for something more.

"I'm the one who's responsible," I said.

Master Benedict's eyebrows shot up. "Yes," he said, sounding pleased. He waved at the herbs, oils, and minerals that surrounded us. "These ingredients are the gifts the Lord has given us. They are the tools of our trade. What you must always remember is that they are *only* that: tools. They can heal, or they can kill. It's never the tool itself that decides. It's the hands—and the heart—of the one who wields it. Of all the things I'll teach you, Christopher, there's no lesson more important than this. Do you understand?"

I nodded, a little awed—and scared—of the trust he'd just placed in me.

"Good," he'd said. "Then let's go for a walk, and you'll get your final lesson for the day."

Master Benedict thrust a heavy leather satchel into my

hands and tied his sash with all the glass vials in it around his waist. I kept looking at the sash, fascinated, as he led me back into the streets, the satchel's strap digging into my shoulder.

He took me to a mansion at the north end of the city. To a boy from Cripplegate, it may as well have been the king's own palace. A liveried servant let us into its vast entryway and asked us to wait. I tried not to gawk at the riches that surrounded us: the satin damask on the walls, edged with golden trim; the chandelier overhead, cut glass glittering in sunlight from crystal windows; the ceiling above it, where painted horses galloped through trees under a cloudless, azure sky.

Eventually, a round-faced chambermaid led us up a curved marble staircase to the parlor. A middle-aged woman waited for us there, wearing a low-cut yellow bodice over a bright orange lutestring dress brocaded with flowers. Her dress opened at the bottom to reveal a frilled, emerald petticoat. She lay draped over a purple velvet daybed, eating cherries from a silver bowl.

The woman's high forehead furrowed as she spat out a cherry pit. "Mr. Blackthorn, you are cruel. I have waited for you in torment."

Master Benedict bowed slightly. Then he made me jump as he shouted at her, as if she was hard of hearing. "I apologize for the delay, Lady Lucy. Allow me to introduce Christopher."

He stepped aside. Lady Lucy assessed me with a critical eye. "Bit young to be an apothecary, aren't you?" she said.

"Uh, no, my lady. I mean, yes, my lady," I stammered. "I'm the apprentice."

She frowned. "Find me a necklace? What in the world do you mean, boy?"

I glanced over at Master Benedict, but his face was blank. I tried again, shouting this time, as Master Benedict had. "I'm the *apprentice*."

"Well, why didn't you just say that? Get to it, then. My back is the Devil's torture." The chambermaid began to untie the laces of Lady Lucy's bodice. Shocked, I looked away.

"Don't be ridiculous," Lady Lucy said. She turned away from me, holding the silk to her chest as her maid pulled open her bodice in the back. The skin all along her spine was red and raw. It looked unbearably itchy.

I glanced over at Master Benedict again, unsure of what I was supposed to do. This time, he motioned toward the satchel I carried. I looked inside to find a thick ceramic jar, its wide mouth stopped with cork. I pulled out the stopper, then recoiled in horror. Inside was a chunky, dark brown cream that looked like the back of a baby's diaper. It smelled like it, too.

"Spread a layer over the rash," Master Benedict said quietly. "Thick enough to cover it, but no thicker."

I shuddered as I slid my fingers into the slime, praying it wasn't what it felt like. Then I smeared a handful of it over Lady Lucy's back. To my surprise, not only did she not complain about the smell, she sagged visibly in relief as the goo slid over her skin.

"Much better," she sighed. "Thank you, Mr. Blackthorn."

"We shall return tomorrow, madam," he shouted, and the chambermaid showed us out.

I put the apothecary jar back in the satchel. As I did, I saw a woollen rag inside, folded at the bottom. I pulled it out on the street, trying to wipe away as much of the foul brown gunk from my fingers as I could.

"So?" Master Benedict said. "What did you learn from that?"

I answered without thinking. "Always bring cotton to stuff your nose."

Suddenly, I realized how that sounded. I cringed,

expecting Master Benedict to beat me for insolence, like the masters at Cripplegate would have.

Instead, he blinked at me. Then he threw his head back and laughed, a warm, rich sound. It was the first time I remembered thinking I'd be all right.

"Indeed," Master Benedict had said. "Well, if you think that was bad, wait until you see what I'll teach you tomorrow." He chuckled. "Come then, Christopher. Let's go home."

He did teach me more that next day, and every day after that. When I'd imagined what being an apothecary would be like, I'd thought working in the store was where I'd end up. But the workshop in the back became my true home. Here, Master Benedict showed me how to mix an electuary of marshmallow root and honey to soothe the throat; how to grind willow bark and infuse it into a tea that lessened pain; how to combine sixty-four ingredients over four months to make the Venice treacle, an antidote for snake venom. He taught me his own secret recipes as well, and the codes to decipher them. In this room I found my future, making miracles that came from God's own creation.

Some days, anyway. Today all I got was some grain, a bucket, and a poop scraper.

With my master and Stubb talking in the next room, I grabbed what I needed and left. The door opposite the giant oven led to the upper floors, with steep stairs so old, the lightest step made them squeal like a frightened donkey. On the second floor was the kitchen, small but functional, and the pantry, which kept the occasional loaf of bread or wheel of cheese, some smoked fish, and a cask or two of ale. The rest of the rooms were stuffed with supplies for the workshop.

Part of the third floor was kept for storage, too, but for Master Benedict's other passion: books. The only thing that compared with my master's obsession with discovering new recipes was his obsession with discovering new books. He passed that on to me, too. Besides our daily lessons, Master Benedict expected me to study on my own, not just recipes and how raw materials reacted, but from his endlessly grow-ing collection of tomes. From these, I learned philosophy, history, theology, languages, the natural sciences, and what-ever else sparked my master's imagination during his weekly trips to see his friend Isaac the bookseller.

A landing at the top of the stairs swung around to

Master Benedict's private rooms. More books lined the walls, making the passage so slight, you had to squeeze against the railing to get to the door. Opposite my master's quarters, a ladder led up to a hatch in the ceiling. I unbolted it and climbed into the evening chill.

The roof of our home was flat. I liked coming up here on hot summer nights, where the air was cooler and, high above the cobbles, not nearly as rank with the smell of the streets. Tonight, unfortunately, I wasn't spared; the winds were blowing from the northeast, sending over the stink of boiled fat and urine from the soap maker's shop four streets away.

We housed our birds up here in a walk-in wood-and-wire coop at the back corner of the balcony. They fluttered their wings noisily as I unlatched the hook to their shelter. A few of the bolder ones poked around my shirtsleeves when I entered, losing interest when they saw the bucket I carried was empty. One pigeon, a plump salt-and-pepper-speckled girl, flapped down from her perch and tapped at my toes.

"Hello, Bridget," I said.

She cooed. I put the scraper on the dirt and picked her up. She was warm, her feathers soft in my fingers. "I got kicked out," I complained to her. "Again."

Bridget nuzzled her head against my thumb in sympathy. I cradled her in the crook of my elbow and pulled a handful of barley from my pocket, watching absently as she pecked the grain from my palm. My mind was still on the conversation I'd been booted out of. Stubb had always been a slimy thing, but after this new murder, the way he'd eyed our shop made my stomach twist. It was no secret that my master's business did well, and it was equally no secret that Stubb didn't like the competition. I knew he'd tried to buy our shop several years back. After Master Benedict refused to sell it, Stubb had accused my master of stealing his recipes. No one took him seriously, but tonight it made me wonder: How far would a man like Stubb go to get what he wanted?

And why was he here, taunting Master Benedict about the murders? Did he know something about them? Six men had been butchered now, three of them apothecaries—and the latest victim knew my master. *Closer and closer*, I thought. Tightening, like a noose.

I shivered, and not from the cold. Important things were being said downstairs. Yet here I was, stuck on the roof! Well, Master Benedict could send me away if he wanted to. But if I finished my duties up here, I'd have to return to the workshop. "And if I happened to overhear something," I said to Bridget, "that wouldn't be *my* fault, would it?"

I took Bridget's silence for agreement and got to work. The floor of the coop was thick with grayish-white gunk. Bridget, flapping from shoulder to shoulder, nibbled the hair behind my ears as I scraped the top layer of poop off the dirt and slopped it into the bucket. When I was done, I lifted Bridget from my collar and set her in the straw at the back, far from the draft, where she could be warm and snug. "I'll bring your breakfast in the morning," I said.

She bobbed her head at me and cooed goodbye.

We didn't keep birds just for fun. Pigeon poop was valuable. Sometimes we sold a bit of it to the market gardeners—it was particularly good for growing asparagus—but we made something out of it much more precious than fertilizer.

Back in the workshop, I unsealed a cask in the corner. The stink that blasted from the barrel nearly made me pass out. Gagging, I dumped what I'd scraped from the coop into the slop inside, then topped the whole thing up by unbuttoning my fly and peeing into it—another job for the apprentice. Afterward, I resealed the cask. I wouldn't open it again for three more months, when I'd wash the nasty mix out and put it into trays in the sun, where it would dry into spiky white crystals of saltpeter.

When I'd finally finished, I crept to the door and put my ear to the wood, half expecting the conversation to be over. But whatever they were talking about must have been really important. Stubb was still here. And he was near to shouting.

"Change is coming, Benedict," he said. "You want to be on the right side this time."

"I don't have a side, Nathaniel," my master said. "These squabbles don't involve me."

"Perhaps gold will, then. With the right connections, the right backing, we could make a fortune—"

"Money is not the issue," Master Benedict said. "I have no part in any of this. You have the wrong man."

Stubb snorted. "Pretend all you like. You'll choose, one way or the other."

There was a pause. "Is that a threat?" my master said.

Stubb's voice became as smooth as oil. "Of course not, Benedict. After all, what do I have to do with this sordid business? Nothing. Nothing at all."

I heard Stubb's heavy footsteps, then the creak and

slam of the front door. For a moment, there was silence. Then Hugh spoke to my master, so quietly that I had to squash my ear against the wood to hear him. "What do we do now?"

"We be careful," Master Benedict said.

"And if Pembroke talked?"

"He wouldn't."

"Not everyone can stand under torture," Hugh said.

"No, but Nathaniel wouldn't know that, anyway. He's just guessing."

"A bloody good guess."

"Stubb's not a problem," Master Benedict said. "It's that apprentice we need to watch out for."

I frowned. What apprentice? What did he mean?

"Three of the six were right, Benedict," Hugh said. "We can no longer tell ourselves this is a coincidence. If Stubb can figure us out, it's only a matter of time before the others do. Simon's already fled the city."

"To where?"

"France. Paris, I think. He'll have nothing to do with us anymore."

There was a pause. "Do you want to leave, too?"

"You know I don't," Hugh said. "But we can't keep this

up forever. Stubb was right about that. We have to make a choice, and soon."

My master sighed. "I know."

When Master Benedict opened the door to the workshop, I pretended I'd just finished with the cask.

"I'm afraid I can't eat with you tonight," he said. "I have to go out."

That wasn't unusual. Master Benedict often left home in the evening, not returning until well after I'd gone to sleep. "Yes, Master."

He heard the catch in my voice. "What's wrong?" he said. "Are you upset about before? Come here."

He put his arm around my shoulders. "I'm sorry I was cross with you," he said. "But God's breath, Christopher, sometimes you make me wonder if Blackthorn will still be standing when I come home. You must think before you act."

"I know, Master. You were right. I'm not upset about that." Though I still didn't want to scrub the floors.

"Then what's the matter?"

"What did Stubb want?" I said.

"*Master* Stubb," he chided gently, "wanted the same thing he always wants. A quick path to riches."

"Then why was he talking about the murders?"

"Ah. So that's what's troubling you."

Now that I'd finally said it aloud, the rest rushed out like the Thames after the spring thaw. "There's a gang of assassins on the loose and no one can stop them and Tom thinks it's the Catholics but his mother thinks it's the Puritans but I think it's worse than either and even the king is scared and you knew the last man they murdered and *they're killing apothecaries.*" I took a breath.

"So?" Master Benedict said.

"Well . . . *we're* apothecaries."

"We are?" He looked surprised. "So we are! How nice for us."

"*Master.*"

He laughed affectionately. "Never mind the murders, boy; your imagination will stop your heart. There is no 'gang of assassins.' No one is hunting apothecaries. And Nathaniel Stubb is harmless."

But he threatened you! I almost cried out, before I realized that would reveal I'd been eavesdropping. I floundered for something to say and finally settled on, "So we'll be safe?"

"As the king's breeches," he said. "Now, settle down.

I'm in no danger. And as long as you don't build any more firearms, neither are you. There's nothing to worry about." Master Benedict patted my shoulder. "I promise."

I wanted to believe him, but I wasn't sure I did. I mean, *someone* was murdering these poor people. And it had sounded like Hugh felt the same.

Three of the six were right, he'd said. *We can no longer tell ourselves this is a coincidence.* What did that mean? Nothing good, I was sure. Whatever it was, they clearly weren't going to tell me. If I wanted to find out, I'd have to do some more eavesdropping.

Either way, I couldn't do anything about it tonight. Hungry, I sliced a hunk of cheese from the wheel in the larder for my supper and downed it with a mug of beer. Then I did my punishment. I wrote out the cannon recipe in English and Latin until my hand cramped, then scoured the floors and the steps, all the way up to the roof. When I finally finished, three hours past nightfall, I barred the front door, shuttered the windows, then crawled under the shop counter to my palliasse and fell fast asleep.

A noise woke me. At first, I thought it came from the street. Then I heard it again, from the other side of the counter. A ceramic jar clinked against the shelf.

I'd sealed up the shop before I'd gone to sleep. I hadn't barred the back door to the workshop so Master Benedict could return, but it was locked, and only my master and I knew where the key was hidden. And Master Benedict always entered the house through the workshop and went straight upstairs. He never came to the front.

But there it was again. A footfall, the gentle creak of the floorboards.

Someone was here.

CHAPTER

I REACHED UNDER THE STRAW, groping for my knife. My heart hammered at my ribs. A plan. I needed a plan.

I thought of several. I could jump out and surprise them. I could run and call for help. Or I could stay where I was and wet myself.

I gave option number three serious consideration. But if this was a burglar, he'd come around the counter. The most valuable remedies we had were here, on the shelves a few feet above my head. And if it was an assassin . . . I gripped my knife as if it were Excalibur. In reality, it was a two-inch blade, loose in the handle and dull as a millstone. The thing had a hard time slicing apples.

I pushed myself to my knees and peeked over the counter. The coals in the fireplace still glowed softly. I couldn't see the intruder, but the dull red light cast a shadow of him on the wall.

A *huge* shadow.

He was a giant. Incredibly, impossibly tall.

All right, then. Fighting was right out. And wetting myself was not a plan. So: option number two. Sneak to the front, unbolt the door, run outside, scream like a girl.

But—Master Benedict! I thought. *What if he's come home?* I couldn't just leave him.

The giant moved away from the shelves. He was carrying a ceramic jar, and not doing a good job of it. He struggled, grunting, and lowered it with a *thunk* on the table near the fireplace. Now that he was closer to the auburn glow of the coals, I could see the intruder better. He wasn't a giant at all. The man was tall, yes, but still human size. And while the shadow made him look broad, he was actually quite skinny. In fact, he looked exactly the same shape as my—

"Master?" I said.

Master Benedict leaned against the table. "Yes. Go to sleep."

Not likely. My heart still whumped like His Majesty's cannons. What was he doing with that jar in the middle of the night?

"Are you all right?" I said.

"Yes, Christopher. I'm fine. Go back to sleep."

I went to the fireplace, using the coals to light the wick on the lamp. When the lantern flared, I nearly dropped it.

Master Benedict looked like he'd just come back from a war. His wig was gone, his short gray hair revealed, spiked and dirty. His clothes were so caked with mud, the blue underneath was only a memory. There was something black smeared all over the right side of his face. It looked like soot.

"Did someone attack you?" I said. "Was it Stubb?" I shrank back. "Was it the killers?"

"No." He tried to turn away, but his movements were clumsy, twitching.

I took his arm. "Let me help you."

"I'm fine," he said.

"Please, Master. Let me take you to your room."

After a moment, he nodded. I lifted his right arm to wrap around me. He cried out in pain. It was then that I saw his coat was torn at the shoulder.

I took him through the back and upstairs, the lantern

lighting our way. His weight, resting on me, seemed to grow with every creaking step. At the top, I nudged the door open with my hip and brought him inside.

Master Benedict's bedroom smelled faintly of Egyptian incense. Against one wall, next to the fireplace, was a narrow bed with plain brown cotton sheets and a single pillow. A simple table stood beside it, one short leg steadied underneath with folded sheepskin. A chamber pot rested on the rose-carved elm chair near the desk at the open window; the desk was covered with papers and ash dust from the incense holder, blown off by the night's breeze. The rest of the space was piled with books, stacks and stacks and more stacks, each one at least a dozen high. *Isaac the bookseller*, I thought, *must be swimming in gold*.

I weaved my master through the books to the bed and laid him down as gently as I could. I looked at him for a moment, unsure of what to do.

Master Benedict trained you, I told myself. *You are ready for this*. It calmed me.

I lit the lantern on the table using my own, closed the window shutters, and poked at the coals dying in the fireplace to give him some warmth. Then I looked him over. Downstairs, I'd thought his coat was torn, but in better light, the charred, crumbling wool and blackened skin underneath gave the truth away. He'd been burned. My heart burned, too, toward whoever had hurt him.

"Rest a moment, Master," I said.

I ran down to the workshop, trying to remember everything my master had taught me about treating burns. I hauled two buckets of water up to his room. Then I went back and searched the shelves for the remedies I needed. One of them, a cream of powdered silver, was already out, the one my master had pulled down when I was asleep. I balanced the jars in my arms, added a small tin pot full of water and a mug on top, then went upstairs.

Master Benedict lay on the pillow, breathing slowly. He watched me place the pot on the fire and line up the jars on the table beside him. I started to pull off his coat, but he flinched when I lifted his arms, so I used my knife to cut it away at the seams. It was ruined anyway, its future value only as rags.

I was relieved to see that while the skin of his shoulder was blistered, he wasn't badly burned. I washed away the soot, and that from his face, too. I scooped dried poppies from one of the jars into the water boiling in the pot on the fire and, after a minute, poured it into the mug beside the bed. The poppy was the best pain reliever God had gifted the world with, and the infusion would relax him as well.

Master Benedict sipped at it as I worked. I smeared the silver cream on his burn, to prevent the flesh from rotting. Then I wrapped a cloth around it, tying it under his arm, and removed what was left of his filthy clothes.

He looked so frail. He'd never seemed old to me, but tonight I saw every year in him, all aged skin and bones. Still, otherwise, he appeared unharmed, except for his palms, which were cracked and raw. The wounds didn't look like burns, so I slathered his hands with aloe sap and wrapped them as I did his shoulder.

"You've learned so much," he said softly.

I flushed, embarrassed, but proud. "Thank you, Master."

He began to speak again, but his voice choked. His eyes were wet, ringed with red. My heart ached. I'd never seen him cry before.

"Can I do anything more?" I said.

He reached out and touched my cheek with his fingertips.

"You're a good boy," he said.

I couldn't find any words. I just bowed my head and leaned into the warmth of his hand.

His eyelids began to droop. The poppy tea was working. I helped him lie down again, and pulled the covers over him. "Sleep well, Master."

I extinguished the lantern on the table. I carried the other one to the door before he spoke.

"Wait."

He stared into the flame of the lantern. It flickered, tendrils of smoke dancing over the glass.

"It's Oak Apple Day tomorrow," he said.

"It . . . yes. The king's birthday."

"And your own."

He remembered.

"Did you and Tom collect your oak sprigs?" he said.

"This morning."

I was wondering why he'd stopped me for that, and then he said, his voice nearly a whisper, "Do I ask too much of you?"

I wasn't sure what he meant. "Master?"

"No one ever gave you the choice," he said. "The orphanage made you study. The Guild gave you the test. I brought you here. No one ever gave you the choice." He looked into my eyes. "If I sent you away, to walk a different path," he said, "somewhere you'd be safe, somewhere you couldn't be hurt . . . would you choose it?"

His question stunned me. Had any master ever allowed his apprentice to choose? I remembered his secret conversation with Hugh.

We have to make a choice, and soon.

When the killings had started four months ago, Tom and I had teased each other that assassins were coming to get us. It didn't take long for our jokes to stop, as the reality of what was happening to our city began to weigh on us. Tonight, alone in the dark, I'd been more scared than I ever had before. I still was. Part of me wanted to go: go somewhere safe, no Stubb, no killers, nothing more to fear. But that was *us*, together. Leave Master Benedict behind? I couldn't. I wouldn't.

I said it with conviction, so he'd know it, too. "No, Master. I'm grateful for the life you've given me. Whatever happens, I want to stay with you."

He didn't say anything. I waited at the door, not sure if he wanted me to go. I got the sense that he wasn't sure, either. Finally, he spoke.

"I have something for you."

He pointed to a small package, wrapped in linen, resting on top of one of the book stacks.

"What is it?" I said.

"A present."

I was stunned. The last two Oak Apple Days, Master Benedict had brought home my favorite, fresh roast pig, for supper. He'd eaten sparingly, mostly watching with amusement as I stuffed my face with the sweet white meat, slurping grease from my fingers. I'd always thought the pigs were special for the holiday. Now I wondered if he'd really bought them for me.

But this . . . I'd never got an actual present before. "Can I . . . can I open it?"

"I suppose it must be past midnight by now. So tomorrow is officially today." He nodded. "Go on, then."

I pulled at the cloth. It fell away.

I lost my breath.

Underneath was a polished silvery cube, slightly bigger than my palm. On the top, engraved in the metal in fine, smooth grooves, was a series of circles.

With trembling fingers, I turned it around. On each of the other faces, a single symbol was engraved, five in all:

♃ ♀ ♄ ⊕ ♂

"It's beautiful," I said.

"Do you recognize the metal?"

I tapped one side with a fingernail. It wasn't silver. It didn't feel quite like tin, either. I bounced it in my hand. It weighed a little more than a plum. "Antimony?"

"Good. Otherwise known as?"

"The Black Dragon. Some say it has mystical properties. But it makes you throw up if you eat it."

"Excellent."

I hugged the cube to my chest. "Thank you so much."

"Don't get too excited." His eyes twinkled. "That's only half your present."

My jaw dropped. "There's *more*?"

"You get the rest if you can open it."

For a moment, I wasn't sure what he meant. Then I realized he was talking about the cube. "It opens?"

I held it close to the lantern. A quarter of an inch below the top, a line traced around it, almost too fine to see. I tried to pry it off, but the top wouldn't budge. "How do I . . . ?"

He smiled. "I told you. You get the rest . . . *if* you can open it."

I shook the cube. Inside, something rattled. "What is it?"

"That would spoil the surprise, wouldn't it? But I do think you might need a little help on this one." He was nearly asleep now, his voice beginning to slur. "I'll tell you this. The key is downstairs, somewhere in the shop. And that"—he pointed to the book the cube had been resting on—"will help you find it."

FRIDAY, MAY 29, 1665

Oak Apple Day

CHAPTER
5

THE POUNDING ON THE FRONT DOOR
made me jump. For a moment, I thought my master's attackers had come to finish the job. Though I doubted they'd be the type to knock.

I twisted in my chair, my fingers on the pages of the book my master had given me. The shutters were still barred, the door was still bolted. I waited.

More thumping. Then: "Christopher! Are you there? Let me in."

I opened the door. Tom stood on the doorstep, hunched over in his coat, trying to shield a package wrapped in wool from the rain. I'd been so caught up in reading that I'd lost all sense of time. The sky was heavily overcast, the clouds a dusky gray, but it was clearly no longer night.

Tom edged past me into the warmth of the shop. "Finally."

"What time is it?" I said.

"I don't know. Eight? Nine, maybe? The cry of six was ages ago." He shivered. "Ugh. I hate the cold." He shook his coat, and ice pellets skittered across the floor.

"Is that hail?" I said. "It's almost June."

"It's an omen." Tom went to the fireplace, where a solitary log burned low. He placed the package he was carrying on the table and stuck his hands near the flame to warm them. "There was another murder yesterday."

"I know." I told Tom about the visit from Stubb and my wounded master's return in the night.

Tom's eyes went wide. "Who attacked him?"

"He wouldn't tell me," I said. "But I don't think it was ordinary robbers. They burned him."

"It could have been the killers," Tom said. "My mother says they're part of a cult."

I stared at him. "A *cult*? Where did she hear that?"

"Mistress Mullens. Her husband's a clerk, and she says he says there are whisperings about it at court. She says the murders might be human sacrifices." Tom shuddered and crossed his fingers. "There are reports of plague in the western parishes now, too. I'm telling you, this weather's an omen. The city's turning bad."

Maybe Tom was right. Hail in almost-June did sound like an omen. Although I wished God's warnings would be a little clearer. You wouldn't think it would be so hard for the Almighty to write STOP STEALING STICKY BUNS in the clouds or something.

I poked at the package Tom had brought. "What's in here?"

He smiled, ill winds forgotten. "Open it."

I unwrapped the wool. The folds fell away, and I was enveloped by the smell of warm apple and cinnamon. Inside was a freshly baked pie, its crust crimped and lightly browned, steam still rising from the flower-petal holes in the center.

"Happy birthday," Tom said.

This day was getting better and better. I hugged him. I think I got drool on his shirt. Then I had a thought. "Did you steal this pie from your father's bakery?"

Tom managed to look offended. "Of course not."

"Really?"

"Well . . . I might have borrowed it."

"Borrowed it? Are we going to return it?"

He thought about it. "In a sense."

"What if your father finds out? He'll hit you."

Tom shrugged. "He hits me anyway. May as well get pie out of it."

"Tom!"

He grinned. "I'm kidding. My mother let me make it for you. Come on, let's eat."

We did, shoveling the sweetness into our mouths by the fistful. I saved a piece for my master, who liked a good pie almost as much as I did; the rest we devoured. I think it was the best I'd ever tasted, and not just because Tom had made it specially for me. He really had the magic touch. When Tom took over his family's bakery, he'd outshine even his father.

As I licked the last of the goop from my fingers, Tom let out an earthshaking belch. I tried to match him, and failed badly.

"A shameful effort," he said. He spotted the book I'd left open on the chair beside the fire, and his expression grew even more disapproving. "Satan's woolly socks. Were you *studying*? On your own birthday?"

"It's not for work," I said. "It goes with Master Benedict's present." Proudly, I showed him the antimony cube.

Tom was impressed. "He gave you this? It must be worth a fortune." He shook it, listening to the rattle. "What's inside?"

"That's what I was working on. Look." I turned the cube so the top was facing us.

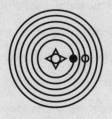

"What is it?" he said.

"Our universe. The Sun, and the Earth, and the other five planets. Each big circle represents an orbit."

"Oh. Oh, I see, they go around." He traced a finger over the figure in the center. "Why does the Earth have these peaks? Are they mountains?"

"That's not the Earth," I said. "That's the Sun."

"Why is the Sun in the center?"

"Because that's where the Sun is."

"It is?" Tom frowned. "Says who?"

"This man." I handed him the book.

He squinted at the cover. "*Sys* . . . *System* . . . What is this?"

"*Systema cosmicum*," I said. "It's Latin. It means 'cosmic

system.' It says the Sun is at the center of the universe and all the planets go around it."

Tom flipped through it, a skeptical expression on his face, until he got to the title page. "By Galileo Galilei. Sounds Catholic to me," he said disapprovingly.

"Just . . . that's what the figure is, all right? The Sun is at the center, and the six planets go around it. Mercury's the closest, then Venus, then Earth—see, this circle on the third ring is us—then Mars, Jupiter, and Saturn. That's all of them."

He turned the cube over. "So what are the rest of these symbols?"

"They're the planets." I pulled out a sheet of parchment that had been slipped inside the back cover of the book, inked with Master Benedict's smooth, familiar handwriting.

Planetary Symbols

⊕ Earth   ♃ Jupiter

♂ Mars   ♀ Venus

☿ Mercury   ♄ Saturn

Tom looked from the parchment to the cube.

♃ ♀ ♄ ⊕ ♂

"But there's only five symbols here," he said. "There's Jupiter, and Venus, Saturn, Earth . . . Mars. Mercury's missing."

"Right," I said. "Now look at the top again. The first circle, closest to the Sun. The black dot on it, where Mercury's supposed to be."

He peered at it. "Oh! It's a hole."

"I think that's where the key goes. And the missing symbol is the clue." I pointed at the shelf behind us. On it was a ceramic jar, smaller than its neighbors. "Can you bring that down?"

Tom rose obligingly and grabbed the jar one handed. He looked surprised. "It's heavy."

I took an empty cup from the rack behind the counter, then unstoppered the jar. "This," I said, "is quicksilver."

I tipped the jar over the cup, draining it carefully. A shiny silver liquid poured out.

Tom was amazed. "How did you melt that?"

"It's already melted. It's not hot." I dipped my finger in it. "Look, you can touch it."

Cautiously, Tom held out a finger. He barely grazed the surface, then pulled away, leaving jittering waves that stilled almost immediately. He tried again, going deeper. "Strange. It doesn't really feel like anything. It's almost like it's not even there. What's it for?"

"Treating diseases. Really bad ones, that you get on your . . . you know. But what we want it for is . . . the key!" I turned the jar over.

Nothing happened.

"Do I applaud now?" Tom said.

I looked into the jar, frowning. "There's nothing in here."

"Why did you think there would be?"

"Because mercury is supposed to be the key." I jiggled the cup, trying to see if anything had slipped out with the liquid. "That's what quicksilver's real name is. It's called mercury. And that hole is where the planet Mercury would be."

"That's clever," Tom said, looking at the cube, "but I don't see how you're going to get a key in here. The hole is too small. And it's round. There's no such thing as a round key."

He was right. A round key didn't make sense; it wouldn't have any teeth. But Master Benedict had promised there was a key, and it was in this room.

That's when it struck me. "Tom! You're a genius."

"I am?"

I pointed at the hole. "How would you get a key in there?"

"I told you, you can't. It's too small. You'd need something that could slip inside . . ." His eyes widened as I swirled the cup, sloshing the mercury around. "A *liquid* key? How is that even possible?"

"Let's find out."

He held the cube steady. Carefully, I tipped the cup. Three drips of liquid metal splashed onto the surface, running along the engraved circles like little silver beads. They drained toward the hole and slipped inside. Still, nothing happened.

"Maybe you need more," Tom said.

I poured again, and a third time.

Click.

The seam around the top opened. Just a crack.

Slowly, I lifted the lid. I looked inside.

I gasped.

CHAPTER
6

TOM LEANED OVER. "WHAT IS IT? What is it?"

I pulled it out and placed it on the counter.

It was a coin, shiny silver. Real silver.

Tom's eyes bulged. "A *shilling*. You got a *shilling*."

A shilling. Twelve whole pennies. I was *rich*.

The coin was brand new, the center stamped with a profile of the king. Around it was inscribed CAROLUS II DEI GRATIA. Charles II, by the grace of God. Oak Apple Day, his coronation day, his birthday. And mine.

I felt like I was glowing.

Tom picked up the shilling, marveling at it. I peered

into the puzzle cube again. "Look at this," I said.

The inside of the cube was antimony, too, except for one face opposite the hinge. Here it was glass, letting us see the lock's mechanism. A channel from the top guided the quicksilver into a well in the front, where there was a lever. When we'd poured enough in, its weight pushed the lever down, which opened the latch.

"Brilliant," Tom said.

It was, even more than it appeared. Master Benedict loved hiding things inside other things. Codes within codes, puzzles over locks. Here, too: inside my birthday gift, a second present. And beneath it all, a lesson in symbols.

No, I thought. *Not just a lesson.*

Last night, before he'd given me my present, Master Benedict had hesitated. He'd asked me if I wanted to stay with him, despite whatever danger he was in. Even when I told him yes, he'd hesitated. He'd prepared this gift for me, yet until that final moment, he hadn't decided whether to hand it over.

The cube, the book, his words, this puzzle . . . it was more than a lesson. It was a *test*.

But of what?

I ran a fingertip along the grooves in the cube. Tom had said the thing was worth a fortune. I didn't care about that. For whatever reason Master Benedict gave it to me, as a gift it meant so much more. I'd starve in the streets before I'd sell it.

"Wait here," I said.

I went upstairs to my master's room. He was still asleep, his chest rising and falling softly. I didn't wake him. Instead, on the table beside his bed, I left the piece of apple pie I'd set aside for him. Back in the shop, I placed the open cube on the counter beside Master Galileo's book, right where Master Benedict would be sure to see it.

Tom was still fondling the shilling. "What are you going to do with this?"

"I don't know," I said. "Maybe I'll go see if I can find a best friend who'll help me spend it."

"I'm a best friend."

"Oh? Well, then, what do you think I should do with it?"

"Buy icy cream?" he said hopefully.

"Today? It's so cold out."

"I love the cold."

"You just said you hate the cold."

Tom looked indignant. "I never said that."

"All right." His face lit up, as bright as the fire. "But we have to save a penny."

"For what?" he said.

"What else?" I grinned. "Eggs."

It may be a lot of money, but on a holiday, a shilling doesn't go as far as you'd think. By late morning, the rain had stopped. The cobbled streets remained an awful muck, and the rain did nothing to ease the clogs in the gutters, so the roads smelled as horrid as ever. But the clouds broke, and the warmth of the sun reflected in the face of the city. Banners hung everywhere, strung from one balcony to another, flashing colors, patterns emblazoned brightly with the king's coat of arms. The crowds pressed, packing every street to see the sights, the gardens, the entertainers: jugglers and acrobats and musicians, even a dancing horse. And though it was officially a day of rest, the street vendors were out, calling like crows, trading on the goodwill of the holiday to charge ridiculous prices for treats people wouldn't otherwise buy.

I'd never bought anything in my life, as I'd never had any money. The few pounds I'd inherited as a baby had been saved by the masters at the orphanage to cover my admission fee to become an apprentice, and apprentices didn't get paid. As for Tom, his family sold a lot of pies, but he never had any money to spend, either, since his father kept his purse strings tighter than a hangman's noose.

So the shilling went. I spent the first four pennies on two orange water icy creams, as promised. The confectioner even let us make it ourselves, Tom furiously cranking the handle that churned the cream, milk, and sugar with the orange water in a bucket immersed in salted ice. It was so tasty, I bought a third icy cream for us to share, dripped this time with honey and lemon. After that went one penny each for walnut sugarplums and a handful of chewy chicle imported all the way from the New World, and two more for a lunch of hot, steaming lamb with spiced potatoes and peas slathered in chive butter. That left us with two: one for half a dozen gassy rotten eggs, the other burning a hole in my pocket.

The eggs, of course, were not for eating. On Oak Apple Day, everyone wore a sprig of oak to honor the return of our king, Charles II, the Merry Monarch, whose life was spared by God when he hid from Puritan traitors high in the branches of an oak tree. After a decade of exile and oppression, our king had regained his rightful place in 1660 after the tyrant Oliver Cromwell died and the city's government of brutal, joyless Puritans fell. Now London was allowed to have festivals—and fun—once more.

Only the most boring of men would stay indoors today—or Puritans, I suppose, who might have found it troubling to see children dancing around the maypoles, the girl in the lead waving a thick oak staff with a Puritan's sun-bleached skull rattling on top. As for everyone else, they'd better sport the oak on their lapel or they'd get pelted. Fruit was a popular choice, and mud was readily available. But I'd always felt that rotten eggs made a real statement.

The problem was that in the five years since our king had returned to us, everyone had learned their lesson. No one dared walk the streets ungarnished. We'd almost got lucky earlier, when an oak apple had fallen off a gentle-man's overcoat, but by the time we got there, he'd managed to pluck it out of the mud after being introduced to four tomatoes and an onion.

By late afternoon, I was getting restless. "This is ter-rible," I said. "What am I going to do with half a dozen rotten eggs?"

"Put them in one of your remedies?" Tom said.

I was just about to retort when I stopped in my tracks.

"What's the matter?" Tom said.

Nathaniel Stubb was the matter. I saw him, on the other side of Lombard Street. He was pushing through the crowd, swiping at children who got too close with his silver cane.

My blood grew hot. Master Benedict had claimed it wasn't Stubb who'd attacked him. I wasn't sure I believed him, and frankly, I didn't care. I wanted vengeance. And I'd have it, on that man over there.

That's when I saw his collar.

I couldn't believe my luck. Another birthday present, this one from God Himself.

I grabbed Tom's arm. "He's not wearing the oak," I said.

"Yes, he is." Tom pointed.

I deflated. He was. An absurdly small—pathetic, really—oak apple was hanging from Stubb's coat. It had slipped down its pin and now dangled loosely from his lapel.

Loosely?

Tom knew that look. "No, no, no."

"Yes, yes, yes," I said.

"That's not fair play."

"Only God may judge," I intoned. "Now go knock it off."

He looked panicked. "Me? No way."

"I can't do it. He knows who I am." Actually, he'd probably forgotten me again, but still.

"If he knows you," Tom said, "he might know me. Forget it."

"Please," I said. "Pleeeeeease. He's getting away."

But Tom folded his arms and wouldn't budge.

Then I had an idea. A *great* idea.

I ran ahead, Tom following reluctantly. Up on the corner, three parish boys, maybe nine or ten years old, were playing at jousting, sprinting at full speed toward each other with badly bent maple branches. A girl of about twelve sat on the stoop of a nearby fishmonger's stall, seemingly oblivious to the smell. She watched the action, twirling a lock of her auburn hair around her finger and petting a gray alley cat that sat purring in her lap.

"Hello," I said.

The boys stopped their game and eyed us warily; me with the eggs, and Tom just because he towered over everyone. One of the boys, thin and wiry, squared off against us with a curious combination of boldness and fear. "Wha'd'you want?"

I pointed at Stubb, on the other side of the street. "Knock his pin off, and I'll give you each an egg to throw."

To his credit, the boy considered it. Unfortunately, the swinging silver cane won the battle. "Nah. He'll hit me."

"Not if you're fast enough," I said. But he shook his head.

This was *so* frustrating. I turned to leave.

"I know you," a high voice said.

I turned back. It was the girl on the stoop who'd spoken.

"You were at Cripplegate," she said.

She surprised me. Few of the orphans at Cripplegate were girls, and they were housed separately. We saw them mostly at mealtimes, when older children were assigned to duties helping the masters and caring for the younger ones. I'd been placed in the kitchen, boiling broths under the supervision of the head cook, Sedley, who liked to crack his charges on the forehead with a long wooden spoon when they made a mistake. I'd taken enough spoons to the skull to eventually become pretty good at seasoning the soup.

In fact, my broths were how I became apprenticed to an apothecary in the first place. Occasionally, men of high standing would tour the school. One Sunday, when I was nine years old, Cripplegate was visited for dinner by the three members of the Apothecaries' Guild Council. As

I served the soup, one of the Council, Oswyn Colthurst, called me over.

I was completely awed by the apothecaries. From what little I'd read of them, they seemed to have talents that were almost magical. And while our headmaster, Reverend Talbot, always treated his guests with deference, the way he fawned over the Guild Council made me realize these were incredibly powerful men.

Though Oswyn was the most junior member of the Council, to me, he was the most fascinating of the three. He'd shaved his head bald, and against fashion, he wore no wig. He looked at me with intelligent eyes and said, "I'm told you're to thank for this delicious meal."

I tried not to stare at his scalp. "Just the broth, Master Colthurst," I stammered.

"The broth is the best part. You have a real talent for herbs."

He was probably just being kind to an orphaned boy—a man of his stature must have eaten at much better places than the dining hall at Cripplegate—but my heart still swelled under his praise. "Thank you, Master."

Reverend Talbot leaned over and said, "Christopher has a small sum left from his inheritance. We're planning to use that money to apprentice him to a cook."

"If he has the funds," Oswyn said, "why not send him to our Guild instead?"

Reverend Talbot seemed just as stunned as I was. Oswyn looked amused.

"You believe only men of high standing can become apothecaries?" he said. "On the contrary. All we require is a disciplined mind, an appreciation for nature, and a keen desire to learn." Oswyn gestured at me with his spoon. "Boys like Christopher, in fact, are exactly what our Guild needs more of: plain and simple Englishmen, who grew up knowing hard work." He returned to his meal. "Think on it, Reverend," he said, and from that casual remark, my path was set. The very next day, my studies—and, to my dismay, the beatings I got when I answered wrong—doubled in intensity. Reverend Talbot wouldn't tolerate my bringing shame to his school by failing the entrance test to the Apothecaries' Guild.

I studied the face of the girl on the stoop. I'd left the orphanage three years ago, so she would have been around nine at the time. She had big green eyes and a slightly upturned nose with a dusting of freckles across its bridge.

I *did* remember her. She'd come to Cripplegate a few years before I'd left, after her parents died on a merchant voyage to France. I'd helped the nurses care for her the last winter I was there, feeding her chicken broth for three weeks when she'd had a terrible case of the flux. Her name was . . . Susanna? Sarah?

It came to me. "Sally."

Her cheeks flushed, pleased that I'd remembered her. "What happened to you?" she said.

"I'm an apprentice. To Master Apothecary Benedict Blackthorn," I said proudly. She nodded, as if satisfied. "How much longer do you have?" I asked her.

"A couple of months, maybe. They've been trying to find me a job. But . . ." She shrugged.

I knew what she meant. The masters did their best to place the children before they turned thirteen, but not everyone ended up with a job or apprenticeship. If you aged out without anywhere to go . . . life on the streets wouldn't be good to you. Especially if you were a girl. I remembered how little I'd had at Cripplegate: nothing, really, but the slightest hope of something better. Sally barely had that.

I reached into my pocket and pulled out the last of my pennies. I held it out to her. "Here."

Her eyes went wide. The three parish boys stared with

her. One even took a step forward, but Sally was off the stoop before him, the cat springing from her lap and bolting around the corner, knocking over a wicker basket as it fled.

Sally clasped the coin to her palm. She stared at her knuckles, as if afraid the silver might leak out. I turned to go.

"Wait."

Sally nodded toward Stubb, who stood in the lane, waiting impatiently for a parade of brightly painted sheep to pass. "What did he do?"

"He threatened my master," I said.

She held out her hand. "Give me an egg."

I glanced over at Stubb's silver cane. I'd felt its sting before. "You don't have to."

"I want to."

I handed her one of the eggs. She rolled it in her fingers, not meeting my eyes.

"You made good soup," she said quietly. Then she wormed her way across the street.

The three boys clamored for an egg of their own. We all inched forward, hiding behind a carriage stopped by the side of the road. Tom, standing farther back, looked disapproving and muttered about there being rules and things.

If I hadn't been watching, I wouldn't have seen Sally do it. She darted in range of Stubb's cane and casually flicked the oak apple away. It fluttered down and landed on the cobbles.

A second later she shouted, "He's not wearing the oak!"

For a moment, Stubb didn't seem to understand what was happening. Then he realized everyone was staring at him. His hands went to his lapel, but all his fingers found was the sharp end of an empty pin. Stubb looked frantically at the ground.

I threw first. The egg shattered on his shoulder, sending yellow goop flying into his ear. He recoiled like he'd been shot with a musket.

Sally's egg hit him right in the neck, spraying all over his ruffled collar. The three boys followed. One missed entirely, hitting an already irritated sheep. The other two were square on, arm and hip.

The rest of the crowd joined in then, pelting Stubb with whatever they had. The most impressive was Tom. He'd slunk back so far I wasn't even sure his egg would make the distance, but it sailed past the fleeing Stubb's raised hands and pegged him right on the crown.

I laughed like I'd gone mad. Even Tom looked pleased. I shouted a joyful whoop as we fled. "Long live the king!"

We pushed through the crowd, running from the chaos. Fun was fun, but now that justice had been meted out, I really didn't want to get caught. Oak Apple Day or not, Stubb was a master of the Guild and I was just an apprentice. If it came to a matter of words, I wasn't going to be on the winning end. Still, there was something especially satisfying about the fact that the eggs that had plastered him had come from a shilling earned by my master's work.

"This is the best day ever," I said.

Tom scanned the crowd, looking for signs of pursuit. "What now?"

"I don't know." I leaned against the shutters of a glass-blower's shop and panted, trying to catch my breath. "We're out of money. Maybe there's sparring in the park. Or we could go to the Tower and see the king's zoo again. No. Wait."

I realized our flight had taken us just outside the borders of our parish. Hugh's home was nearby. "He left with Master Benedict last night," I told Tom. "Maybe Master Hugh knows who attacked him."

"Traitors!" a ragged voice cried out from behind.

I whirled, terrified that Stubb had tracked us down. Instead of the waddling apothecary, however, I saw a madman, his face cracked and weathered, his hair wigless and wild. His torn and tattered clothes barely covered his scabby limbs.

He stared goggle eyed at me. "Traitors!" he said again.

The man lunged forward and grabbed my arms. The stink of rotting meat came from between his blackened teeth. "There are traitors in our midst!"

I felt the crowd's eyes on me. I tried to pull away, but the man's grip was like iron. "Get off!" I said.

"Do you know them? Do you see?" The man shook me. "The Cult of the Archangel hunts. Who is its prey?"

Tom tried to push between us, but even his strong hands on my captor's stained jacket couldn't pry the man off. The lunatic leaned in farther. I thought I might throw up from the stench.

"They are not who you think," he whispered, sending furtive glances at the curious crowd. "Those are not their faces."

Tom finally managed to shove the man away. He sprawled across the cobbles, the mud adding more stains to his filthy, threadbare breeches.

"Guard yourself," the man said beseechingly. "Change is coming. God's wrath will burn us all. Look! His general rides!"

He pointed behind us, but Tom had had enough. He pulled me protectively into the shelter of the crowd, which had begun to jeer at the madman on the ground.

"Thanks," I said. I rubbed my arms. They still hurt where the man had gripped me.

Tom glanced over his shoulder to see if the man was coming back. "Are you all right?"

In honesty, I was rattled. "What was that about?"

"What do you mean? The man was mad."

"Didn't you hear what he said?"

The Cult of the Archangel. Though the day had turned warm, I shivered. I thought of my master's burnt shoulder, and of Stubb's visit to our shop last night.

Change is coming. The apothecary had said exactly the same thing.

Tom scoffed. "So what? I'm surprised he didn't warn us the Moon was made of cheese."

A buzz passed through the crowd around us. At first, I thought it was because of the madman, but it seemed like it came from the opposite direction. Tom craned his neck, peering over everyone's heads. Suddenly, he grabbed my elbow. "Look!"

I stepped onto a nearby crate and spied what Tom was

seeing. It was a pair of soldiers. They were armored in padded leather, broadswords on one side, flintlock pistols on the other. Their beige tabards were emblazoned in the center of their chests with the king's coat of arms. Though the press of the crowd was heavy, they pushed through roughly, opening a space for the man who followed them.

His clothes were finely made, obviously the work of a master tailor. Yet the tightly fitting satin seemed out of place on him, as if someone had tried to dress up a panther. Like the King's Men before him, he carried his own pair of weapons, a heavy, battle-worn sword and a pearl-handled pistol. But it was the dark black wells of his eyes that made the crowd fall silent as he passed. His left cheek was a mess of scars, a gnarled trail of flesh from nose to neck.

"That's him!" Tom whispered. "That's Lord Ashcombe." He pulled my arm. "Come on."

We followed in his wake, Tom's bulk pushing our own path through the crowd. The soldiers guided Lord Ashcombe to an alley that wound behind a row of enormous houses and opened into a long, airy space. Most of the clearing was blocked by a tall, ornate wrought-iron fence. Behind it was a private garden, well tended.

Five men waited on the stone path beside a dug-up

flower bed, under the drooping branches of a willow tree, in front of a large statue of an angel. One of the men held a shovel. Another paced. A third gripped the leash of a hunting dog, its paws and muzzle covered with mud. The dog barked madly at the ground. It looked like it had discovered something.

When Lord Ashcombe reached the gate, a man wearing the sash of the parish constable straightened himself in salute.

"Open it," Lord Ashcombe said. His voice grated, like a demon's whisper.

The constable turned the key in the padlock that held the gate closed. Lord Ashcombe went inside. The constable locked the gate behind him as the trailing throng pressed against the fence. I squeezed through to the front and grabbed a railing. Tom managed to make it behind me, his hands gripping my shoulders, holding himself in place against the jostling crowd.

Lord Ashcombe moved to where the others waited. The flower bed had turned to mud in the morning's rain. The man with the shovel had finished what the dog had started, digging a long hole in the dirt. The stone angel behind it looked down, wings folded, an expression of sorrow on his face. The King's Warden stared with him, then crouched down and reached inside.

He came up with what looked like a muddy club. It wasn't.

Lord Ashcombe brushed off the dirt. The men beside him backed away. The crowd gasped. Lord Ashcombe's expression stayed as still as the angel's.

It was an arm. A man's arm, torn from his body, mangled, blackened, and burnt.

CHAPTER
7

TOM AND I BURST INTO THE SHOP, tumbling over ourselves.

"Master!" I said. "There's been another mur—"

I broke off. Master Benedict was kneeling beside the counter, trying to gather cream-covered pieces of pottery from a shattered jar with his bandaged hands. A second, smaller jar, fallen beside the first, had cracked a chunk off at the bottom and was pumping out the last of the boar's blood. The scarlet liquid ran in rivulets down the seams of the floorboards and stained the knees of his breeches.

I went to him. "Are you all right?"

He held up his hands, fingertips poking through bulky

cloth. "These bandages are decidedly inconvenient."

I knelt beside him. "I'll take care of this, Master. You should be resting."

"I'm fine." He continued to collect the slippery shards until I placed my hands on his. He sighed, then nodded. "We'll need more burn cream."

"I'll make it tonight," I said.

I began to collect pieces of the broken jars. Tom came to help, dodging the boar's blood that tracked across the floor as if it hunted his shoes.

"I'll get some sand," Tom said.

"Bring the sawdust instead," I said. "It's in a tub next to the oven in the workshop."

Tom hauled the heavy tub from the back a lot more easily than I could have. We scooped up handfuls of sawdust and dumped them on the floor. The sawdust clumped, turning red, soaking the blood up quickly.

Master Benedict watched us, curious. "This is why you collect sawdust?"

I nodded. "The masters at the orphanage used it. It's better for spills than sand. Gets rid of the smell, too," which was a blessing when fifty sick children were squirting fluids from every end.

It was funny how fascinated Master Benedict seemed by the sawdust. Cleaning spills was the apprentice's job, so it's not something he'd given any thought to since I'd joined him. Still, using sawdust instead of sand was so ordinary; it hardly seemed to deserve my master's interest. It was just a simple technique I'd grown up with. And I thought he knew everything.

He stared out the window, lost in thought. Then his eyes widened. He grabbed my shoulders.

"Master?" I said, startled.

He shook me. "Magnificent, boy. Well done. So very well done."

Without even stopping to clean the cream off his shirt, he grabbed his coat from its hook and threw it on. Then he ran into the street.

"Wait! Master! I need to change your dressing!" I shouted after him, but he'd already darted behind a rattling carriage and vanished into the holiday crowd. He hadn't even taken his sash of ingredients with him; it still hung on the hook behind the counter.

Tom gave me a sidelong glance. "Madmen everywhere today," he muttered. For once, I couldn't disagree.

SATURDAY, MAY 30, 1665

The Feast of the Burning of
Joan of Arc, Heretic

CHAPTER

8

I DIDN'T KNOW WHAT TO DO.

After cleaning up the spill, I'd made a new batch of Blackthorn's Soothing Burn Cream as promised. Then Tom and I went up to the roof, where we sat, legs dangling over the edge, with fistfuls of corn. Half of it we fed to Bridget, who hopped between our shoulders. The rest we dropped over the side, trying to catch the kernels in the wigs of gentlemen passing below. When Tom finally had to go home, I curled up by the fire in the shop with Master Galileo's book, waiting for my own master to return.

I must have drifted off, because I awoke with the cry of six, still in the chair. The fire long dead, the chill had settled into my bones, and my back ached like I'd spent the night shackled to the Tower of London's least comfortable rack.

I prepared the shop for opening, sweeping the floors of yesterday's now-dried mud. I checked the stocks and made a note of what we needed from Monday's market. Then I went up to the roof to feed the pigeons. While coming back down, it struck me: With all of London outside for yesterday's holiday, the cobblestone streets had been thick with mud. But there were no new tracks on the stairs.

The door to Master Benedict's quarters was closed. "Master?" I called.

No answer.

I knocked, lightly. "Master? It's morning."

Still no answer.

Normally, I would have left him alone. But there was nothing normal about Master Benedict sleeping in on a workday. I went inside. His room was empty, his bed still made.

He hadn't returned.

I knocked next door, at Sinclair the confectioner's, and on the other side, at Grobham the tailor's, but neither master nor apprentice had seen him. The servers in the Missing Finger, the tavern across the street, where we sometimes ate supper, hadn't seen him either.

Worry fluttered in my stomach. I thought about the body Tom and I had seen yesterday, burned and buried beneath the angel in the private garden, and it wasn't until I got hold of myself that I remembered I'd seen my master well after that poor man had been murdered.

A voice pulled me from terrible thoughts. "Boy. Boy!"

Outside our shuttered shop, a pudgy woman in a faded green dress waved a ceramic jar at me. I recognized her: Margaret Wills, one of Baron Cobley's servants.

"I need a refill," she hollered.

Syrup of ipecac, an emetic. I crossed the street, grumbling inside. I had bigger worries than Baron Cobley's vomit.

I let her into the shop, then donned my blue apron and refilled her jar. I made a note of it in the ledger, adding the cost to the baron's tab, which was already the size of a whale. I'd planned to lock up and go look for my master again, but as Margaret left, Francis the publican came in with a nasty bottom rash. I took care of him—the prescription, anyway; he'd have to put the ointment on himself—and then Jonathan Tanner arrived, and before I knew it the shop was packed.

And then finally, finally, finally, Master Benedict stepped in from the workshop.

I felt like a sack of lead had been lifted from my back. He was all right. In fact, other than the bags under his eyes, he looked very pleased indeed. I didn't get the chance to speak to him; he barely got a pace inside before he was swarmed. He sent a weary smile in my direction and got to work.

By lunchtime, we'd whittled the horde down to five; me with William Fitz and his seeping earlobe, Master Benedict with Lady Brent's swollen hand, and three more waiting before we could break. I'd just finished writing up Mr. Fitz's account in the ledger when Lady Brent said, "Are you listening to me, Mr. Blackthorn?"

My master, standing behind the counter, stared past her out the front of the shop. I tried to see what he was looking at, but there was a customer blocking the window: a stocky boy of around sixteen, wearing his own blue apron, smirking at the still-unrepaired bear in the corner.

"Mr. Blackthorn?" she said again.

He blinked. "One moment, madam. I need to check our stock."

When he returned, a minute later, he looked pale.

"Well?" Lady Brent said. "Can you make it?"

Master Benedict wiped his forehead. "Yes. Yes, of course. It will be ready Monday."

He really didn't look well. I tried to catch his eye, but he barely glanced at me. He turned away, scanning the shelves, then went to the ledger on the counter.

"Christopher!" he barked.

I jumped.

"Come here," he said.

I went around the counter. My master no longer looked ill. He looked furious.

He stabbed a bony finger at the ledger. "Did you serve Baron Cobley this morning?"

"Yes, Master," I stammered. "His maidservant."

"And did I not ask you—twice—to collect his account the next time she came?"

Had he? "I . . . I'm sorry, Master, I don't remember—"

He hit me.

He smacked me on the side of my jaw, an open-handed blow that cracked like a thunderclap. I stumbled into the shelf hard enough to make the jars rattle.

"You are *useless*," he said.

I stayed there, hunched against the wood. My cheek burned. It hurt worse inside. I felt all the customers' eyes on me, Lady Brent watching curiously, the boy by the door freshly entertained by the show behind the counter.

"Do something right," Master Benedict said. "For once." He snatched a handful of pennies and a few worn shillings from the strongbox. "Go to the Exchange and purchase all the natron they carry. And don't return until you have."

"But—" His narrowing eyes stopped me. I bowed my head. "Yes, Master."

"And get Lady Brent her electuary. And the lemon juice."

I brought him the jars. He huffed. "I apologize for my apprentice, Lady Brent," he said.

"Not necessary, Mr. Blackthorn," she said. "Servants need firm correction. My husband purchased a bamboo whip from the Orient for just this purpose."

"Did he buy an elephant as well? It would take a kick from one to fix this boy."

She laughed. So did he.

I fled.

I barely saw where I was going. I was so blind, I almost walked straight into an older boy twice Tom's size throwing dice with a long-haired friend in the alley behind our house. I mumbled an apology and went around them, each step echoing the pounding in my head.

He'd hit me.

My cheek still stung. My hand hurt, too. It wasn't until I looked down that I realized it was because I was clenching the coins he'd given me so tightly, they'd cut into my skin.

I didn't understand. I'd swear on my life he hadn't asked me to collect Baron Cobley's account. And sending me for natron . . . natron came to market on Wednesdays. They'd be out of stock by now.

Something had to be wrong. I'd seen Master Benedict angry before, made him angry before, but never like this. I wanted to go back, talk to him, plead with him to tell me what I'd done. But he'd ordered me not to return.

And he'd hit me.

I wiped my eyes on my sleeve.

The Royal Exchange was packed. Traders, jammed shoulder to shoulder, hawked their wares, shouting, haggling, arguing. I went to every stall and each time got the same answer.

"Nothing today, lad. Try next Wednesday."

I hunted for hours. I even considered going to another apothecary, but they'd mark the cost high, and Master Benedict wouldn't be pleased. In the end, I gave up and went home while it was still light. I was afraid of what my master would say. But I needed to know what was wrong. And I wanted to speak to him, say I was sorry, go back to the way things were.

I came in through the workshop, too scared to show up in the store empty handed. Strangely, the back door wasn't locked, and the shutters on the back windows were closed. In the furnace, dying embers gave off just enough light to see. I frowned when I saw the tongs left in the ashes. I moved to pull them out, then jerked my hand away with a curse.

I sucked my fingers. The tongs burned. They must have been sitting in the fire for ages.

A small glass jar sat open next to the oven, its lid on the floor. Scattered nearby were a handful of tiny, black, kidney-shaped seeds. I picked one up, rolled it between my fingers. It smelled faintly of rotten tomatoes.

Madapple. The first remedy Master Benedict had ever taught me. In small doses, it helped asthma patients breathe. Any more than that, it became a deadly poison. What was the jar doing left open?

I couldn't hear any conversation from the shop. The light in the open doorway was as dim as in here. I frowned again. Sunset was still a few hours away. The shop shouldn't be quiet.

I moved toward the door. My shoes squelched. I lifted a foot and saw a pool of liquid underneath. Streaks led away from it, long dark tracks, as if something heavy had been dragged, leaking.

I followed them. The shop's shutters were closed, the fire dead in here, too. The front door was locked, the bolt thrown. The sodden trail smeared across the floorboards, turning crimson. A smell, hot, metallic, filled the room. And there, in the middle of it all, was my master.

They'd left him slumped against the front of the counter, his wrists and ankles bound with rope. His shirt was ripped apart. His stomach, too. His eyes were open, and he stared back at me, but he couldn't see me, and he wouldn't, never, ever again.

CHAPTER
9

THEY ALL CAME. SINCLAIR THE
confectioner, and Grobham the tailor, and Francis the
publican and his servers. Others came too, neighbors and
strangers. Crammed in. Gawking.

By the time they'd arrived, I'd already cut the ropes that
had bound my master and laid him out on the floor. The
scraps of rope lay beside him, next to the woolen blanket I'd
used to cover his body, now stained red. I was stained, too,
from when I'd held him.

Now I sat beside him, my hand over the blanket, resting on top of his chest. Everyone else stood around, useless.
Just like me.

Sinclair leaned over. "Come, lad," he said gently. "Let's get you out of here."

I swatted him away. I didn't want them here. This was our home.

So many, staring. I wanted to lie down, to sink into the floorboards, to go to sleep. To never wake up.

Someone else cleared the room for me. Bad news travels on wings.

It was the King's Men, the two soldiers I saw yesterday. They pushed through the crowd, the same man following them. Everyone went silent.

Lord Ashcombe stepped forward, stood beside me. Up close, his scarred cheek twisted like a map of hell.

He tilted his head toward the mob. "Get out," he said.

For a moment, no one moved. Lord Ashcombe turned, barely a glance over his shoulder. He didn't have to ask again.

I stayed with my master while the others shuffled out. One of the King's Men put a hand on my collar. I smelled oiled leather and sweat.

"Leave him," Lord Ashcombe said.

The soldier took his place beside his partner, guarding the door. Lord Ashcombe crouched and pulled the woolen blanket away. His eyes flicked over my master's body, his face, his blood. I traced a thumbnail in the grain of the wood.

"You found him?" Lord Ashcombe said.

I nodded.

"You are?"

"Christopher Rowe," I said. "He was my master."

The King's Warden looked at the ropes I'd sliced from Master Benedict's body. The ends, frayed and feathery, had already begun to soak up his blood. "Why did you cut these away?"

I looked up at Lord Ashcombe. "What was I supposed to do?"

For a moment, he didn't respond. Then: "Say what you know."

I told him. Most of it, anyway. Opening the shop. Master Benedict's return. Being sent for natron. Coming back. I didn't say he'd hit me. I didn't tell him the last words he'd said.

Kneeling next to me, Lord Ashcombe scanned the room. I could feel his heat. "Did your master often stay out all night?"

"Never," I said. "He went out most evenings, but he always came back around midnight."

"Why not yesterday?"

"I don't know."

"Was he in a dispute with anyone?"

"Nathaniel Stubb," I said. "The apothecary. He wants our shop. He threatened my master." I told him about Stubb's visit on Thursday night. "And someone attacked him that evening." I pulled the dressing from my master's shoulder to show the burn underneath. His flesh was so cold.

"Was your master especially devout?" Lord Ashcombe said.

The question threw me. "I . . . yes. He took me to services on Sunday, and he honored the festivals."

"Church of England?"

"Of course."

"And how did he feel about His Majesty?"

That made me angry. "He was loyal. Always. Like every true Englishman."

Lord Ashcombe stood. He stepped over to the shelves. Slowly, he traced a finger across the spines of the books. Then he stopped.

"I thought you said your master was Church of England."

"He was."

Lord Ashcombe pulled a tome from the shelves. It was large, and bound in light brown leather. He held it out so I could see the cover: *The Saints of Roman Catholic Virtue*.

Master Benedict had given me that to read, three months earlier. "It's just a book," I said. "Part of my studies. We're Church of England. Ask Reverend Wright."

Lord Ashcombe flipped through the pages, studying the illustrations. "Do you have any more works on religion?" he said. "Or the worlds beyond? On heaven, or hell?"

"Master Benedict has books on everything." *Had*, I thought. Not *has*. Not anymore.

"Did he talk to you about what he was reading?"

"Every day."

Lord Ashcombe looked up from the book. "And did he ever talk about the Cult of the Archangel?"

The words of the madman echoed in my skull. *The Cult of the Archangel hunts*. I wrapped my arms around myself. My bloodstained shirt stuck wetly to my chest.

Bitterness swelled inside. Lord Ashcombe was His Majesty's protector. Where was *our* protector? Where was the King's Warden when we needed him? Why had they come after us? Why did they have to hurt my master?

And where had *I* been, while he was dying? When Master Benedict needed me?

I bowed my head.

"Well?" Lord Ashcombe said.

"Master Benedict didn't believe there was a cult," I said.

Lord Ashcombe grunted, as if I'd just said something incredibly stupid. Sitting beside the Cult's obvious handiwork, I guess I had.

"So," he said. "Lady Brent was the last customer he saw before he sent you out?"

"No," I said. "William Fitz was here, and Samuel Waltham. There were two more. I don't know who they were."

"Describe them."

I tried to picture them. "There was an apprentice, about sixteen years old. A little taller than me. Big. Muscles, not fat. Reddish hair. The other was a man, maybe thirty or so. I didn't really look at him. He was wealthy, I think. His coat was nice. He had a long black wig, the kind with the curls over the ears. His nose was crooked, like it had been broken."

"Anyone else waiting around outside? Casing the shop?"

I didn't remember seeing anyone casing the shop. Then

again, I hadn't been paying attention to anything when I'd left. I'd been too busy feeling sorry for myself. Now I felt so ashamed.

"You were gone for the afternoon," Lord Ashcombe said, and I nodded. "So others could have come in."

Suddenly, I stiffened. "The ledger." Lord Ashcombe looked blank. "We keep track of everything we sell," I said. "If there were other customers—" I broke off.

"What's wrong?"

"The ledger," I said. "It's gone."

It wasn't on the counter anymore. The inkwell was still there, unstoppered. There was blood, too, already drying a crusty brown, smeared on the side of the wood. Otherwise, the counter was empty. I walked around it to see if the ledger had fallen behind it, but the book wasn't there, either. Just my straw mattress and pillow, my puzzle cube and knife resting on top, and the empty strongbox. I turned it over.

"They took our money," I said.

Lord Ashcombe pointed. "What's that?"

There it was. The ledger was on a shelf, under the jar of lemon juice, the one Master Benedict had ordered me to bring him before I left. The quill was on top of the leather cover, or at least the pieces of it were. Someone had snapped it in two.

Lord Ashcombe got there first. He tugged the ledger from under the jar, leaving the ceramic rattling on the wood. He laid the book on the counter and opened it, flipping pages until he got to the end. I could still smell the citrus tang of the lemon.

He studied it for a moment. "I can't read this," he said.

I hadn't expected him to. In the ledger, Master Benedict wrote names and remedies in shorthand, and often in Latin. He'd taught me the same code. We did it partly because it was faster, and partly because it was another way to keep our business secret.

Most of the day's entries were mine. The last three were in my master's hand.

†∆ *esid.* A: *rapf.* O *set. age* Htsn. *oil eh. two leb.* Ht4: *shg. Uh.* ←

↓Mo8→   *end.swords*

neminidixeris

I stared.

Lord Ashcombe watched me. "Something wrong?" he said.

"I . . . no." I felt my face grow hot. "These are . . . notes. Reminders to buy more ingredients we're out of. Oil of vitriol, and . . . others. The numbers say how much." I left my hand on the page. "He didn't write down Lady Brent's sale. Or anyone after."

The black wells of Lord Ashcombe's eyes seemed to bore right through me. *He knows*, I thought. *He knows you're lying.*

He was about to speak when the front door creaked open. He turned. So did the guards.

I did it without thinking. My fingers clenched around the page and pulled just before I snapped the ledger shut. With the commotion at the door, and the noise from the street, no one appeared to notice I'd ripped it out.

CHAPTER
10

I STUCK MY HANDS BEHIND MY
back and folded the paper. Then I lifted my shirt and
slipped the crumpled page under my waistband.

An ancient man limped through the door, leaning on a
gnarled wooden cane. One of the soldiers put a hand on his
chest, stopping him. The man waited calmly.

The paper from the ledger slipped a little down my back.

"Let him in," Lord Ashcombe said.

I recognized him, and the two that followed, though I
hadn't seen any of them in three years. They were the members of the Apothecaries' Guild Council.

The limping man, dressed from waistcoat to breeches

in emerald silk, was Sir Edward Thorpe, Grand Master of Apothecaries. He'd been the head of our Guild since before I was born. There were whispers that he'd kept himself alive by discovering the elixir of youth. If he had, then he must have walked the Earth with Moses, because Sir Edward looked a few thousand years old. Even his wig was gray.

The men with him were the Guild Wardens, Valentine Grey and Oswyn Colthurst. I barely knew Valentine, more by rumor than anything. He was the Guild Secretary, and was said to be the wealthiest apothecary in the city. Certainly, the gold chain around his neck was thick enough to see all the way from heaven. He was also said to be a bit of a scold, and there was a sourness in the downturn of his lips that made me suspect the rumors were true.

Oswyn, I remembered well. He was the one who'd encouraged the headmaster at the orphanage to send me to the Guild. He'd also given me the Apothecaries' Guild entrance test. Since he'd wanted me to join, I'd figured he'd go easy on me. Instead, I'd ended up trembling in front of him as he grilled me with a stern voice and sharp eyes on science, mathematics, history, theology, and especially Latin. He'd thought to trip me up there, but I'd earned enough beatings at the orphanage to speak Latin like

Julius Caesar. At the time, sweating through the exam, I'd thought the man was a tyrant. But after I'd passed the test, while Sir Edward and Valentine had merely nodded their congratulations, it was Oswyn who'd smiled and welcomed me warmly to the Guild.

No smiles today. He nodded to me sadly before joining the rest of the Council over my master's body. Valentine breathed, "God preserve us," and made the sign of the cross. Oswyn folded his arms and turned away.

Sir Edward shook his head gravely and spoke to Lord Ashcombe in a voice fuller than I'd imagined his ancient body could hold. "Our Guild is under attack, Richard. We beg His Majesty's aid."

"And I'm here, Edward," Lord Ashcombe said.

"Doing what, precisely?" Oswyn said, his voice filled with scorn.

Lord Ashcombe's retort was just as hostile. "My job, Puritan."

I'd seen Lord Ashcombe darken at the sight of Oswyn. Now I knew why.

I hadn't realized Oswyn was a Puritan. His dress was simple compared to the other two Council members', certainly, just an ordinary brown wool coat over plain clean linen, and his shaved head, wigless, set him distinctly apart from the other men. There was also a definite severity to him: His stinging rebukes when I failed a question on the Apothecaries' Guild entrance test landed as harshly as Reverend Talbot's quick fists ever had. But when I'd spoken to him afterward, I'd realized he hadn't come at me so strongly just to be mean. He'd needed to make sure I was ready to be an apprentice. "There are many here who won't be happy to count an orphan among them," he'd said, waving at the other boys and masters milling around the hall. "They'll be waiting for you to fail. But don't doubt yourself, Christopher. The measure of a man has nothing to do with where he comes from." After that, I'd felt a lot better about growing up at Cripplegate than I ever had before. So, Puritan or not, he didn't seem so awful to me.

Still, I supposed Lord Ashcombe, who'd been exiled for nine years with King Charles in France and the Netherlands, had plenty of reasons to feel differently. When our king returned, Lord Ashcombe had spearheaded the purge of Puritans from the ranks of power. Those who were proven traitors—and some who weren't—were executed. The way he glared at Oswyn now made me think the King's Warden wanted to add another head to the pikes on London Bridge.

Sir Edward placed a soothing hand on Oswyn's arm. "Forgive my colleague's abruptness, Richard. But his point has purpose. Benedict Blackthorn is the fourth of our Guild to fall."

"Then maybe one of you could tell me about the Cult of the Archangel," Lord Ashcombe said.

Sir Edward frowned. "You think the killer is an apothecary?"

"Our Guild members are honest men," Valentine said, managing to look even more sour. "And loyal to the Crown."

"Some of you," Lord Ashcombe said.

Oswyn stiffened. Before he could respond, the door slammed open, and in stepped Nathaniel Stubb.

Rage boiled inside me. My blood was on fire. To have this rat in my home twisted the knife already stuck in my heart.

The King's Men grabbed him. "Unhand me!" he said.

"Who is this?" Lord Ashcombe said.

Stubb tried to pull away. "I'm here to register a claim against the assets of this shop."

"Not now, Nathaniel," Oswyn said, looking irritated.

"I have a right," he said.

I knew I shouldn't say anything, especially in front of

the Guild Council. An apprentice wasn't allowed to speak without permission. But something broke inside me. Or maybe it was already broken. "You have no rights here," I spat.

The Council stared at me, shocked. Even Lord Ashcombe raised an eyebrow.

"How dare you!" Stubb said. He turned to the King's Warden. "Arrest him, sir! This boy assaulted me."

"What are you talking about?" Oswyn said.

"Yesterday. He and some hooligan children attacked me in the street."

Everyone looked at me questioningly. It appeared Stubb had seen me with the eggs after all. "He wasn't wearing the oak," I muttered, and once it dawned on the Guild Council what I meant, they actually looked embarrassed. Under normal circumstances, there would have been trouble. Standing over my master's body, no one cared.

Especially Lord Ashcombe. "This is Stubb, then." He turned to the apothecary. "You had an argument with Benedict Blackthorn on Thursday."

"What are you saying? Let me go!" Stubb finally managed to pull away from the footmen. I could tell by their crinkled noses they didn't really mind not touching him anymore.

Valentine seemed to be losing patience with Stubb, too. "What's the basis for your claim against this shop?" he said, frowning.

"My dispute with Benedict is well known, sir. He was stealing my secrets. By the laws of our Guild, I'm entitled to fair compensation."

"You're a liar," I said.

Valentine's jaw dropped. "Watch your mouth, boy."

"Everyone be *silent*." Sir Edward spoke softly, but even Stubb, his face beet red, went quiet. "We are perfectly aware of our own laws, Master Stubb. As *you* should be aware, any claims against a member's assets are for the *Council* to decide." He glared at Stubb, who shrank under the old man's gaze. "First, we will need to determine who now owns this property."

"Benedict's will should be in our records," Oswyn said. "I'll have the clerks pull it."

"Is this acceptable to the Crown?" Sir Edward said.

Lord Ashcombe shrugged. "Your business isn't my interest."

Sir Edward turned to me. "You. Er . . ."

"Christopher Rowe," Oswyn said.

"Present yourself to the Guild Hall on Monday, Rowe. We'll address your situation if time permits."

I wanted to rage, at all of them. But I still had enough sense left to know yelling at the Grand Master would be very, very bad. So I just ground my teeth and said, "May I speak, Grand Master?"

"You'll have leave to speak on Monday," he said. "And when you do, apprentice, it would serve you to remember your place." He looked around the shop. "For now, you'll need to find somewhere to live."

My stomach twisted. As I'd sat beside my master on the floor, a question, dirty and shameful, had wormed its way into the back of my mind. *What's going to happen to me?* I guess I had my answer. "*Blackthorn* is my home," I said.

"You can't stay here, boy," Valentine said. He waved at my master's body. "Not with this . . . evil."

"But . . ." I struggled to find a reason. "I . . . have to feed the pigeons," is the best I could come up with.

"Someone from the Guild will care for them," Oswyn said. "This shop is no longer your responsibility."

His eyes flicked from me to the Grand Master, a warning. *Hold your tongue.* I could only do that by biting it. Silently, I went behind the counter and grabbed my puzzle cube.

"What's he doing?" Stubb said. "Stop him!"

Lord Ashcombe did. "What's that?"

I showed it to him. "Master Benedict gave it to me for my birthday."

"He's stealing it," Stubb said.

"He *gave* it to me!" I shouted. "It's *mine*!"

Valentine held out his hand. "Let me see it." The Guild Secretary inspected it, then handed it to Oswyn, who turned it over curiously.

"Is it silver?" Sir Edward asked Valentine.

"Tin, I think."

Oswyn shook his head. "Antimony."

If Stubb touched it, I'd scream. "It's mine," I said again.

Sir Edward regarded me sternly. "An apprentice has no possessions." He took my cube from Oswyn and placed it on the counter. "It stays here. Ownership shall be decided by the will."

He was right. According to law, everything, even my bloodstained clothes, belonged to my master. I wondered bitterly if they were going to dump me naked in the street.

Clearly, Stubb had considered it. "Search him. He might have something else."

I froze. In my rage, I'd forgotten. I *did* have something else. Suddenly, the paper slipping down the back of my waistband felt like a blade against my skin. If they found it, there'd be questions I couldn't answer. And Lord Ashcombe would try to make me. In the Tower dungeon. With hot coals.

But the Guild Council looked disgusted that Stubb had even suggested it. "Oh, do shut up, Nathaniel," Oswyn said, and I could breathe again. I wasn't going to the Tower.

But the Cult of the Archangel had taken my master. And now the Council had taken my home.

CHAPTER
11

TOM'S FATHER STOOD IN THE DOOR-
way and folded his doughy arms. "Absolutely not."

"But, Father—" Tom began.

William Bailey jerked a sausagelike thumb at the five small girls peeking from behind him. It made his whole body jiggle. "I have enough mouths to feed. Can he pay for his lodging? Will he work?"

"He works harder than anyone," Tom said.

"Well, I don't need more hands."

My heart sank. It was no accident that Tom and I rarely spent time at his place. His father was just plain mean.

Tom's younger sisters tugged at their father's flour-crusted apron. "Please, Father, let him stay, please." They were kind girls, like Tom, taking after their mother. They also knew that if I stayed, I'd read them stories for bed.

In fact, it was Tom's mother who settled it. Mary Bailey, half as tall as her husband but just as round, leaned out the window on the third floor and hollered. "Let him in, Bill. We can afford this charity. It's the Christian thing to do."

Tom's father pointed down the street. "The church is right over there."

A soggy towel landed on his shoulder with a splat. "William Bailey! Shame on you." Tom's mother snapped her fingers at me. "You come up here this instant, Christopher."

William Bailey glared at me, but he let me pass. Tom got a slap across the head.

Trailed by a gaggle of Baileys, I went up to Tom's parents' bedroom. Mrs. Bailey shooed her giggling daughters back down the steps and sat me at the table by the window.

An old wooden bed, its mattress squashed with the weight of years, was pressed against the wall. There was a worn velvet settee in one corner, and a set of drawers, faded yellow paint flaking off, in the other. The table in front of me was the only concession to wealth, with intricately carved cherry legs that curved upward to a thick slab of white stone. On top was a tin basin; beside it, a rough, mottled towel. A silver mirror was set into the back.

"I was just about to wash," Tom's mother said. "You can have my water." She sized me up. "I haven't thrown away Tom's old things yet. I'm sure some of them will fit you." She left, and I was alone.

I pulled off my apprentice's apron. It cracked with dried blood. My shirt, equally ruined, joined the apron on the floor. The folded page I'd torn from the ledger came loose from my waistband and tumbled down to land beside my clothes.

I looked in the mirror. My reflection stared back. It seemed so still, so calm.

Everything's fine, it said.

But it, too, was painted with blood, streaked across my cheek. I remembered the softness of my master's chest, where I'd pressed my face against him.

I dipped a finger in the basin, sending ripples across the surface. I brought my hand up and drew a line through the blood. A drop of crimson water trickled down my palm and fell from my wrist. It splattered on the marble, an ugly pink blot.

I was alone.

For the first time since I'd found him, I was alone.

I couldn't speak. I couldn't breathe. All I could do was sob.

Despair swallowed me, like a demon. It howled in my head, crushed my chest, spiked claws into my soul and pulled. *Come,* it said. *It's peaceful here.* I wanted to go. I wanted to die. I wished so much that the Cult had taken me, too.

A breeze from the window brushed my hair against my eyelids. At my feet, I heard the rustling of paper. It was the page I'd torn from the ledger. Pushed by the wind, it fluttered and scraped across the floorboards.

Despair chanted, reached for me, called me back.

No, I said.

I punched the table. Hard. It echoed like a hammer. The skin on my middle finger split at the knuckle. Blood oozed out, dripped down, mixed with my master's in the water on the stone.

My hand throbbed. The pain brought me back to life.

Because you are *alive, Christopher. He kept you alive. That's why he sent you away.*

And he left you a message.

The paper trembled in the breeze, then stilled. I straightened in the chair, pressed against it. The oak dug lines in my back.

I wanted to go to sleep, to sleep forever. To see my master again. And I would.

But not yet.

Master Benedict had left me that message in the ledger for a reason. Whatever was on that page was so important that he'd stayed to write it down instead of running for his life.

He needed me. Three years ago, I'd needed him, and he'd saved me, brought me to Blackthorn, gave me my first real home. That life was gone now, stolen along with his. It didn't matter. He needed me. Even in death.

I wiped my eyes, my heart still burning. I shouted from the flames, so he'd hear me all the way in heaven. *I promise you, Master. Whatever you asked of me, I'll do. I won't cry. I won't rest. I won't fail.*

And I'll find whoever killed you. I'll make them pay. Before God and all His Saints, I swear it.

There was a knock on the door. Tom's mother called through it. "Christopher? Is everything all right?"

I looked in the mirror. My reflection spoke back.

"Everything's fine," it said.

CHAPTER

12

TOM'S MOTHER ADJUSTED MY COLLAR.
"There," she said. "That's not so bad."

Tom had grown so big so quickly, she'd had to go back three years to find something of his that fit me. Now I was kitted in a pair of brown wool and linen breeches and a white linen shirt with a burgundy stain down its sleeve. I remembered the shirt. Tom had been wearing it the day I'd met him.

It was three months after I'd first become an apprentice. Master Benedict had given me a book on ancient warfare to study. After reading about catapults, I became fascinated with the idea of building one. Master Benedict let me use some spare wood from the workshop and a fresh set of maple branches to do it. On Sunday, after service, I'd lugged my miniature siege engine north to Bunhill Fields to test it out, carrying a selection of rotting fruits as ammunition in a burlap sack over my shoulder.

As it turned out, the catapult launched things very well. It just wasn't especially accurate. I stared with horror as the first thing I fired—a profoundly overripe pomegranate— careened wildly to the left and bonked a rather large boy on the top of his head, squirting juice all over his shirt.

Puzzled, he looked up at the clouds, as if wondering why God was pelting him with pomegranates. Then he spotted my little catapult on the grass. He came toward me holding a very young girl in his arms, who laughed with delight as small, burgundy seeds dripped from the boy's hair onto his collar.

My first thought was to run as fast as I could possibly go. I'd grown up surrounded by bigger boys in Cripplegate, so I expected a severe pounding. Instead, he spoke rather calmly, especially considering he now smelled like compost.

"Why are you attacking me with fruit?" he said.

"I'm so sorry," I said, a phrase I'd end up repeating many times over the next three years. "I wasn't aiming at you, I swear."

The girl in his arms thrust her tiny fists in the air and cheered. "Do again!" she said.

I pointed at the branch I'd used for the catapult's launcher. "It's supposed to go straight. I think I broke it on the way here."

The boy studied the bent launcher. "Is that maple?"

I nodded. "It's all I had. I probably should have made it out of yew."

The boy tilted his head and thought about it. "There's yew trees by the cemetery," he said. "Do you have a knife?"

We used the new branch of yew to fix the launcher while the girl, Tom's youngest sister, Molly, dug her little fingers into the grass. Then we fired off the rest of the fruit, the three of us cheering every shot. Afterward, I ran home to show Master Benedict my catapult, and to tell him about Tom, my new friend.

I remembered Master Benedict listening, smiling gently. "Very good," he'd said.

I turned away so Tom's mother wouldn't see my face.

By the time I came downstairs, Tom's father had already hauled his children back to work. The girls were in the side room doing laundry, splashing their baker's aprons with soapy water. Cecily, at twelve years old the most senior of the girls, blew suds into my hair as I passed. The rest of them laughed and scooped up their own fistfuls of bubbles.

I ran out of there before they covered me in foam.

I found Tom at the back door, scrubbing the steps. He shook his head when he saw what I was wearing. "I should've run away."

"From me or the catapult?" I said.

"You *are* a catapult," he said, but his heart wasn't in the joke. He sighed. "I'm really sorry about Master Benedict. I liked him."

"You were afraid of him."

"Yeah. But he was good to you." Tom scanned my face, then sighed again, more deeply. "All right," he said.

"All right what?"

"I'll help."

"Help with what?"

"Whatever your new scheme is."

I pulled the ledger page from my pocket and held it up. "We find Master Benedict's killers."

Tom stared at the last three lines on the page.

†Δ esid. A: rapf. O set. age Htsn. oil eh. two leb. Ht4: shg. Uh. ←

↓Mo8→   *end.swords*

neminidixeris

We'd come inside to read them, smoothing the paper over an empty worktable in the bakery. Though the day's business was done, the smell of freshly baked dough still filled the air like a cloud.

"It's a message," I said. "For me. Master Benedict wrote it when—" My voice caught.

Stop it, I scolded myself. *You said you wouldn't cry. You made a promise.*

I cleared my throat. "Master Benedict must have known his killers," I said. "He wrote this for me when he knew he was going to die."

Tom's eyes went wide. "The murderers' names are in here?"

"I think so. I haven't worked it out yet. The codes—"

"Wait," Tom said. "If this says who the killers are, why didn't you give it to Lord Ashcombe?"

"Master Benedict said not to."

"He did?"

"In the last line," I said.

Tom read it. Or tried to. "*Nemi* . . . uh . . . what? Is this a word?"

"Two words. It's Latin. It says '*nemini dixeris.*' Master Benedict didn't hide this in code so that when I saw it, right away I'd know what to do."

"Steal this page?"

"Keep it secret. *Nemini dixeris* means 'tell no one.'"

"Why would he want to keep his killers' names a secret?"

"I don't know," I said. "But if you have any paper, we can find out."

We started with the first line of the message. It was hidden by one of the first codes Master Benedict had ever taught me.

†∆ *esid*. A: *rapf*. O *set. age* Htsn. *oil eh. two leb.* Ht4: *shg. Uh.* ←

"It's gibberish," Tom said.

"Actually, it's English," I said. "Plain old English."

He frowned. "I see *some* words. Set . . . age . . . oil. And two."

"That's the trick. It looks like those are words, but they're only there to throw you off. Same with the dots. The arrow's the only thing that matters. It tells you what to do."

He pointed to the left. "Go that way?"

"Yes."

"I don't get it."

"On the line," I said. "Go that way on the line."

It dawned on him. "You mean go *backward*."

"Right. Get rid of the dots and capitals . . ." I wrote it down.

esidarapfosetagehtsnoilehtwolebht4shguh

". . . and then go backward . . ."

hughs4thbelowthelionsthegatesofparadise

". . . and you'll get the words," I said.

Hugh's 4th below the lions the gates of paradise

Tom looked impressed. Then: "That doesn't mean . . . was it Master *Hugh* who killed him?"

"What?" I stiffened. "Of course not."

"But you said Master Benedict would name his killers. Although I did kind of expect more of an 'Arthur Quacken-bush did it, curse his eyes.'"

"It doesn't say 'Hugh.' It says 'Hugh's.' Hugh's fourth."

"Hugh's fourth what?" Tom said. "And what lions? The ones in the king's zoo? In the Tower?"

"I'm not sure," I said. "Maybe it's on the second line."

"I remember this," Tom said. "It's the same code as the gunpowder recipe. But aren't there supposed to be numbers?"

"There are." I held the page out. "Smell it."

Tom looked puzzled. "Is that a joke?"

"I'm serious."

Suspicious, he leaned over and sniffed the paper. "Is that . . . ?" He sat up. "Lemons. It smells like lemons."

"Before Master Benedict sent me out of the shop," I said, "he asked me to bring him the lemon juice. I didn't understand why, since lemon juice is the treatment for scurvy, which none of our customers had. Then, when I came back, he'd tucked the ledger under the jar on the shelf. It wasn't until I saw the message that I realized what he was doing. He wrote the numbers in lemon juice. He's hiding codes inside codes."

"Why would he do that?" Tom said.

"Because whatever this is, he *really* doesn't want anyone but me to see it."

"How do *we* see it?"

"Fire," I said. "The heat will cook the lemon juice. We need a candle or something."

Tom used the still-smoldering coals in the baking ovens

to light a wax taper. I asked him to hold it steady. "If the paper gets burnt . . ."

He gripped the wax so tightly, I thought he was going to squash it. I had to steady my own hands as I brought the paper close, hovering above the flame. Slowly, I dragged it across. I smelled the tang of burning citrus. Like magic, dark brown marks appeared on the page.

↓M08→ 0514202022220720160108042021011 5 *end.swords*

For a moment, we just looked at it. Then I wrote out the key to the code.

A	B	C	D	E	F	G	H	I	J	K	L	M
22	23	24	25	26	01	02	03	04	05	06	07	08

N	O	P	Q	R	S	T	U	V	W	X	Y	Z
09	10	11	12	13	14	15	16	17	18	19	20	21

We translated the message. We sat back in our chairs. "What does *that* mean?" Tom said.

CHAPTER
13

I STARED AT IT. "I . . . I DON'T KNOW."

JSYYAALYUFMIYZFT

Tom scratched his head. "Is it Latin?"

"It can't be," I said. "There's no letter J in Latin. No U, either."

"Maybe this is another code, like you said. Maybe this one's really, *really* secret."

Another code made sense. "But how do I decipher it? Where's the key?"

"Well . . . maybe those symbols mean something. At the beginning."

†Δ

"Is that a cross?" he said.

I peered at it. "I think it's a sword."

"A sword? Oh!" Tom pointed to the end of the second line. "There. 'End swords.' There's another sword."

A sword. A triangle. Another sword.

Hugh's fourth. Lions and gates. And a jumble of unreadable letters. That was the message.

I didn't understand *any* of it.

Master Benedict had taught me backward writing the very first summer I'd joined him. He knew I'd figured out the number code from the gunpowder recipe. And he'd pointedly stuck the lemon juice in my face. He obviously expected me to decipher this message. But now I didn't know what to do.

I slumped in my chair. Tom put a hand on my shoulder. "Don't worry. You'll figure it out. Master Benedict believed in you."

I felt like throwing up.

. . .

I helped Tom finish scrubbing the back step before his father returned. Tom kept up a chatter, but I wasn't listening. I was thinking about what he'd said before.

When the Guild Council threw me out of my home, I'd wanted to run to Hugh right away. The last line in Master Benedict's message had stopped me.

Tell no one.

When I'd first seen that page in the ledger, I'd thought Master Benedict had left it behind to name his killers. Now, after what Tom and I had deciphered, I wasn't so sure that was the case. Something else was hidden behind these codes.

That's what puzzled me. Codes were designed to fool strangers, as they'd fooled Lord Ashcombe. Hugh was no stranger. He'd been Master Benedict's apprentice, too. He'd decipher this message faster than I ever could.

So why not tell me to go see him?

I shook my head. Hugh couldn't be in the Cult of the Archangel. He wasn't a killer. I was sure of it. Master Benedict would have warned me.

Then again, maybe he did.

Tell no one.

I finished scrubbing and sat on the step. I didn't have

a choice. Hidden in that message was something that mattered more to Master Benedict than his own life. It meant everything to him. To decipher it, I'd need Hugh's help.

I decided I wouldn't tell Hugh about the message. I'd talk around it instead, maybe mention one of the symbols. Say I saw it in a book or something. I had to take the chance. Whatever his 'fourth' was, Hugh Coggshall was the only one who knew what it meant.

Hugh didn't have a shop. While still with Master Benedict, Hugh had become friends with Nicholas Lange, an apprentice in the Royal College of Physicians. According to my master, the two had spent almost as much time together as Tom and I did. They both became journeymen the same year, both married nearly identical girls, and both became masters a few years after that. As a physician, Dr. Lange needed someone to fill his patients' prescriptions, so he contracted his friend Hugh as his exclusive apothecary. That way, Dr. Lange got a trusted preparer of medicaments, and Hugh—who'd loved every minute in my master's workshop and hated every minute in the store—never had to stand behind a counter again.

That the contract brought Hugh a lot of money didn't hurt, either. His home on Chelsea Street—next door to

Nicholas Lange's—was narrow, but of quality. It was solid brick, and tall, a story higher than most of its neighbors. His workshop was on the ground floor, with living quarters on the three floors above.

Tom and I reached his door, brightly shellacked oak banded with a curled, wrought-iron frame. Though it was growing dark, there were no lights in the house, not even from a fireplace.

Tom peered in the window. "Is he not home?"

I knocked. When there was no response, I knocked again, harder.

A door opened, but not the one I was in front of. From the house beside us stepped Dr. Lange, accompanied by his wife. Both were dressed for a night on the town.

"Dr. Lange!" I ran over to catch him before he stepped into the carriage waiting at the end of the path. "Dr. Lange!"

He turned and pushed his long brown wig away from his eyes. "Yes? Oh. Uh . . ." He wagged a finger, trying to place me.

"Christopher Rowe, sir," I said. "Benedict Blackthorn's apprentice. We met last Christmas, at his shop."

"Yes, of course." He frowned. "I'm glad I ran into you. Have you seen Hugh?"

"No," I said, surprised. "I was just going to ask you the same."

He huffed. "I haven't. I'm quite cross about it, actually. Hugh was to join us for supper on Oak Apple Day, and he left us all waiting. Our lamb was cold." He said it like he'd been forced to swallow hemlock. "Worse, I had several prescriptions to be filled today. I had to send my patients to that idiot on Cornhill instead. He's not with Mr. Blackthorn?"

Obviously, Dr. Lange hadn't heard the news yet. I just shook my head. "You haven't seen Master Hugh since Thursday, then?"

He stroked his beard. "Yes, that sounds right. We had breakfast on Ascension Day. If he's gone to see his wife without informing me, I'll plant my boot in his backside." He poked a finger at me. "And when you see him, you tell him that."

I stomped on the cobbles as we walked back to Tom's house. Tom wouldn't meet my eyes.

"Master Hugh didn't do it," I said.

Tom held his hands up. "I didn't say anything."

"I can read your mind."

"All right," Tom said. "I believe you. But then where is he?"

Maybe it was as Dr. Lange said. Hugh's wife couldn't stand the noise—or the smell—of the city. She often spent months away with their two daughters at Hugh's country house. Maybe he'd gone to be with his family. I remembered the conversation I'd overheard Thursday night.

Hugh, worried: *Simon's already fled the city.*

Master Benedict, resigned: *Do you want to leave, too?*

And then my master was attacked.

Maybe that pushed Hugh over the edge. So he ran away. But then wouldn't he convince Master Benedict to leave with him?

Well, no. Master Benedict had wanted to stay. And of all my master's qualities, "easily persuaded" was not one of them. I shook my head. If Hugh had already left London, then I had no way of finding out what my master's message meant.

We got to Tom's street, but instead of going down it, Tom took us through the narrow alley that led behind his house. His mother was waiting at the back door, a burlap sack in her hand. "Did you break the news to Master Coggshall?" she said.

"He wasn't home," I said.

"That's a shame. It's always better to hear this sort of

thing from friends." She handed the sack to Tom. "Dinner in five minutes."

Tom stopped me from following her into the house. "We have to wait."

"For what?" Inside the sack was half a loaf of crusty bread, a hard rye, and a few sweet buns. "Is this what we're eating?"

"No." He nodded toward the end of the path.

A man turned into view. From a distance, he looked as if he was well off, which was odd, because while this wasn't a bad street, it also wasn't the kind of place you'd find wealthy men strolling through alleys. But when he got closer, I saw he wasn't what I'd thought at all.

His clothes had once been fine, but not anymore. His wig was a bird's nest. His thin wool jacket was ragged and frayed at the edges. His shirt had become so stained, its original color was long forgotten. And his soft doe-leather breeches had worn so thin, you could see his knees.

This was Dr. Parrett. He used to come to our shop. Then, last summer, his house burned down. He hadn't repaired it. He hadn't moved out, either. He still lived there, alone, among the charred timbers and ashes of his former life.

"Pleasant evening, Dr. Parrett," Tom said.

"Pleasant evening, Tom. And to you . . ." He cocked his head, as if he were listening to something. ". . . Christopher."

He came closer. He hadn't washed his body any more than he'd washed his clothes. "Good to see you again, sir," I said.

He looked at me sadly. "I'm so sorry about your master, lad. If you need anything, my home is yours, for as long as you need to stay. And James would love the company."

I felt my spine freeze. James—Dr. Parrett's twelve-year-old son—had died in the fire.

"That's very kind," I stammered.

Tom held out the sack. "Here you go, sir. Bread and sweet buns."

"That'll please James," Dr. Parrett said. "He adores your sweet buns. It's a task to get him to eat anything else." He tapped at his torn pockets. "I . . . I'm afraid I forgot to bring my coin purse again. I could go and—"

"Don't worry," Tom said. "I'll put it on your account, like usual."

Dr. Parrett took the sack with a trembling hand. He held it to his chest like a baby. "Thank you," he said quietly.

"See you Monday."

We watched him go. On our way inside, Tom put a hand on my arm.

"Don't tell my father," he said.

Tom called for his sisters. Within a second, the five of them came thundering down the stairs. Then we sat down for dinner. Under different circumstances, I would have savored the beef, roasted to perfection with pepper and sage, but with every bite, Tom's father pinched his lips as if I were eating his future. And I couldn't stop thinking about poor Dr. Parrett. It scared me. I'd lost everything, too. One year later, would that be me? Living among my own life's rubble, begging for scraps, imagining Master Benedict was still alive?

After dinner, Tom and I were ordered to clean the table and scour the pots. Normally, the Bailey girls would have been assigned their own tasks, but Tom's father seemed to feel he'd get his money's worth out of my staying there if I did all the chores. Free from their usual duties, the girls decided to hang around the kitchen and use us for their own amusement.

Cecily, delighted at this turn of events, decided she'd be taskmaster. She kept up a steady stream of orders as we worked, telling us how *this* pot needed more scrubbing, and how *that* pot should be scraped *just* so. Plump and cheery Isabel sat on the countertop, swinging her legs under her frilled orange petticoat and chattering away at us— something about a duck who had a sheep for a friend— not seeming to care whether anyone was listening or not. The other three, Catherine, Emma, and little Molly, found a ball of yarn and played some game called stick-tock. I don't know what the rules were, but the girls appeared to score points each time the ball hit me or Tom. Double if it bounced off our heads.

As Tom and I finished with the pots, the three youngest girls clamped onto my legs, declared I was their prisoner, and refused to let me go until I paid for my freedom with a story. So upstairs we went to the girls' bedroom, where the Baileys kept their only book, a dog-eared copy of *Le Morte d'Arthur*.

We all piled onto Cecily's bed as I opened the cover. Cecily, sitting behind me, seemed more interested in braiding feathers into my hair than listening to the story. Isabel amused herself by smearing rouge on my cheeks and giggling a lot. The other three listened, ears pricked like wolves, as I read them the tale of "King Arthur and the Giant of

Mont Saint-Michel." The giant terrorized the countryside, killing its people and pillaging the land until the villagers begged King Arthur to save them. Molly, the youngest at four years old, hid her face in my lap as the giant ate twelve children like roast chickens on a spit. And she and gentle Emma both clutched at my waist during the final battle, when the two rolled down the hill to the sea, until the Great King of Britain smote the monster with his dagger.

Cecily leaned her slender frame against me, her head on the back of my neck. "I wish he were here," she said sadly.

"King Arthur?" I said.

"Uh-huh." She rested her chin on my shoulder and locked her arms around my chest. "He'd stop the Cult of the Archangel. Then they wouldn't have hurt your master." She sighed. "But I guess he's just a story."

She held on to me as Molly and Emma turned to the next page in the book, pleading with me to keep reading. Tom, watching from the doorway, hushed them and tucked them in. "That's enough sport for one day. You'll get another tale tomorrow."

Tom and I blew out the candles and went outside, sitting on the well-scrubbed step in the back alley. Tom handed me a woolen rag so I could wipe the rouge off my cheeks. As I did, he kept looking at me out of the corner of his eye.

"What?" I said.

"You've gone all quiet," he said.

"Have I?"

"Uh-huh." He sighed. "So what are you getting me into this time?"

"What do you mean?"

"I've seen that look in your eyes before."

I don't suppose I could have kept this one inside. Cecily was right: King Arthur was just a story. No one was coming to save me. But that didn't mean I had to let everything I cared about get taken away. I might not know how to solve Master Benedict's riddle, but I did know what I could do tonight.

The Cult of the Archangel took my master. The Apothecaries' Guild Council took my home. I had only one thing left of my life: my puzzle cube. And I'd burn in the pits of hell before I'd let anyone take that, too.

CHAPTER
14

"THIS IS MADNESS," TOM HISSED.

"You said that already," I whispered.

"And yet, here we are, still doing it. So, if you don't mind: This is madness."

He had a point. Sneaking through the alleys of London at midnight wasn't the smartest idea in the world. At best, you'd meet a parade of drunks. At worst, you wouldn't see the sunrise. And if you ran into a parish constable on patrol, he'd be as likely to crack your skull as question you, since he'd just assume you were up to no good.

No lanterns hung in the streets. City regulations forbade them after nine p.m. There were torch boys you could hire to light your way, but that obviously wasn't an option for us. We traveled instead by the half-moon, which cast the city in a foggy silver glow. Fortunately, my home wasn't far, just three streets away from Tom's. We dodged behind the clattering cart of the night-soil men, bolted through one more alleyway, then hopped a stone fence, and we were outside Blackthorn's workshop at the back.

"How are we going to get in?" Tom said. "I thought the Guild Council took your key."

They had. Except they didn't know about the key Master Benedict kept hidden, and I hadn't told them where to find it. At the back corner of the house, a column of cracked brick led up the side of the chimney. I dragged my fingers along it, feeling for the symbol. I found it, etched near eye height on the left side, camouflaged by the brick's natural pattern.

Tom cocked his head. "Isn't that a planet?"

He was right. This was the symbol for Mars. I wondered why Master Benedict had used it to mark his key. I was still thinking about it when a frenzied fluttering burst in front of my face. I jumped. Tom gave a little squeak I didn't know a boy his size could make.

My heart started up again when I saw it was just a pigeon. It flapped its wings and landed next to me. In the moonlight, it took me a moment to recognize her. "Bridget!"

She cooed.

I knelt and scooped her into my hands. She nuzzled against my fingers. "What are you doing out here?" I said.

Tom pointed upward. "Look."

Right above us, at the edge of the roof, the door to our pigeon coop swung open in the breeze. I cursed. Whatever idiot the Guild Council had sent to feed the pigeons hadn't latched it behind him. All our birds would be gone. And out in the wild, Bridget could have been hurt.

She wriggled in my fingers, alarmed by my voice. I stopped swearing and stroked her feathers to calm her. She still managed to look offended.

Tom looked around nervously. "We can't stay out here all night."

Right again. I cradled Bridget in one arm and pulled on the brick with the symbol of Mars. It slid outward, scraping on the masonry. Behind it was a small nook. Inside was the key to our house.

When I went to the back door, however, it was already unlocked. The same idiot who'd lost our birds hadn't even secured the house when he left. I was about to start swearing again, but when we went inside, I couldn't find my voice.

Our workshop had been ransacked.

A low fire left burning in the oven in the corner gave enough light to see the damage. Pots and cookware were scattered across the benches. Books, flipped open, had been tossed aside like garbage. The ceramic jars were overturned, leaving rainbow powder starbursts on the floorboards. Even the ice vault in the floor was open, the precious chipped chunks left exposed to melt.

It wasn't until Bridget made a strangled cry that I realized I was squeezing her.

Tom tugged on my sleeve. "We need to go."

I couldn't. Against Tom's urging, I went forward, trembling, into the shop. I expected bad. I got even worse.

Half the jars were off the shelves, some tipped over, some shattered, herbs and powders blown everywhere. Here, too, the books were torn apart, pages fallen across the room like an ink-stained blanket of snow. Even the stuffed animals hadn't been spared. Every one was sliced open, straw sprayed over the rest of the mess.

My shoulders shook. The horrible, hateful monsters. Were they going to destroy everything I cared about? For a moment, I wanted to collapse. But I didn't break my promise. I just wiped my eyes and stamped the swell back down, let it fuel the anger inside.

My master's sash lay in the corner, partly covered in blackberry leaves. I dropped the key on the counter and put Bridget there, too. I picked up the sash. It still smelled faintly of Egyptian incense, reminding me evermore of him. I shook the leaves away and wrapped it around my waist. It held me tight.

I hadn't returned for this, but I wasn't going to leave it. Not now. I tied it on over my shirt. Then I searched through the wreckage, fingers sifting through multicolored grains, until I finally spotted what I came for, hidden on the floor under a mound of cinnabar.

My puzzle box. My birthday gift from Master Benedict. Mine.

I held it, letting its weight press into my palm. For one small moment, it felt like everything was all right again.

"Should she be eating that?" Tom said.

I turned. Bridget, on the counter, was pecking away at a pile of fine white crystals.

"Bridget! No!" I ran over. She marched away, flapping her wings.

I dipped a finger in the powder and touched it to the end of my tongue. I tasted sweetness, and breathed a sigh of relief. It was only sugar. Harmless, thank goodness. Though I imagined what Master Benedict would say if he caught me feeding valuable sugar to a pigeon.

That's when it hit me. It *was* valuable.

Sugar, blackberry leaves, saltpeter, cinnabar . . . apothecary ingredients traded for a fortune at the market. Even if the burglars didn't understand what all the goods were worth, we had jars of powdered gold and silver, obvious prizes to take. Instead, we stood in a king's ransom scattered like sand.

Then I realized something else. It was the *dry* ingredients that littered the shop. Powders, minerals, leaves. All of them. Not one of the jars left on the shelf contained something solid. And none of the jars with liquid had been touched.

Books torn apart. Stuffed animals shredded. Dry goods dumped.

Whoever had ransacked the shop hadn't come here to steal. They were *searching* for something. Something specific, hidden by my master. Something so valuable, they were willing to throw away hundreds of pounds' worth of ingredients to find it.

And they could read the labels on the jars.

I jammed the puzzle cube under my master's sash and picked up Bridget. "We need to go."

Tom sounded exasperated. "That's what *I* said." He half jogged toward the workshop door. I followed him, then ran straight into his back.

Bridget squawked and ruffled her feathers. I stepped back. Tom stood frozen in place. "What are you—" I began, but he held his hand up, eyes wide.

Then I heard it, too.

CHAPTER
15

A SLOW CREAK, FROM THE STAIRS
to the second floor. A foot on the dirt. A voice, low and
rough.

"Who's there?" it said.

I pulled on Tom's shirt. We ducked under the second
display table, the one farthest from the light of the fireplace.

Footsteps came to the door, slowly, cautiously.

"Master? Is that you?"

He took another step forward. I could see a boot, covered in muck and fine white grains, a shred of parchment
stuck to its heel. The leg of his breeches, gray wool, was
tucked inside.

He came closer, and I could finally see his face. The light was dim, but it was enough to place him. Close-set eyes, sloping brow. Red hair, muscles. About sixteen years old. This time, no blue apron.

It was the apprentice. The one who had been in the shop this morning. The one who'd blocked out half the window, who'd laughed when my master had hit me.

I pushed farther back against the legs of the table. I prayed that the fact that I could barely see Tom cowering at the other end meant we were still in shadow. I also prayed that Bridget wouldn't make a sound. She nestled against me, trembling. I wondered if she could smell my fear.

Another voice came, whispering from the workshop. "Wat? Where are you?"

"In here," the apprentice replied.

The second man came into the shop. "Did you leave the back door op—" He gasped.

I knew that voice. I knew it well; I knew it before he stepped into view.

It was Nathaniel Stubb.

He gaped, aghast, at the mess. "Wat! What in the Nine Hells have you done?"

"What I was told to do," Wat said, sounding annoyed. "Look for the bloody fire."

Stubb cracked Wat on his ear. "Do you not understand what this is worth?" His eyes bulged. "Is that *saffron*? You idiot!"

Stubb scrambled to the end of the counter and tried to pluck the golden strands of saffron crocus from the vermilion it had mixed with. He didn't see the look Wat gave him. Or the way the boy's fingers gripped the handle of the broad, curved blade in his belt.

"Have you even found anything?" Stubb said. "Or are you just destroying this shop for the sake of it?"

Wat ground his teeth. "It isn't here."

"It has to be here. If you hadn't killed Benedict so quickly, he would have told you where it was."

The words pierced my heart like an arrow. Part of me already knew that Stubb had had something to do with my master's death. Hearing it made it hurt all the same.

"It wasn't my fault," Wat said, sullen. "He'd already poisoned himself before I could get anything out of him."

"Because you gave yourself away."

"I didn't!"

Stubb looked scornful. "Yes, I'm sure Master Apothecary

Benedict Blackthorn chewed madapple by accident."

The madapple. I'd forgotten all about it. Now I remembered the black, kidney-shaped seeds scattered around the glass jar in the workshop, just before I found my master's body. I'd thought maybe the Cult of the Archangel had taken them, to use on future enemies. But Master Benedict had poisoned *himself*.

My mind raced. Why would he do that? To spare himself from the torture Wat was going to put him through, like the Cult's other victims? Or was it more than that? Wat had wrecked my master's shop searching for something. Had Master Benedict poisoned himself so he couldn't tell the boy where it was?

I thought of the hidden message my master had left for me in the ledger. I'd left the page back at Tom's place, stuffed under the mattress of his bed. It occurred to me that that was probably the best idea I'd had all day. Because whatever they were looking for, the secret to finding it had been given to *me*.

It was as if Stubb had heard my thoughts. "Why didn't you at least stay to question the apprentice?" he said. My chest turned to ice.

Wat folded his arms. "He doesn't know anything.

Blackthorn hated him. He wouldn't teach that boy how to wipe his own backside."

In the darkness, I put my hand to my cheek. *You are useless*, Master Benedict had said, and he'd hit me. But all the time, he knew Wat was watching.

Master Benedict had struck me in front of Wat to *save* me, to throw the boy off my trail. The cruel sting of the memory evaporated, leaving an aching emptiness inside. *Oh, Master*, I cried out to him. *Why did you stay when you knew they would kill you? Why didn't you come with me instead? Why didn't you take my hand and run?*

"I don't care what Benedict thought of his apprentice," Stubb said. "The boy might have seen something, heard something, read something. Find him and question him. Then get rid of him, same as the others, whether he knows about the fire or not. We can't risk keeping him alive."

I felt like I was frozen. I think Tom had stopped breathing, too.

Wat shrugged. "Fine," he said, and he moved to go.

"Not now, you fool," Stubb said. "How are you going to find where he went in the middle of the night? Do it tomorrow. Finish checking the books."

Wat scowled. "Do you have any idea how many books this old man had?"

Stubb brought his hand up to strike the boy. "Watch your tongue."

They locked eyes. For a moment, I was sure Wat was going to pull his knife. Instead, slowly, he reached down and took a leather-bound tome from the floor. He slapped it on the counter, puffing a cloud of orange powder into the air. Stubb coughed. Wat smirked, then started flipping pages.

Stubb returned to the saffron, trying to rescue as much of it as he could. Both of them were facing away from us. That wouldn't last forever.

We needed to get out of here. Now.

Stubb was blocking the door to the workshop. The front door, behind me, was bolted shut. Maybe I could slip that open and unlock the door while their backs were turned. I almost crawled out from under the table before I realized I'd made a terrible mistake.

The key. I'd left the key to the shop on the counter.

It was still there, dull gray iron in a pile of sugar. I cursed. I might be able to crawl around the far side of the room without getting spotted, but getting to the counter unseen was never going to happen. There was only one way out.

I needed to get Stubb away from the workshop's door.

I tried to think. A corner of the puzzle cube tucked under Master Benedict's sash poked into my stomach. I shifted, trying to adjust it so it would stop. Across from me, Tom curled up even tighter. He looked so scared, I thought he was going to cry. I knew exactly how he felt.

But it was looking at Tom that gave me the idea.

I held Bridget out to him. Fingers trembling, he gathered her in massive, gentle hands and held her close. His eyes widened as I slipped away.

I moved around the table, keeping the wood between me and the intruders. There was a gap in the middle of the room I'd need to cross, but I hoped if I stayed in the shadows, they wouldn't notice me.

I crawled slowly to the other table, close to the fireplace. My heart thumped all the way there. Huddled behind the display, I searched through my master's sash. Fortunately, Wat hadn't broken the vials inside when he'd dumped it. I had to pull half of them out to read the labels before I found the three I was looking for.

Sulfur. Charcoal. And saltpeter.

Wat's ransacking of my master's books had left torn

paper everywhere. I could use that. Quietly, I worked the cork stoppers out and emptied the vials on one of the pages. My fingers mixed the gunpowder as best as I could. Without the pestle, it wasn't going to be as good as our cannon. I prayed that it would still do.

This close to the fire, I'd have only a few seconds to get it right. I put the paper with the gunpowder on it next to the fireplace. I took a second page and laid it on top, one corner on the gunpowder, its opposite in the blaze.

It caught instantly. The fire curled the paper faster than I'd expected. I scrambled into the open and dived behind the table that hid Tom and Bridget.

Stubb spun around, eyes narrowed. "What was th—"

Suddenly, the fireplace flared. There was a terrifying hiss. Then flame burst outward from the stone, burning pages shooting upward in its draft.

"Fire!" Stubb screamed. "Put it out! Put it out!" Frantic, he scanned the shelf behind the counter for water. Wat ran through the smoke to the fireplace and stamped at it, trying desperately to stop the smoldering paper from catching anything else.

I grabbed Tom by the collar. I pulled. We ran.

• • •

Tom sprinted through the London night, clutching the panicked Bridget. I ran behind him, twisting at every corner to see if we were followed.

Either we lost them or they hadn't seen us, because we made it to the alley behind Tom's house without sight of Wat or Nathaniel Stubb. We nearly crushed ourselves at the back door—or, more accurately, Tom nearly crushed me—trying to scramble inside at the same time. I slammed the bolt shut and bent over the table, panting. Tom leaned back against the plaster and slid down, gasping for air.

Poor Bridget struggled in his hands. I had to coax her from him, and hold her to my face until she quieted. She was made of sturdy stuff, that pigeon, because she calmed down well before either of us did.

I went to the window. I looked for a glow, for smoke, for something to announce that the gunpowder I'd set off had flared out of control, that I'd burned my own home to the ground. But I saw nothing, and I knew that by now, if the fire had caught, the alarm would have been raised. Still, I watched, waiting.

Tom looked out next to me, his arm pressed against my shoulder. "Are we safe?" he said.

I didn't know how to answer that.

SUNDAY, MAY 31, 1665

The Visitation of Mary

CHAPTER
16

I COULDN'T SLEEP.

It wasn't just that the floor of Tom's bedroom was a forest of splinters. It wasn't the fear lingering in my guts, either. Tom had been as scared as I was, yet ten minutes after his head hit his pillow, he was snoring louder than carriage wheels on cobbles.

I couldn't sleep because I knew who'd murdered my master. I couldn't sleep because his killers were now coming after me.

And I didn't know what to do about it.

I wanted to run to Lord Ashcombe, tell him what I'd seen. I couldn't. Even if he believed me—and the King's

Warden didn't really seem like the trusting type—I had no actual evidence that Stubb and Wat had killed my master. It would be my word against Stubb's, and I wasn't stupid enough to not know how that would turn out. He was a master, I was an apprentice. No one would listen to me.

Tom could back me up, of course, but he wouldn't be taken any more seriously than I would. Plus, we'd committed a serious crime. Breaking into a house—even if it *was* my own—was bad enough. Taking the cube and the sash, both now hidden under Tom's bed with the page from the ledger, was theft. The penalty for stealing either was death. We'd both end up swinging from the gallows, murdering cult or not.

Tom's bedroom door creaked open. His youngest sister, Molly, padded in on bare feet, curled up on the floor, and snuggled into me, clutching a well-loved blanket to her chest. I listened to her breathe as I lay awake and thought. To see Stubb and his apprentice hanged for their crimes, I'd need to go to Lord Ashcombe with hard evidence, or the support of someone with higher standing than Stubb. Someone respected, whose position placed him above ordinary men. I didn't know how to get the first. But the second, maybe I could do.

· · ·

I slipped out from under Molly's arms and crept out of the house with the dawn. Most days, the streets would already be jammed with traffic: tradesmen on their way to work, merchants hauling goods to market, coachmen swearing at pedestrians. But today was Sunday, the Lord's day of rest. Though there were a few souls out to greet me with a pleasant morning, the city felt empty.

I still didn't feel safe. On the one hand, empty streets made it easier to keep an eye out for Stubb or Wat, either of whom might be hunting me. On the other hand, there were fewer witnesses to scare off potential kidnappers. The best I could do was stay far away from any streets near Stubb's apothecary. I hoped that spending all night ransacking our shop meant they would need the morning to get some sleep.

I took my master's sash with me, tied underneath my shirt so no one could see it. I also took the ledger page, and my puzzle cube, which made a bulge in my pocket. What I really wished I could take was Tom. Bridget, too. I'd had to let her go before we'd gone to bed, since if Tom's father found a bird in his house, he'd bake her in a pie. She'd flapped away into the night, toward the shining moon, before disappearing behind a distant roof. I scanned the skies for her as I walked, wishing she'd come back.

It took some time to get where I was going. I knew the house I was looking for was on Cornhill, but I wasn't sure which one it was. I asked directions from a passing rag-and-bone man with a greasy sack slung over his shoulder. He sent me to the corner, where I called on the home of Grand Master Apothecary Sir Edward Thorpe.

"He's not available," said the gangly servant girl who answered the door.

"When can I speak to him?" I said.

She looked me up and down. *Never*, her eyes said. I hadn't had the chance to clean up after last night. I must have looked like a beggar.

"Please, miss. It's urgent Guild business. I'm an apprentice."

She pinched her lips but gave me an answer. "He's gone to the Hall."

I was surprised. "On a Sunday?"

She shrugged. "Not my place to ask." I stepped back before she introduced the door to my nose.

I hadn't returned to Apothecaries' Hall in three years. After passing my entrance exam, Master Benedict had taken me to my new home, and neither one of us had ever gone back. That wasn't unusual for someone like me. Technically, apprentices weren't yet Guild members, so unless facing discipline or assigned to the Guild laboratory, there wasn't anything for an apprentice at the Hall. Sometimes, though, I'd wondered about my master. He hadn't had many friends. Only Hugh ever came to the house. There was Isaac the bookseller, of course, but I'd never met him. I wouldn't even have known he existed if it wasn't for the book stacks growing like cornstalks in my home. Once, I'd asked Master Benedict why he never went to the Hall. "Politics bore me," was all he said.

As I walked there, I wondered if it was actually the stench that kept him away. The Hall was near the Thames, down on Blackfriars Lane. The river stank something awful, especially during low tide, when the mud on the banks smelled like rotting . . . well, *everything*. The streets were no better, choked as they were by the patrons of the nearby Playhouse, where actors, writers, and other low persons spilled drunkenly from shadowed doorways to relieve themselves, clogging the gutters with filth.

But the Hall itself was impressive. It had once been a monastery—the home of the Black Friars, which gave its name to the street—and it showed, with dark brick walls three stories high. The first time I'd come here, I'd stood outside, peering into the tall, narrow windows. I'd watched the men coming and going, imagining what their life— soon to be mine, I'd hoped—was like. I'd studied their faces, wondering who would be my new master, hoping for this one, hoping against that one, for no real reason other than whether I liked the look of them. I remembered meeting Master Benedict for the first time, still flushed from passing my test. He'd held out his hand and said, "Pleased to meet you, Christopher Rowe." As if I were a real person.

And that front door. Back then, the entrance to the Hall had made me nervous. It was a grand thing of oak, twice my height, flanked by two pillars with an arch at the top. THE WORSHIPFUL SOCIETY OF APOTHECARIES, it said, with the blue shield of the Guild's emblem above it. On it was Apollo, the Greek god of healing, standing over the black wyvern of disease, supported by two golden unicorns. A scroll unfurled beneath, bearing the Apothecaries' motto: OPIFERQUE PER ORBEM DICOR. *I am called throughout the world the bringer of aid.*

Today, the massive door was barred. I thumped a fist against it.

A minute passed before it creaked open. A young man with slate-gray eyes stuck his head around the crack and said, "Guild Hall's closed Sundays. Candidates for apprenticeship apply to the clerk during the week." He began to close the door.

"Wait," I said. "I'm already an apprentice. I need to speak with Grand Master Thorpe."

"Either way. Come back tomorrow. He'll address business then."

"It's about Benedict Blackthorn's murder."

The man looked me up and down. I wished again that I looked a little cleaner. "One moment," he said, and he shut the door.

It was several minutes before he returned. "Come with me."

He took me through the arched passageway into the courtyard, which was paved with stone. In the center was the well, which supplied water for the Guild laboratories and workshops. Around the sides, set against walls freshly painted with yellow ocher, sat riveted iron benches. Windows from the upper offices looked down on the space. They all appeared empty, which was to be expected on a Sunday.

A set of stairs led up from the courtyard on the south side, to the right. Those went to the masters' offices, and to the Great Hall, where I'd been tested. The door to the labs was in front of us.

For a moment, I thought that's where the man was taking me. Instead, he turned left at the end of the courtyard. We went northward into a chamber with a door to the clerks' offices and a pair of simple chairs.

He waved at one. "Someone will be with you shortly."

I waited.

A hand shook me awake.

I blinked. Through bleary eyes, I saw the bald head of Oswyn Colthurst gazing down at me.

"You're drooling," he said.

"Sorry." I wiped my mouth with my sleeve. My shirt still smelled of gunpowder.

Oswyn folded his arms. "If I recall, Christopher, you were asked to show up on Monday. You do know your days of the week?"

I stood. "I apologize, Master Colthurst. I need to speak to the Grand Master right away."

Oswyn managed to look both annoyed and amused

at my presumption. "You must have driven poor Benedict mad," he said. He ran his hand over his scalp. "Sir Edward isn't here."

"I was told he came to the Hall."

"He left an hour ago for Sunday services. I expect him to return this afternoon. I expect *you* to return tomorrow." He put a gentle but firm hand on my shoulder and began to steer me out.

"Wait, Master, please," I said. "It's about Master Benedict's murder. I know who killed him."

"Everyone knows who killed him," Oswyn said. "The Cult of the Archangel."

"Yes, Master, but I meant, I know *who* it was."

He stopped, surprised. "Go on."

"It was Nathaniel Stubb."

Oswyn's jaw dropped. Then he grabbed my ear, twisted it, and opened the door to the clerk's offices with my head.

CHAPTER
17

OSWYN APPARENTLY THOUGHT MY
skull did such a good job on the first door that he used it
to open the next one, too. He dragged me down a narrow
hall and rammed me into an empty office. I fell against the
desk, toppling a paperweight ceramic goose.

"Have you completely lost your mind?" Oswyn said.
"Stubb is a *master*. If he heard what you said, he'd have you
thrown out of the Guild. Then he'd have you flogged. By
rights, I should do it myself."

I put my hand to my forehead. Oak really hurts. "But
it's true."

I worried that, this time, Oswyn might use my head to

open the window. But he just snorted and said, "Ridiculous. Nathaniel Stubb may be a weasel, but he's no killer. He doesn't have the stones for it."

"He didn't do it himself," I said. "It was his apprentice."

Oswyn was taken aback. "His apprentice?"

"He was in the shop, right before Master Benedict's murder. His name is Wat." I described him.

Oswyn frowned. "That's not Stubb's apprentice."

"He called Stubb 'master.' And he was wearing the blue apron."

"'Master' is a common title. And anyone can wear a blue apron."

"But—"

"Nathaniel Stubb has two apprentices," Oswyn said, irritated. "Edgar Raleigh and Adam Horwath. Edgar's the right age, but his hair is black, not red, and 'muscly' is not how anyone with eyes would describe him. Adam's a year younger than you, and half a head shorter. Stubb has no other apprentices. I know this for a fact, since—as I'm sure you recall—I've personally tested every candidate for apprenticeship in the past ten years. Who told you this nonsense?"

"I heard them," I said. "Last night. In my master's shop."

"What on God's blessed Earth were you doing in your master's shop?"

My cheeks flushed. I tried not to look down at the bulge in my pocket. Or the sash under my shirt, which was looking pretty bulgy itself.

It didn't matter. "You went back for that cube, didn't you?" he said. I responded by looking guilty. Oswyn sighed. "Oh, Christopher. What am I going to do with you?" He waved for me to sit. "All right. Tell me."

I described our ransacked shop. He didn't care about our lost birds. He did care about the conversation I overheard.

Oswyn was stunned. "Why would Nathaniel kill Benedict? Had things really got so bad between them?"

"He was looking for something," I said. "Wat called it the 'fire.'"

"The fire? Is that one of your master's remedies?"

"I don't know," I said. "He never mentioned it."

Oswyn looked puzzled. "There's *Greek* fire. But every apothecary knows that recipe." He tapped his chin, thinking. He frowned. "Hmm."

"Master?"

"Benedict's will is missing," Oswyn said. "He registered

a new one with the clerks three months ago. Someone's taken it from the vault."

Another outrage. "Why would they do that?"

"I assume they didn't like what it said."

"But then what's going to happen to the shop?" *Our* shop!

"Benedict bought the property from the Guild some thirty years ago. With no will, and no family, the shop will revert to the Guild. Stubb's claim against its assets will likely be rejected, but he was Benedict's closest competitor, and he has more than enough gold to buy it. If he wants Blackthorn, he'll get it."

I felt sick.

"But money is all Stubb's ever cared about," Oswyn said. "Are you sure he wasn't looking for that? A stash your master kept hidden somewhere?" I shook my head. "Then we have to consider that this really was another strike by the Cult of the Archangel."

"Master Benedict told me there was no such thing as the Cult," I said. "But there is, isn't there?"

"Oh, yes. Although, Stubb, in the Cult . . ." Oswyn blinked. "I can't even imagine it."

"Why are they doing this? What do they want?"

He shrugged. "The same as everyone else. Power."

"I don't understand."

Oswyn straightened in his chair. "Tell me. From where does the healing force of our remedies come?"

I felt like I was eleven again, sweating through the Apothecaries' entrance exam. "From God."

"Correct," Oswyn said. "The herbs and oils and ointments we mix have no power of their own. They're merely the channel through which God's holy blessings may work. But our remedies, though miraculous, are drawn only from the truths that God has given to man. There are other truths, greater truths, that Our Lord reserves for His heavenly host alone. And those wonders, Christopher, would make our earthly miracles hide in shame.

"That's what the Cult of the Archangel is looking for," he said. "The power of God Himself. Whatever this 'fire' is, clearly, they believe it's the key to unlocking it." His eyes narrowed. "So *that's* why the Cult is torturing its victims. These aren't sacrifices, they're interrogations. They must think these men know where the fire is."

"But what will they do if they find it?" I said.

"What anyone would, with such power in their hands. Shape the world as they see fit."

Shape the world, I thought.

I remembered the madman, back on Oak Apple Day. *The Cult of the Archangel hunts. Who is its prey?*

I remembered Lord Ashcombe, interrogating me in the shop. *And how did Master Benedict feel about His Majesty?*

Now I understood. "King Charles," I said. "They're trying to overthrow the king."

Oswyn nodded. "There's always been a struggle for the Crown, and as you're well aware, it's been particularly contentious of late. Kill the king, force Parliament to fall in line, and England will be theirs." He sighed. "It's not so difficult to understand, really. You and I may be loyal, Christopher, but this nation is hardly paradise. Your master was a good man, with no patience for scheming nobles, so you've been shielded from the worst of them. But you can't imagine the corruption that inhabits the ruling classes. Even our own Guild—which is supposed to be about knowledge and healing—isn't free from such things. It's no surprise there are men who believe they can do better." He arched an eyebrow. "Oftentimes, they're the ones who profess their loyalty the loudest."

I thought about Master Benedict. He was faithful to God, and he'd sought deeper truths, too. But he'd never wanted power, never wanted to rule over others. He'd loved knowledge for its own sake.

I missed him.

"Regardless," Oswyn said, "we have more pressing matters. We need someone who can verify your story."

I couldn't tell Oswyn about Tom. It would make him as much of a target for the Cult as I was. It wouldn't help, anyway. Oswyn needed an adult witness, not a baker's apprentice.

"I was alone," I said.

Oswyn pursed his lips. "Then we have a problem. The first time we met, I told you the Guild needed more men from humble backgrounds. Not everyone shares that view. The Grand Master's an honest man, but he's a bit blind when it comes to seeing the truth about certain members. Plus, there's the shame that such a discovery will bring. He simply won't want to believe an apothecary is in the Cult of the Archangel.

"And you've already dug yourself quite a hole. Sir Edward was *not* impressed when you spoke without permission yesterday. Cursing a master was even worse. Valentine thinks you should be flogged." He looked at me warily. "Please tell me you haven't further blackened Stubb's name."

Not *after* the murder, I hadn't. "No, Master. I promise."

"Then we may salvage this yet." He stood. "I'll send someone to look over Benedict's shop. And I'll speak to Sir Edward—without Valentine—this afternoon. That should be around four o'clock. If the Cult really is after you, you'd better keep off the streets until then. You may hide in here." He pointed a finger at me sternly. "And I mean *here*, Christopher, in this office. Don't wander the grounds. If Stubb is looking for you, he may very well come to the Hall."

I swallowed. That hadn't even occurred to me. "Yes, Master."

"After I've spoken to the Grand Master, I'll ask you to tell him your story. Be brief. Be respectful. Don't say anything that isn't plain and simple fact. And for the love of Our Blessed Savior, keep your temper under control this time. Do you understand?"

"Yes, Master."

He turned to go. Suddenly, he stopped. His eyes narrowed. "If you're lying to me, boy . . ."

I held up my hand. "I swear, Master Colthurst. Everything I said is the absolute truth."

All right. So. *One* little lie.

CHAPTER
18

ACTUALLY, TWO.

Head peeked out the door, I watched Oswyn go. He stopped at the steps in the courtyard to speak to the clerk who'd let me in. The man nodded, then went upstairs. Oswyn left through the main entrance. I waited as long as I could stand it—which was somewhere less than a minute—then ran after him into the street.

Forget what I'd promised Oswyn. The streets might not be safe, but the Hall sounded even worse. I couldn't believe I'd come here without realizing Stubb might show up, even on a Sunday. *He's an apothecary, too.* I cursed myself. *He has more right to be here than you.*

Besides, it was midmorning. It would be at least six hours before I had to meet Sir Edward. And I still had a job to do.

The Baileys returned home from service to find me sitting on their stoop. The girls were happy to see me, the younger ones twirling to show off their Sunday dresses, but Tom's mother wasn't pleased. "I don't know what your master got up to, Christopher, but if you're staying in this house, you're going to church like a proper Christian."

"Sorry, Mistress Bailey," I said. "I had to report to the masters at the Guild Hall. I'm going to the twelve o'clock service at Saint Peter's. May Tom have permission to come with me?"

She seemed satisfied by that. "Of course. A second helping of the Lord's wisdom would do him good."

Tom frowned. When we were alone, he said, "I don't want a second helping. Reverend Stills is so *boring*."

"We're not going to church." I prayed a silent apology, hoping the Lord would understand. "We're going back to Master Hugh's."

Hugh's home was locked and shuttered, same as yesterday. I'd hoped he'd returned, but I hadn't really expected it.

"Then why are we here?" Tom said.

"We need to search his place," I said.

"But nobody's—" He folded his arms. "Christopher. We are *not* breaking in there."

"Is it really breaking in if we have a key?"

"Yes!" He frowned. "Wait. When did we get a key?"

We hadn't. But we were about to. I took him around the back corner of the house, where the brick from the chimney ran up the side. I peered at it, running my fingers over the pattern until I found it.

Just like my master's shop. I took the key from behind the brick and held it up to Tom, triumphant.

He wasn't nearly as pleased. "What if Master Hugh comes home?" he said.

"I think he left the city."

"You think. What if he's—" Tom's eyes went wide. "Oh, no. No, no. No, no, no."

"Calm down," I said. "He's not in there. I'm sure of it."

Well, *almost* sure. It was possible that Hugh had been murdered. Yet I didn't think he had. The Cult's murders were . . . showy, I guess. As if they wanted everyone to see what they'd done. If they'd killed Hugh, they would have left a grisly sign of it, as with all the others.

Or so I believed. As much as I tried to hide it from Tom, I was just as scared. I didn't want to find another body. I . . . couldn't. But I didn't have any choice.

I dragged Tom to the back door. I had to drag myself, too.

The house was dark. Slivers of sun slipped through cracks in the shutters, letting in just enough light to see. There was no front or back room on the ground floor, like there was in our home. Just one long, cluttered space for Hugh's workshop.

It hadn't been ransacked. And, praise the Blessed Baby Jesus, there was no butchered body to find. Otherwise, the workshop was laid out exactly the same as Master Benedict's, right down to the onion-shaped oven in the corner. I thought about the future I'd dreamed of, owning my own shop. Of course I'd set it up the same way. *If I still have a future*, I reminded myself.

No one had worked in here for a while. Both fireplace and oven were stone cold.

"What are we looking for?" Tom said.

"Hugh's fourth." I pulled the ledger page from under my master's sash. "Like it says in the message."

"His fourth what?"

I didn't know. Master Benedict had clearly expected me to figure out the answer, but he was a genius at this sort of thing. Sometimes he forgot that others—namely, me—weren't quite as good at deciphering puzzles as he was. Worse, his brain worked in odd ways. I was hoping that once we'd got inside, the solution would come to me. But other than the somewhat jarring feeling that I'd been here before, all I could see was a plain old workshop.

With nothing leaping out at me, we went upstairs. The second floor held Hugh's wife's parlor. There was also a kitchen, a half-stocked pantry, and a dining room. On the dining table, a single bowl rested, crusty streaks of brown stew congealed with the spoon at the bottom. The stub of a candle remained; its purple wax bled over the polished walnut below.

The third floor had three bedrooms and a sewing room. Two of the bedrooms were stuffed with dolls and frilly things: his daughters'. The other bedroom was plain and cramped; for Mistress Coggshall's maid, I guessed. I couldn't imagine whatever my master wanted me to see was in here.

There were two more bedrooms on the top floor. One wasn't quite as girlish as the chambers below, but was just as frilly, with a four-poster bed draped in aquamarine velvet. The other was clearly Hugh's.

Like the workshop, the bedroom was laid out nearly identical to Master Benedict's. Simple bed, side table, desk by the window, covered in paper. Even the furniture looked like it was made by the same carpenter. And here, too, stacks of books grew like trees from the floorboards, though nowhere near as many.

The bedsheets were crumpled. On the floor, next to a teetering pillar of tomes, were the last few bites of a loaf of bread. I tapped it with a fingernail. It ticked back, hard as a rock.

"No one's been here for days," Tom said. He looked at the papers on the desk. "Are we going to have to go through all that?"

It did seem like the best place to start. I sat at the desk and began to shuffle through Hugh's papers. Tom searched the clothes in the closet, turning out pockets.

There were lots of notes, recipes, and thoughts on herbs and mixtures in general. Looking for "Hugh's fourth," I scanned the fourth page, the fourth line on each page, the fourth word. Nothing looked promising. It was getting harder to concentrate, too. The puzzle cube in my pocket was poking my leg, and while I liked wearing my master's sash, its seams were starting to chafe my waist. The thing was designed to be worn on the outside, not hidden next to the skin. I untied it and flopped it on the bed.

After last night, Tom had as much reason to like the sash as I did. "This is really something," he said. He sat on the floor, legs splayed like he was still a little boy, and began poking the vials one by one out of their straps. His stomach growled like a taunted tiger. "I don't suppose any of this is food," he said hopefully.

"That's food," I said, nodding at the vial he was holding. "Sort of. It's castor oil."

Tom made a face. "Gives me the trots."

"It's supposed to." I put aside Hugh's papers and stared at the page from the ledger. "There's ipecac next to it, if you prefer. That makes things come out the other end."

"If you're trying to ruin my appetite," Tom said, "it's not working."

I was hungry, too. I'd left Tom's house so early, I hadn't even had the chance to eat breakfast, and now we'd missed lunch, as well. I thought about raiding Hugh's pantry, but I forced myself to stay at the desk, reading the ledger page over and over again. We still hadn't figured out what everything in the message was for. In particular, we'd barely paid any attention to the words "end.swords" in the second line. Master Benedict wouldn't have written that for no reason. It had to be part of the clue.

The question was how to decipher it? The period might separate the words, as it appeared. Or it could mean something else, like a starting point, or a stand-in for a comma or an apostrophe. It might even be nothing, a distraction to throw a would-be spy down the wrong path. End swords. Sword's end. End's words. Send words. Send them? Send them where?

"What's in this?" Tom said curiously.

He held up a vial from my master's sash. The liquid inside was clear and yellow. Unlike the others, the top was sealed with wax and bound tightly with twine. "Oil of vitriol," I said.

"Is that like castor oil?" He began to pull at the twine.

"Don't touch it!" I shouted.

He froze.

"That's not something you eat," I said. "Oil of vitriol dissolves iron."

He blinked. "Really?"

"It also dissolves people. If you get it on you, it'll melt your flesh."

He jerked his fingers away from the stopper. Still, he said, "Can we try it on something?"

"If you want." I stared out the window, trying to think. Hugh's bedroom, four floors up, was a story taller than the townhouses that faced it, giving him a nice view of the city. I could even see right into the forest green of a private garden nestled off an alleyway two streets over.

And there was a pigeon sitting on the windowsill.

"What the . . . ?" I began.

Tom looked up.

"It's Bridget," I said, amazed.

She bobbed her head and pecked at the glass.

"She followed us here?" Tom said. "What do you feed that bird?"

I unlatched the window. It was hinged at the top, swinging outward, so it began to push her off the sill. She flapped her wings accusingly.

"I can't open it unless you move," I said. Then I stopped.

I grabbed the ledger page. I reread my master's message. My heart was pounding.

Hugh's 4th below the lions the gates of paradise

"Is something wrong?" Tom said.

"I . . . I think I know where Hugh's fourth is."

"Where?"

"Here," I said. "Right here. We're standing in it."

"Hugh's bedroom?"

"What floor are we on?"

Tom counted. "The fourth." He looked surprised. "Hugh's, fourth. But how do you know that's the right answer?"

I pointed out the window. "Look."

Bridget tried to stick her head through the crack at the bottom of the frame. Tom followed my stare past her to the private garden beyond. It was walled off from the alley by a gate with pillars of stone, linked together by an iron fence. On top of the pillars were two statues, facing away from us. Their tails curved around the base.

Tom looked at me quizzically. I pushed the ledger paper over to him. He read it, then looked back at the garden. His eyes widened. "The statues."

I nodded. "They're lions."

CHAPTER
19

I STOPPED SHORT WHEN I ROUNDED
the corner. I stared at the brick wall that blocked our way.
Again.

"We should've turned left," Tom said.

I looked back the way we came, seeing nothing but
more brick. "Left would take us to the street."

"No, right is the street. Left is the houses."

"This place is a maze," I said.

"I think that's the point."

It sure seemed to be. We'd left Hugh's house and made
our way to the alley that led to the statues of the lions. We
should have been in a nice straight path to the private gar-

den. Instead, someone had laid a confounding pattern of walls between the houses, fifteen feet high, complete with sharp turns and dead ends. There were iron spikes set in the top of the walls, to stop anyone from climbing over. "This thing has more twists than a pretzel."

"What's a pretzel?" Tom said.

"It's a kind of dough the cook at the orphanage made. You dip it in butter and—it doesn't matter. We go right."

"It's *left*," Tom said.

"It's *right*."

Bridget flapped by overhead, going left. Tom glared at me.

"All right, fine," I said. "It's left."

Tom folded his arms. "We should put the bird in charge."

The bird was right. Going left led us along a path through the maze that exited directly in front of the pillars. Behind the wrought-iron fence was the private garden, which looked a lot like the one where Lord Ashcombe had found the buried body on Oak Apple Day. The gate here was closed, too, but not padlocked. At the top of each pillar that flanked it, the stone lions faced the mansion beyond, one paw raised.

"What now?" Tom said.

I held out the ledger page.

below the lions the gates of paradise

He looked at me. "And that means . . . ?"

There was a gate between the statues. Were these the gates of paradise? I couldn't see anything special about them. The pillars looked like large gray slabs stuck together with mortar. I ran my hands along them. They remained large gray slabs stuck together with mortar.

Beyond the fence, a path of cracked slate led from the gate and forked around a boxy granite structure, eight feet high and twelve feet across, ivy crawling up its walls. A plain stone cross adorned the top. Bridget waited for us there, preening an outstretched wing.

The path ended at the rear door of the mansion. On either side of the slate, the grass grew unkempt. The once-cared-for bushes had lost their trimming, their branches sticking out in misshapen lumps.

I unlatched the gate. "Let's check it out."

"We're not allowed in there," Tom said. "It's private."

The house's windows were dark. The only sound in the

garden was Bridget, cooing at us from atop the cross. "I don't think anyone's lived here for weeks."

We walked along the path to the other side of the stone structure, which turned out to be a mausoleum. The front, facing the house, had a wooden door with an iron latch. Vines crawled upward around the sides, sprouting bright white flowers that flared out like horns. Above the door was a brass plaque, tarnished to a mottled green by centuries of weather.

IN MEMORIAM

GWYNEDD MORTIMER A.D. 1322

REQUIESCAT IN PACE

I frowned. "Mortimer. Why do I know that name?"

"Henry," Tom said. "Lord Henry Mortimer. He was the third man killed by the Cult." Tom went over to the mansion and peered in the window. "You think this was his house?"

Bridget flapped down to the grass. When I picked her up, she stuck her beak into my fingers, looking for food. "I didn't bring anything," I told her.

"Christopher."

Tom stared back the way we came, head cocked to one side.

"Come here," he said.

I did. He turned me so I was facing the garden. "Look."

From where we stood, the mausoleum blocked most of the iron gate that led back to the maze. We could still see the lions on the pillars above it. The way they were posed, they appeared to be guarding the corners of the shrine. Behind the houses that backed onto the enclosure—all of whose windows had been bricked up, I noticed—was the window to Hugh's bedroom, where we'd first spotted the hidden garden. Beyond that was the steeple of a church. Even from this distance, I could make out the statue on the spire. It was a bearded man with a halo, right hand raised in blessing, his left hand holding a key.

"That's Saint Peter," Tom said. "Keeper of the Pearly Gates."

Saint Peter hovered directly above the mausoleum, lions at his feet on either side. Vines trailed around the door, flowers blooming white.

Below the lions, the gates of paradise.

We'd found it.

• • •

The mausoleum was dark and cramped inside. A marble sarcophagus, six feet long, rested in the center. It had no markings except water stains and a Latin inscription on the side.

DOMINUS ILLUMINATIO MEA

The Lord is my light.

Three of the walls held an alcove. Inside each was a statue, eighteen inches high, made of the same marble as the sarcophagus. On the left, a man with a round face and downturned lips held a tower in one hand and a book in the other. Facing him on the right was a bald man with a long beard, holding the paw of a lion lying peacefully at his feet. I was surprised to realize that I recognized them both. I'd seen their images in that book my master had given me to read three months ago, the book Lord Ashcombe had questioned me about in the shop. They were Catholic saints: Thomas Aquinas on the left, Jerome on the right. The patron saints of knowledge and learning.

The statue opposite the door was an angel. His sharp cheekbones and blank eyes were framed by long flowing hair. His wings were spread, every feather carved in such detail that they looked almost real. In his right hand he held a sword turned downward, its tip hovering just above the stone. His other hand was open, palm forward, fingers pointed toward the ground.

Bridget poked her head in the mausoleum's entrance, one foot stepping cautiously into the dark. Tom leaned over and peered at Saint Jerome's lion. I couldn't take my eyes off the angel.

End swords.

I went around the sarcophagus. My fingers traced the angel's blade to its tip.

Sword's end?

I pulled on the stone, gently, so as not to break the statue. I prodded the tip, and looked at the hilt. The angel stared back, unmoving.

Tom came over to join me. He touched the angel's open palm. "It's like he's trying to show you something."

Below the statue was nothing but rough stone. I looked behind us, at the sarcophagus. In the dim light, at the bottom of the casket, a shape caught my eye.

"Tom," I said.

He turned, and stared at the same place.

To anyone else, it would have looked like just another water stain on the marble. But we'd seen this shape before.

I knelt, searching. I didn't see any seams around it, any brick to move. I ran my fingers along the symbol, tracing the ripples of lightly corroded stone all the way around. The groove fit the circle perfectly.

I pressed it. The loop of stone slid in.

There was a low *click*.

A hollow grinding echoed in the chamber. I fell back, Tom pulling me by the collar. Bridget flapped her wings and flew for the light.

The sarcophagus shifted three inches toward Saint Jerome. Then it stopped.

Below the casket, dug in the floor, was a hole.

CHAPTER

20

I PEERED INTO THE DARKNESS. IT smelled musty.

"This is bad," Tom said.

"This is good," I said.

Tom shook his head. "I'm pretty sure this is bad."

I couldn't see anything, but the way the hole swallowed my voice made it clear that whatever was down there, there was a lot of it. There had to be a way to fit inside.

Bridget came back and peeked into the hole. I nudged her aside and pushed the casket toward Saint Jerome. It slid another inch. "Help me."

Reluctantly, Tom came over and gave the sarcophagus a

shove. It ground against the floor until it stopped with a jolt. The hole underneath was square, three feet wide. On the side nearest the angel, a notched wooden ladder descended into the dark.

"We need light," I said.

"We're not going down there," Tom said.

"But this is what we came here for."

Tom threw his hands up. "I didn't know there'd be a pit under a coffin."

An unlit torch hung in the corner by the door. I used the flint and tinder from my master's sash to ignite its oil-soaked end.

The torch flared brightly in the cramped chamber. I held it over the hole and was barely able to see the bottom.

"About twenty feet," I said. "Come on."

I swung onto the ladder. Bridget marched around the hole, poking her head in and ruffling her feathers. She trilled, alarmed.

"Listen to the bird," Tom said.

I went down. The air grew noticeably more damp with each rung. Grumbling, Tom followed. Bridget flapped her wings at me, but she wouldn't come.

We were in what looked like an ancient crypt. The

passage, eight feet wide, tracked away from the ladder, back toward the house. On either side, in narrow ledges dug into the rock, were skeletons.

Tom stepped off the ladder. "Oh, of course there are bodies."

The remains had clearly been here for ages. Their clothes and wrappings had disintegrated, leaving nothing but the occasional rusted buckle among time-stained bones.

"This crypt must have been built centuries ago," I said. "Let's see where it goes."

Tom clasped his hands together and mumbled a prayer. "Jesus, in Your mercy, please protect fools like us. Amen."

The passage continued, skeletons lining the sides, for about fifty feet before it turned sharply to the left. It narrowed, just enough to fit a man, then widened into a smooth, square chamber.

Unlike in the passageway, the items in here were new. On both sides were workbenches. The one on the left held about thirty glass jugs, each one labeled with a liquid: water, mercury, aqua vitae, oil of antimony, and more. The other bench supported an equal number of smaller glass jars, also labeled, containing powders. Salt, natron, sand, clover, all familiar. But what really drew my eye was what faced us.

The wall opposite the entrance was covered with a mural. At the top, an angel drove his sword downward into the belly of a dragon. The dragon twisted and writhed, roaring in agony, about to gobble a small black ball. Below the beast were two more dragons, their own serpentine bodies coiled, each snapping at a ball identical to the one above. The scene was ringed by an enormous snake with a red back and a green stomach, its head above the angel's, swallowing its own tail.

Tom yanked at my sleeve so hard, he nearly tore my shirt. "We have to go. Christopher. *We have to go.*"

I could barely keep my balance. "What are you doing?"

"Don't you realize where we are? This is the lair of the Cult of the Archangel."

"It isn't," I said.

Tom stabbed a finger at the mural. "Cult." Then he pointed at the figure at the top. "Archangel." He shook me. "Now put them together. How hard is that?"

"This can't belong to the Cult," I said. "Master Benedict wanted me to find this. He wouldn't send us into the lair of his killers without any warning." I would never believe that.

Tom wasn't as confident, but at least he stopped trying to tear my arm off. "Then . . . what is this place? Some sort of secret apothecary workshop?"

"It's not a workshop." Other than the ingredients in the jars, there wasn't any equipment. There were just a couple of glass beakers with long narrow spouts on the table with the liquids, and a long-handled metal spoon on the other. "It looks like a storeroom."

"For what?"

I wasn't sure. There were a lot of ingredients, but nothing you wouldn't find in any apothecary. I couldn't imagine why anyone would hide them down here.

Tom, still staring at the mural, pulled me close and whispered in my ear. "But what if we're being watched?"

"Tom," I said. "It's a painting."

"Then what are the holes in it for?"

For a moment, I had no idea what he was talking about. Then I realized he was right.

The black spots, in the dragons' mouths. I'd thought they were paint, like the rest of the mural. But up close, I could see each one was actually a small hole in the wall, the three of them together forming the corners of a perfect triangle. I peered into the one being eaten by the dragon on the left, but even with the torch, it was too dark to see anything. Against Tom's urging, I poked my finger inside.

I couldn't feel anything, either. There was a gap behind the wall, but the end—if there was one—was at least far enough away that my finger couldn't reach it. I could tell one thing, though. From the smoothness of the hole, and its coolness on my skin, the wall wasn't stone. It was iron.

Up close, the mural was even more remarkable. Hundreds of shapes and symbols were inscribed around the dragons. Some were simple, like circles and squares. Others looked more like alien letters of a forgotten language. As I stared at them, I noticed something. Near each of the holes in the dragons' mouths, some of the glyphs were ringed with gold, so faint you could barely see it.

Gilded next to the serpent at the top was a triangle with a line across it, like the peak of a snowcapped mountain.

The dragon in front of Tom had three highlighted symbols: a triangle, upside down; a curious ladder with a strange zigzag at the bottom; and a circle with a horizontal line through its center.

The final dragon, in front of me, had a single golden glyph.

☿

I stopped. I'd seen this one before.

This was the symbol for the planet Mercury. I looked back at the workbenches, and the ingredients that sat upon them. I took my puzzle cube out of my pocket and turned it around.

"What is it?" Tom said.

I touched the wall. "I think I know what this is. It isn't just a painting." I traced my fingers from the dragon to the hole. "I think this is a *door*."

CHAPTER
21

TOM INCHED AWAY FROM THE
mural. "A door?"

I pointed to the symbols above the holes. "I think this
is what the ingredients on the tables are for. The liquids and
powders, the beaker, the spoon. It's like my present." I held
out the antimony box. "You pour the right thing in and it
opens."

"What's the right thing?"

"Well, this symbol here is for Mercury, so I'm guessing
it's quicksilver."

There was plenty of mercury in one of the jars on the
table, more than I'd ever seen in one place before. I took one

of the notched beakers and poured some of the quicksilver into it. The glass grew heavy as I filled it to the mark.

At the door, the beaker's nozzle fit cleanly into the hole in the dragon's mouth. I tilted it, letting the metal run out. With the last few drops, a faint *thunk* came from behind the mural.

"It worked," Tom said.

But nothing else seemed to happen. I pushed on the wall. Tom joined me, putting his shoulder to it. It didn't budge. We heard another *thunk*, as if something clicked back into place.

I stepped away from the mural. "There are two more holes," I said. "We must have to put something in all of them to open the door." And from the sound of it, we didn't have much more than a minute to make it happen.

The symbols, with the right ingredients, were the key. I was amazed at how clever this was. It was much better than an actual key of iron or brass, which could be lost or stolen. With this door, if you were allowed in, you'd already know how to enter. Which we didn't.

"What about the rest of the message?" Tom said. "Those letters, from the code in lemon juice. Maybe they tell you what the ingredients are."

I pulled the parchment with the code from my pocket.

"Look," Tom said. "Say the *M* is for 'mercury.' Then *J* is for . . . uh . . . 'jam.' Or something."

If you ignored the part about jam, Tom's idea was a good one. But there were two more holes, four more symbols, and my master's message had enough letters to start a new alphabet. Even if Tom was right, I couldn't count how many different combinations we'd have to try. We were lost.

Again.

We returned to the surface and pushed the sarcophagus back into place. Bridget had already gone. Though I wanted desperately to remain below a little longer, I couldn't stay either. The afternoon was passing quickly, and I needed to get back to Apothecaries' Hall.

We stopped at Tom's house on the way. Reluctantly, I left the puzzle cube in his room. My master's sash could be more or less hidden under my shirt, but the cube was too bulky to carry well concealed, and the last thing I needed was Grand Master Thorpe asking what was in my pocket. I did keep the ledger page and the scrap with the translation, which I tucked safely underneath the sash.

As we left Tom's bedroom, Cecily appeared in the doorway to hers. Her eyes were wide with fear.

"Run!" she whispered.

Little Molly slipped past her sister, her mop of curls bouncing as she ran. She threw her arms around me, buried her face in my stomach, and sobbed.

I looked at Tom, puzzled. He knelt beside his sister. "Molly? Cecily? What's wrong?"

A meaty fist grabbed the back of Molly's dress and pulled her away. She landed on her backside, wailing.

Tom looked shocked. "Father!"

William Bailey grabbed me, next. I'd never been dragged by my hair before, much less while bumping down a flight of steps. Catherine and Isabel, playing in the front hall, dropped their dolls and scrambled behind their mother, who watched her husband pull me away.

"Father!" Tom ran after us. "Father, please! Stop!"

William Bailey kicked the front door open and tossed me into the street. I skidded across the cobblestones. My shirt—Tom's shirt—ripped at the shoulder. My skin ripped with it.

I lay in the gutter, too hurt to move. My hand pressed

against my wounded arm. The piercing pain in my scalp made me wonder if Tom's father had torn out enough hair to leave me as bald as Oswyn.

Tom moved to help me. His father punched him across the cheek before he could even get out the door. Tom crashed against the wall and held his hand to his face, stricken.

William Bailey loomed over me. "You abused my trust, boy."

It was true that Tom's father had allowed me to stay at his house, but I was pretty sure trust had nothing to do with it. "What did I do?" I croaked.

"The constable came looking for you."

The constable? My mind whirled with possibilities, none of them good. Had someone seen us break into Hugh's house? Did he know I took the puzzle cube? The sash?

Neighbors in the street watched curiously as Tom's father stabbed a pudgy finger at me. "The constable said Lord Ashcombe wants you. Said he heard you were staying here. I told him we didn't let strangers in the house. We don't know you. We don't want to know you. Don't come near my son again."

He stormed toward the house. Tom ran back inside in

front of him. I heard scuffling, then the thumping of Tom's feet bolting up the stairs.

Tom's mother filled the doorway. She looked less angry than sad. "I'm sorry, Christopher. But my husband is right. I have to protect my family. Please don't come here anymore."

She closed the door.

CHAPTER
22

A COUPLE OF MONTHS AFTER I'D turned twelve, I'd nearly broken open my skull. I'd been playing handball in Bunhill Fields when another boy tripped me, sending me sprawling headfirst into a tree. I couldn't walk—I couldn't even stand—so Tom had carried me all the way back to the shop. He'd laid me down on my palliasse, where Master Benedict had leaned over me.

I hadn't known where I was. Terrified, I'd struggled to run away.

Gently, Master Benedict had held me down in the straw. "It's all right, Christopher," he'd said. "It's me. It's me."

My senses returned. "I thought I was back at the orphanage," I'd said, still shaking.

"You don't have to worry about that anymore," Master Benedict had said. "Blackthorn is your home. It always will be."

But that was a promise he couldn't keep. And now everything else was falling apart, too.

My shoulder burned with the sting of a dozen hornets. Tom was probably getting it even worse from his father. I'd never be allowed to see him again. And now I didn't have anywhere to stay. I thought about throwing myself on the mercy of the Guild, but I might not even have that option. If Grand Master Thorpe didn't believe my story, I'd be all alone—no home, no food, and no friends, left to fend for myself against the Cult of the Archangel.

I wouldn't have thought anything could be scarier. But if Lord Ashcombe really was looking for me, my crumbling life had got even worse.

I felt sick.

The man with the slate-gray eyes let me into Apothecaries' Hall again. He looked annoyed that I'd returned. "Come on, then," he said, waving me past him impatiently.

I stepped inside cautiously, irritating him further. "Is Stubb—uh, Master Stubb here?" I said.

The man barred the door behind me and walked away. "Hasn't been here all day." I was relieved, although the fact that the man knew whom I was talking about meant Stubb was a regular. He could still show up any minute. I prayed this meeting wouldn't take too long to start.

I crossed the courtyard, planning to return to the clerk's office on the main floor where Oswyn had told me to wait this morning. An apprentice with long dark hair lounged on the main steps to the upper levels, tossing a small dagger into the air and catching it clumsily. I watched, half cringing, sure that any minute, fingers would go flying.

The dagger thrower looked to be about sixteen. He noticed me watching him while the knife was in midair. The dagger missed his fingers and bounced off his blue apron, right in a spot you don't want daggers to go. Flustered, he stood.

"Who are you?" he said.

"I'm here to speak to Grand Master Thorpe," I said. "Master Colthurst told me to return at four o'clock for a meeting."

The apprentice looked back at the windows. "Oh. All

right. You can wait in Master Colthurst's office, then."

"I don't know where that is."

He slid his dagger into his belt. "I'll show you."

The stone steps in the courtyard led to burnished cherry floors inside. I hadn't been up here since three years ago, when I'd gone to the Great Hall to take my entrance test. The same finely woven tapestries hung from the walls, just as they had back then. On one side was the blue shield of the Apothecaries' Guild. On the other, a man gathered herbs while a unicorn looked on. The light of heaven shone down on him through parted clouds.

The apprentice led me past the landing that went to the Great Hall and up to the third floor. As we climbed the stairs, I had a vague impression that I'd seen the boy before. I wondered if he'd been here when I'd taken my entrance exam. He was probably too old to have tested with me, but he could have been assigned to the Hall at the time.

"Are you Master Colthurst's apprentice?" I asked him.

"Me? No." He flicked his hair from his face and walked me down a long hallway with chestnut paneling. At the end, we reached a simple door with the key still in the key-hole. The apprentice knocked on the door and listened for a moment. When no reply came, he opened it.

"Wait here," he said. "I'll tell the masters you've arrived."
I stepped inside. He closed the door behind me, the latch
clacking shut.

So this was Oswyn's office. It was tidy—I'd expect that
from a Puritan—but smaller than I thought it would be. A
simple desk was in the center. An uncomfortable-looking
wooden chair sat behind it, its back to the courtyard window. An identical chair faced it. The desk was covered with
neatly stacked papers, one sheaf stained with oil that had
leaked from an unlit lantern perched on the nearby corner. The plaster walls were stark and colorless, undecorated
except for a series of vellum pages pinned to them, some
with writing, some with drawings of various figures and
icons. A handful of empty pots were arrayed on one side,
half a dozen books on the other.

I sat in the chair opposite the desk and waited. There
was a curious sketch on the wall beside me. Two men and
two women rode magical beasts: a griffin, a manticore, a
centaur, and a winged horse. Each figure was labeled in
Latin with one of the four elements, the building blocks
of all creation. *Aer, ignis, aqua, terra.* Air, fire, water, earth.

The beasts in the drawing reminded me of the mural
below the Mortimer house. I thought of the lock hidden

behind it, the crypt under the sarcophagus, the statues of saints in the alcoves.

Secrets under secrets, I thought. *Codes inside codes.*

The Cult of the Archangel had begun its murderous campaign four months ago. One month later, Master Benedict had shown me the book of saints. At the time, I'd been confused. Catholic saints?

"It's important to understand history," my master had said. "You never know when you'll need it." And I had.

Then he gave me my puzzle cube. It wasn't just an incredible birthday present. It was a lesson in symbols, and liquid keys. I'd seen those, too, in the mural below the crypt.

Now I understood.

He'd been training me. Even in secret, Master Benedict had never stopped training me. He'd wanted me to find the chamber in the crypt. He'd led me every step of the way. To do that, he'd taught me everything I needed, except one essential thing: what the symbols in the mural meant.

He had to know I didn't understand them. He wouldn't bring me to the edge and just leave me there. He must have given me the solution.

It had to be in the message in the ledger.

I put my ear to the keyhole in Oswyn's door and listened for a moment. Hearing no footsteps, I returned to the desk and pulled the ledger paper and scrap from under my master's sash.

That line. That one line I couldn't understand.

JSYYAALYUFMIYZFT

What had I missed? I looked at the original message, the whole thing together.

†Δ *esid.* A: *rapf.* O *set. age* Htsn. *oil eh. two leb.* Ht4: *shg. Uh.* ←
↓M08→ 0514202022220720160108042021011S *end.swords*
neminidixeris

Each line hid something different. The first, with the sword and triangle I didn't understand, told me how to find the crypt, where I'd seen similar symbols I didn't understand. The last line was the warning, in Latin, to keep it secret.

That left the middle line, from which Tom and I had generated the jumble of letters. The key to deciphering the symbols *had* to be in there. It occurred to me that we hadn't yet figured out what "end.swords" meant. It had to be related to what came before.

End swords. How would that help me decipher the code?

I'd seen a lot of swords lately: the symbol on the first line of the message, the angel statue in the mausoleum, the mural on the iron door below. Had I overlooked something on one of them? Was there another sword somewhere I hadn't found?

I shook my head, feeling like I was missing the point. Swords didn't make any sense here. This line was a cipher. It hid words.

Ends words. End's words.

End's words? What words? What end?

Of the message?

What was special about the end of the message?

Nemini dixeris, it said. *Tell no one.*

I thought about it. It was a warning. It was two words, written as one. It was in Latin.

Latin?

Master Benedict, apothecary. Latin, the language of apothecaries.

Secrets under secrets. Codes inside codes.

Was the cipher supposed to be in Latin?

I frowned. Tom had already asked if the message was in Latin. I'd said it couldn't be. The Latin alphabet had only twenty-three letters. There was no *J*, you used *I* for both. There was no *U*, either; *V* took its place. And there was no *W*. So JULIUS CAESAR would be written as IVLIVS CAESAR. You'd never even get a *J*.

I froze.

A mistake. I'd made a mistake.

You'd never even get a *J. Because it's not part of the alphabet.*

I'd translated the message as if it were English. But if the message was in Latin, then the code was wrong from the start. With a different alphabet, the letters wouldn't come out the same.

I grabbed a quill from Oswyn's desk. I wrote out the cipher, starting as before with 08 for *M*, but this time in Latin.

A	B	C	D	E	F	G	H	I	K	L	M
20	21	22	23	01	02	03	04	05	06	07	08

N	O	P	Q	R	S	T	V	X	Y	Z
09	10	11	12	13	14	15	16	17	18	19

I began the new translation. After five letters, my fingers began to shake. I had to use my left hand to hold them steady.

I got the new message. I stared at it.

ISAACCLAVEMHABET

Tom was right. It *was* Latin.

Isaac clavem habet, it said.

Isaac has the key.

CHAPTER
23

I PACED AROUND OSWYN'S OFFICE, my shoes slapping the floorboards. My mind raced along with me.

Isaac has the key. Isaac the bookseller, Master Benedict's faceless friend. I'd never met him, but Master Benedict had told me where his shop was. I wanted to run there right away, but I couldn't. I still needed to see the Guild Council. It wouldn't have done any good to leave, anyway. It was Sunday. Isaac's shop would be closed.

None of this made me any less impatient. Restlessly, I paced faster, round and round Oswyn's desk, feeling like a dog herding sheep. On one loop, my eye caught a figure through the window, down in the courtyard. It was another apprentice, exiting the door to the laboratories.

I'd thought Tom was big. This young man was twice his size, a true living giant. His barrel chest strained against his blue apron. The way he lumbered across the stone, it looked like an elephant had escaped from the king's zoo.

He plopped down on one of the benches in front of the steps to the Great Hall. The iron groaned under his weight. Like with the long-haired apprentice, the Elephant looked familiar, too. Again, I thought back to my test, but that didn't feel right at all. I got the sense I'd seen him recently. I tried to remember where.

It was while I was trying to place him that Oswyn entered the courtyard. He was with the Grand Master, steadying the old man's elbow, helping him slowly down the main steps. Sir Edward looked upset. Oswyn didn't seem much better. They were saying something, but two floors up, with the window closed, I could barely make out the words.

". . . shop . . . torn apart," Oswyn said. "Stubb . . . looking for . . . vanished."

". . . you think . . . ," Sir Edward said. ". . . have to stop . . . find Lord Ashcombe . . ."

Oswyn nodded. ". . . already sent . . . Christopher . . . murders . . . Cult . . ."

Oswyn guided Sir Edward across the courtyard. The clack of the Grand Master's cane on the stone came through better than their words. I opened the window, trying to catch the rest of what they were saying, but their backs were to me now as they made their way toward the entrance to the Hall. The little I could hear came in equally frustrating fragments.

". . . Archangel . . . ," Oswyn said. ". . . can't believe . . . we do?"

". . . Stubb . . . ," the Grand Master said. ". . . apprentice . . ."

The wind blew the rest of their conversation away. They disappeared under the arch to the exit to Blackfriars Lane. It brightened with sunlight as the outer gate opened, then went dark again. I blinked.

Did they just leave the Hall?

I'd been trying so hard to hear what they were saying, it didn't even occur to me where they'd been going. I waited a moment to see if they'd return. They didn't.

The long-haired apprentice was supposed to tell Oswyn and the Grand Master I was here. Had he not found them? I moved to chase after them, and was stopped dead in my tracks.

Oswyn's office door wouldn't open.

I rattled it, but the knob was frozen, the latch trapped in the jamb. I peered into the keyhole to see if the key was stuck. I saw right through to the opposite wall instead. The key wasn't stuck. It just wasn't there.

The apprentice had locked me in.

I stared at the door for a moment, my heart beginning to pound. Then I ran back to the window. The Elephant was still sitting on the iron bench, tossing pebbles disinterestedly at a flock of swallows that had congregated by the well. I almost called down to him for help, but the way he threw the stones unburied a memory.

Dice.

That's where I'd seen the Elephant before. I'd nearly tripped over him as I'd fled the shop yesterday, after Master Benedict had hit me. He'd been behind our house, in the alley, throwing dice. Another boy had been with him. I hadn't seen his face, but he'd had long dark hair. I'd been so upset at the time, I'd barely even noticed. Now I remembered both of them.

They'd been in the alley behind our shop, right before my master was murdered. The Elephant and the long-haired apprentice, the one who'd brought me up here.

My guts began to twist. The apprentice hadn't gone to tell Sir Edward and Oswyn I'd arrived. He'd gone to get them to leave the building. They'd left without even knowing I was here. And now I was trapped.

I finally understood why my master hadn't run that day. He'd been trapped, too, the same enemies surrounding him. They'd wanted Master Benedict's secret. If he'd fled with me, they'd have taken us, if not in the streets, then after following us to wherever we'd have run. The best Master Benedict could do was send me away. He'd sacrificed himself to save me. Now, locked in Oswyn's office, I'd squandered that. I'd let them trap me, just like him.

Movement from the courtyard pulled me from swelling despair. It was Valentine Grey, the third Council member, the one who apparently thought I should be flogged for my insolence. His giant gold chain bounced off his stomach as he hurried down the steps. He skidded to a stop at the bottom and, out of breath, addressed the Elephant. "Where's Sir Edward?"

The apprentice pointed toward the entrance. "He just left, Master."

Valentine ran after them, holding on to his necklace. Like the rest of the Council before him, he disappeared under the arch and didn't return.

The masters were gone. I prayed I was wrong, that this was a misunderstanding. When I saw the archway brighten again, I held my breath. They've come back, I thought. Then I saw who it was.

It was Wat.

He strode across the courtyard, untying his blue apron. He threw it on the bench beside the Elephant.

"Blackthorn's apprentice is here," the Elephant said.

Wat's fingers played along the handle of his knife. "Where?"

"Martin took him upstairs."

The long-haired apprentice—Martin—appeared at the top of the steps.

"Where is he?" Wat asked again.

"I locked him in Master Colthurst's office," Martin said.

The three of them looked up at the open window. I leaped to the side, hoping they hadn't seen me—as if at this point that would somehow make a difference.

"Why would you put him there?" I heard Wat say, sounding angrier than usual.

"He said he was here to see Master Colthurst," Martin said defensively. "What was I supposed to do?"

"Hide him somewhere. No one's supposed to see him. What if the masters had gone up there?"

"Why would they do that?"

"Enough." The Elephant's voice rumbled. "It doesn't matter. The masters left. No one's going to find him now."

"Let's finish this, then," Wat said, and I swore I could hear his blade leaving its sheath.

"Not yet," the Elephant said. "The doorman's still here. Go get rid of him. No, not *that* way. Send him on some errand that will keep him away for a while. Martin and I will check the rest of the Hall, make sure no one else has come."

"Just ask the doorman," Martin said. "He'll know."

"Our master told us to be sure," the Elephant said. "So we make sure. Once the Hall's cleared, bring Christopher to the basement. We'll deal with him there." I heard the iron bench creak, the scuffing of leather on stone. "It's not like he's got anywhere to run."

CHAPTER

24

MY HEART POUNDED LIKE A HAM-
mer, echoing the throbbing in my skull. Each beat came
with a question.

How could I have been so *stupid*?

If I hadn't been so wrapped up in my own head. If I'd
just looked at the two of them outside our shop for one
second more. If I hadn't followed Martin up here blindly.
It's not like I'd thought Stubb was the only one in the
Cult.

I shook my head. I could beat myself up later. Right
now, I needed to get out of here.

The window, I thought. Cautiously, I peeked outside.

The courtyard was empty. I stuck my head out farther, look-ing to see if I could climb down.

Not a chance. I was three floors up, with solid stone directly below. Climbing out the window was not an escape, it was a good way to break my legs.

I wanted to scream for the doorman. I would have if I hadn't known Wat would readily kill him to keep him quiet. Instead, I went back to Oswyn's door and pulled on the knob, rattling it as hard as I could. No use. The door jamb was solid oak, the latch was iron. The best I'd do is snap off the handle.

I scanned the room for a weapon, anything I could use. The chairs were sturdy. They might have made good clubs, except Oswyn's office was so small, there was barely any space to swing them. The books were useless, unless I planned to paper-cut my way out of here. The lantern, maybe. The base was solid brass, heavy enough to do some damage. It had oil, too, which could be dangerous. Unfor-tunately, I didn't have any way to light it.

Then it occurred to me: I *did* have a way to light it. In fact, I had a lot more.

My master's sash. I was still wearing it. That not only had flint and tinder, it was packed with useful things. I pulled up my shirt and looked at the dozens of vials in their pockets, cork tops poking above the cloth.

My first thought was to make gunpowder again, try to blow open the lock. But the vials with the ingredients I needed were empty. I'd used them up escaping from Stubb and Wat, and I hadn't thought to refill them when we'd searched Hugh's workshop. I twisted the sash around, searching for something else. That's when I spotted it: wax seal on top, tied with twine. I pulled the vial from the sash, the one that had fascinated Tom so much back in Hugh's bedroom.

Oil of vitriol. That magical liquid that dissolved iron—like the lock on Oswyn's office door.

I had to hurry. I tore the twine from the wax and broke the seal. The sour stink of the vitriol rose from the glass. I could see the latch between the door and the jamb, but I couldn't fit the vial into the crack. I ripped one of Oswyn's sketches from the wall, hoping desperately he'd forgive me for desecrating his office. I folded the parchment into a channel, wedging it into the gap. Then, carefully, carefully, I dripped the thin yellow oil down it onto the metal.

Immediately, the iron began to fizz. The invisible vapor that rose from the bubbles dried my throat, making me choke. I had to step back, coughing, while the oil of vitriol worked on the latch. I let the few drops I'd poured eat away at the iron for a minute, then dripped a little more.

The latch corroded slowly—too slowly—but I was scared to go any faster. The lock wasn't very thick, but there wasn't a huge amount of vitriol, and I couldn't afford to waste any. I'd already lost some to my parchment funnel, which was dissolving even faster than the iron. I'd hoped the vellum, being resistant to liquids, might last long enough to finish the job, but before I could pour the third batch, it crumbled into flakes of blackened calfskin.

I went for another page from Oswyn's wall. Then a better idea struck me. I pulled the silver spoon from my master's sash and rammed it between the door and the jamb, using its handle as a guide to drip the oil down. I wished I'd thought of that before I'd ruined Oswyn's work. Though breaking his door wouldn't exactly endear me to him, either. If I didn't get the chance to explain what had happened, I'd lose the only ally I had left.

Still, the latch disintegrated. I'd worn the iron down to a narrow strip of pitted metal when the vial ran out. There was nothing more I could do about it. I grabbed the handle with both hands and pulled.

The latch still wouldn't budge.

Come on, I thought. I put one foot against the wall and tried again, straining. My fingers throbbed, grew numb with pain.

The iron bent.

Once more. I pulled with all my strength. I prayed just as hard, sending a silent plea up to heaven. *Please, God. Please, Master. Please help me.*

It broke.

The latch snapped with a metallic twang. Its pitted end flew from the jamb and bounced dully on the floor, trailing little yellow drops behind it. I fell backward, landing hard on my side, setting my scraped shoulder to stinging again. I didn't care. I was free.

Or not.

Martin stared at me, wide eyed, from the other side of the open doorway. "How did you . . . ," he began.

I scrambled to my feet. I grabbed the chair closest to me. Before I could swing it at him, Martin was there.

He gripped my arms, shoved me backward into the desk. The corner drove into my spine, just below my ribs.

Pain. Incredible, unbearable pain. It felt like the wood had stabbed me, piercing my back like a spear. I howled and fell to the ground. Martin toppled with me.

His weight crushed the wind from my chest.

For a moment, I couldn't move. I just lay there, groaning in agony. I opened my eyes in time to see Martin's fist flying toward my mouth. His knuckles cracked into my teeth. My head slammed against the floor. I tasted blood, sour and metallic.

"You little rat," he said.

His punch dazed me, but he wasn't finished. Martin drew back to hit me again. I reached into the sash at my waist, more by instinct than anything else. I grabbed a vial, any vial, and drove it into his cheek.

The glass shattered in my hands, its jagged edge slicing open Martin's flesh. He screamed as I dragged the broken vial down to his chin, umber powder spilling out all over me. I twisted my hand as I pulled, sending a sharp stab of pain into my own finger. Martin shoved me away and rolled to the side, holding his face.

I rolled the other way. Martin turned toward me, fingers to his bloody cheek, unbridled rage in his eyes. There was still some powder in the vial. I threw it right in his face.

"Ahhh!" he cried. He fell back, his arm shielding his stinging eyes. I flung the remaining glass at him. It bounced harmlessly off his blue apron. Crimson drops from my cut finger trailed after it, dripping blood all over the wood.

I'd got Martin off me for the moment, but my head was still spinning. I used the side of the chair, now lying on the ground, to push myself up. Dazed, I stumbled, jamming my knee painfully against its oak rungs. My back spasmed horribly, threatening to seize up on me.

On the floor, Martin blinked away tears. His eyes had gone flaming red, the umber powder still dotting his cheeks. He bled badly from the wound I'd given him, scarlet running down his jaw and staining his collar. He began to pull himself up, too. His hand groped in his belt for his knife.

I grabbed Oswyn's lantern, now toppled over on his desk. I swung it wildly. Martin ducked. The lantern whistled past him harmlessly, but it put him off balance for a moment. He stumbled and fell into the corner.

I ran.

I'd planned to go back the way I came. Instead, I skidded to a stop. Thirty feet down the passage, the Elephant stopped in his tracks, too. We stared at each other for what seemed like forever. Oswyn's lantern swung from my hand. A knotted rope swung from his.

I turned and ran the other way.

CHAPTER
25

MARTIN DARTED OUT OF OSWYN'S
office as I fled past it, eyes wild, face bloody. I sprinted
forward to the end of the hall. There was another exit right
by Oswyn's office. I had no idea where it went. On the
other hand, "where" was "elsewhere," which had to be better than "here."

The arched door sheltered a narrow spiral staircase. I
bounded down as fast as I could go, each step shooting pain
across my injured back. Martin followed, his leather heels
scraping on the stone, the Elephant's footsteps clomping
farther back.

As I ran, I realized the lantern I was carrying wasn't

going to be much of a weapon. But I could use it for something else. Halfway down the stairs, I threw it behind me. The glass shattered. Oil splashed everywhere, amber dripping over the steps.

It worked even better than I'd hoped. Martin leaped after me, trying to close the distance. His heel slipped in the oil. He slid off the steps and pitched face-first into the wrought-iron railing. It gonged, like someone was ringing a church bell. He tumbled down.

I didn't stop to watch. Martin was out of it for a moment, but the Elephant was still stomping after me. At the bottom of the stairs, the narrow passageway opened into another corridor on the second floor, going north. I ran, trying every door. All of them were locked.

I heard voices behind me. Martin, swearing. The Elephant, shouting back. I turned to the right, down one hall, then left, into another. I found more steps and went down them.

I ended up on the ground floor, in a chamber I recognized. The clerks' offices, where Oswyn had told me to stay. And past that, the courtyard. I ran outside and skidded to a stop.

Wat was waiting at the entrance to the Hall.

I froze. He coiled, as if to chase me. He didn't. Instead, he scanned the empty windows. "He's here! Down here! In the courtyard!" he shouted.

It took me a second to realize why he wasn't coming after me. He didn't have to. He'd covered the only exit. All he had to do now was wait for Martin and the Elephant. And he wouldn't have to wait long. I could already hear them on the steps.

There was nowhere else to go. I turned and ran into the laboratory.

I'd been here once before, after my test, when the masters had shown us around the Guild Hall. There was one main entrance to the lab complex, which contained three different rooms. The central chamber, for general preparations, was a cluttering of workbenches covered with bins, casks, barrels, and pipes. A doorway on the right led to the distillery, which pumped the scent of alcohol into the prep room. Another doorway on the left held the ovens of the cook room. Each of the three main chambers, I recalled, had a smaller storeroom attached to it, holding various ingredients.

What I hadn't recalled, unfortunately, was that none of the chambers had any windows through which I might escape. Most of the light in the workshop came from the candles set in the walls, already burnt down to nubs. More light spilled from the door to the cook room. I fled in there, hoping someone was still working.

No such luck. The only sign of life was the fires left blazing in the dozen massive ovens. The masters had put pots on the grills to simmer long-cook recipes while they took their day of rest. I was alone.

And I was trapped once again.

"In there!" Wat shouted from the courtyard. "He went in the lab!"

It was over. They'd cornered me. And, I realized, I still had the secret to the crypt in my pocket.

Isaac has the key.

I pulled the scrap with the deciphered code from under my master's sash and threw it into the nearest oven. It curled instantly, crisped to ash. I almost cast in the page from the ledger, too, but I couldn't. I saw my master's handwriting on the paper and I . . . I just couldn't.

I crammed the paper back under the sash and hunted desperately for a weapon. Here, at least, I had better choices than I'd had in Oswyn's office. A heated plate of iron, say, cooking on the fire. Or a poker, to use as a spear or a club.

I shook my head at my foolishness. I wasn't King Arthur. I wouldn't be slaying any giants today. The Elephant alone could crush me just by thinking about it. And even if I got past him and Martin, Wat still guarded the exit with his knife. I'd never get out of here in a straight-up fight.

What I needed was a distraction, like the last time I'd run away from Wat. Well, this was a laboratory. And if there was one thing I *could* do, it was make distractions.

I ran to the storeroom at the far side of the cook room. It was so stuffed with ingredients, I could barely get inside. I'd never seen such a selection. Five-, ten-, twenty-gallon glass jugs held a dizzying rainbow of liquids. The ceramic jars were so big, they looked like they were built for whales.

The first thing I needed to do was buy some time. I found two ingredients: sugar and saltpeter. Together, they were the best distraction makers in the world.

I dragged the jars into the cook room, ceramic scraping along the stone, ignoring the howling pain in my back. My plan would work better if I could melt the ingredients first, but I didn't have the time. So I just tipped both jars over near the doorway that led back to the prep room and tossed their spilled contents together with my fingers.

Voices carried from the central chamber.

"He broke my tooth," Martin whined.

"Quiet," the Elephant said.

"I'm going to kill the little worm."

"You're not going to touch him. Now shut up and let me listen."

I crept to the nearest oven and used a set of tongs to grab a glowing coal.

"Games are over, Christopher," the Elephant said. "Come on out."

Footsteps came closer to the doorway, moving cautiously.

I dropped the coal in the heap of white on the floor.

There was a hiss.

"What's that?" Martin said.

Then the powder burst into flame. Smoke poured from the mound as a rose-red wall of fire erupted, keening like a banshee.

"Back!" the Elephant shouted from the other room. "Get back!"

I fell to the stone and scrambled away, just as scared as the others. I'd never mixed so much sugar and saltpeter before. The inferno spattered hot caramel drips at my shoes until the grains were spent, leaving a charred splotch on the flagstones. Smoke filled the room, a fog of white. I could barely see inches in front of my face.

"God's breath. He set the Hall on fire," Martin said.

"Christopher!" the Elephant called. "Get out of there! You'll kill yourself."

He wasn't half wrong. The smoke was what I'd wanted; the haze would hide me, and keep the others out for a minute or two. But the cloud billowed everywhere, stinging my eyes and choking my lungs. I ran back to the storeroom, hacking and heaving, gasping for air. I grabbed a spare apron and tied it around my face, covering my nose and mouth, hoping it might filter some of the smoke. It helped a little, but I couldn't stay in here much longer.

Still, I'd bought myself a bit more time to work. I'd have loved to make another cannon, but I'd burned up all the saltpeter. I couldn't mix gunpowder anymore. I needed something else.

The smoke was so thick, and my eyes watered so badly, I could barely read the labels on the jars. But there, among the other white powders, was natron. And there, on the other side in a twenty-gallon glass jug, was vinegar.

I grabbed another of the apprentice's aprons from one of the pegs and dumped the natron into it, twisting it at the top to form a heavy pouch. Then I overturned the jug and let half the vinegar inside glug out onto the floor. It splashed everywhere, soaking my shoes, drawing up into a row of burlap sacks of wheat by the door, staining them maroon. *If I survive this*, I thought, *there won't be a master in the Guild who won't have me flogged.*

The sour scent of vinegar mixed with the smoke and made me cough even worse. I squeezed the pouch of natron into the wide, open mouth of the jug. Then I pressed the giant stopper back in so it trapped the top of the apron in the neck of the bottle. A stomp from my shoe drove the cork deep enough to hold.

It took a second for the remaining vinegar in the jar to start soaking through the canvas. The liquid started to fizz.

"Christopher." The Elephant called out, still waiting for me by the doorway in the central chamber. "You can't get away. Come on out, now. We just need some information. We won't hurt you if you tell us what we want to know."

Did I really look that dumb? He was right, though. It was time to come out. The jug wouldn't hold forever; the cork stopper was already straining against the glass. And the smoke was making me dizzy.

I hefted the jug, sending another scream down my

back. Now, one more weapon, that's all I needed. I found it through the fog in a small pot with a long handle, bubbling on the stove with a sticky brown goo that smelled like Satan eating beans. I pulled the pot from the fire. The iron bottom scraped across the grill with a metallic screech.

"Christopher," the Elephant said.

The weight of the pot set my whole arm wobbling, bringing new cries from my wounds. I crept to the doorway that led back to the central chamber, the jug with natron and vinegar still weighing down my other hand. It was gray everywhere. I couldn't see them. I needed to see them.

I coughed. "You promise you won't hurt me?"

"Absolutely," the Elephant said.

There.

I threw the steaming goop toward his voice. I heard it splash on stiff linen. He screamed.

I bolted from the door, jug in one hand, the now-empty iron pot in the other. The smoke was thin enough here to see the goop had hit the Elephant square on. He was soaked, a nasty brown starburst on his chest and neck. He trumpeted, arms flailing, trying to pull his clothes from his scalded skin. Martin, his mangled lip and cheek covered in blood, backed away from his comrade in fright.

He spotted me coming from the smoke, but too late. I swung the pot at his head. It clanged against his skull hard enough to wrench from my hand, bouncing across the floor, ringing over the stone. Martin crumpled like a sack of meal.

That's for Master Benedict, I thought.

I ran out through the prep room back to the courtyard. I carried the glass jug in both hands, now, all my muscles joining my back in howling against its weight. The vinegar inside had already turned into a bubbly pink foam. The cork squeezed upward in the neck.

Wat was waiting. He drew his knife, that long, curved, wicked blade.

But I didn't intend to fight him. Halfway across the courtyard, with the last of my strength, I hurled the jug toward where he stood. Wat watched it fly through the air, surprised. It was a clumsy thing, easily sidestepped. He did, just like I'd hoped.

I dived, skidding across the stone to slam into the back of the well, putting it between me and Wat. The jug hit the ground.

It exploded. The glass shattered with an earsplitting bang, sounding like the biggest cannon in the world. The fearsome pressure from the mixture of vinegar and natron blew shards so far, they plinked off windows on the third floor, pitting the courtyard brick like a thousand Saracen arrows.

Chips of glass, flecked with pink foam, rained down beside me, where I lay protected from the blast behind the cover of the well. I stuck my head over the rim to see what had happened.

Wat writhed on the ground, still gripping his knife, the blade scratching against the stone. His right side, from boots to hair, was plastered with red. I didn't know if it was vinegar or blood. I didn't stay to find out. I sprinted past him, flung open the door to the Hall, and fled into the street. After what I'd just done to the place, I knew I'd never get to return.

CHAPTER
26

I RAN, LUNGS BURNING ALL THE WAY.
It seemed like the whole of London stared as I sprinted past, stinking of smoke and vinegar, coughing to hack up a lung. Still I ran, on the edge of panic, only one thought in my mind.

Blackthorn.

Home.

It didn't matter that the shop wasn't mine anymore. I didn't know where else to go. Even if it hadn't been Sunday, Isaac's place was too close to Apothecaries' Hall for me to go there now. Plus, I didn't know how much I could trust the man. And I wasn't welcome at Tom's.

I gave myself an excuse to go home again: ingredients.

I'd used up two more of the vials in Master Benedict's sash in my escape. Without those, and the ingredients in the lab, Wat would, at this very moment, be slitting me open like a Sunday pig.

That wasn't my only excuse. Tom's place was on the way home from the Guild Hall. Maybe he'd be outside, and I could see him for a moment without his family around. He'd got in trouble because of me. I wanted to see him, say I was sorry. Say goodbye.

I had to be careful. I shuddered to think of what Tom's father would do if he saw me. I'd have to be even more cautious about going home again. There was a good chance the shop was being watched. Wat and the others might be back at the Hall, but Stubb wasn't. And if I'd learned one thing today, it was that anyone, anywhere, could be part of the Cult.

In the chaos, I'd forgotten that Lord Ashcombe was looking for me, too. I didn't forget for long.

By the time I'd neared Tom's place, I was so out of breath, I could barely walk. My back, protesting all the way, spasmed with every step. *Just a few more streets to go*, I told myself, and then I could rest. I was concentrating so hard on staying on my feet that I nearly ran into the lion's den.

Tom *was* outside his house, but he wasn't alone. Lord Ashcombe was there, too.

I nearly tripped on the cobbles. I stumbled to the safety of the doorway of a nearby jeweler and pressed my back against the wood, panting heavily, lungs on fire.

Lord Ashcombe wasn't saying anything. Tom, on the other hand, was babbling. I was too far away to hear a word of it, but he looked terrified. Lord Ashcombe stared at him, black eyes piercing.

Keeping my head down, I crept into a nearby alley between the jeweler's workshop and the ironmonger next door. Under better cover, I peeked my head out again. Lord Ashcombe was still listening as Tom ran his mouth. One of the King's Men stepped from Tom's home, carrying something. He gave it to Lord Ashcombe. The King's Warden held it out wordlessly to my friend.

I caught the glint of sunlight off silvery metal. Lord Ashcombe was holding my puzzle cube.

Tom's eyes went wide. He started babbling again, even faster than before. Slowly, Lord Ashcombe reached out with his free hand and grabbed Tom's hair. He twisted, forcing Tom to his knees.

Tom's mother ran from inside her home. She knelt in

the mud next to her son, begging Lord Ashcombe, babbling as fast as Tom was. Tom's father started in, too, face red and sweaty, gesturing angrily down the street, the way I'd left his house when he'd thrown me out. The King's Warden barely acknowledged them, his eyes never leaving my friend's.

Lord Ashcombe had to know *I'd* taken my puzzle cube, not Tom. According to the law, that didn't matter. Finding it in Tom's house marked him as a thief. The penalty for that was death.

I bowed my head. I couldn't just leave Tom to Lord Ashcombe. If the King's Warden was going to make someone take the blame for the theft, it had to be me.

I stepped into the street.

"Hello, Christopher," a small voice said.

It came from behind me, back in the alley. I turned.

It was Molly. She smiled at me from the shadows, her mop of soft curls tumbling into her eyes. At four years old, she was young enough that she had trouble pronouncing some of her letters. *Hewwo, Chwistophuh.*

I blinked. "Molly?"

Her smile widened. "Come with me," she said. *Come wiff mee.*

"I . . . I can't," I said, though I wished so much that I

could. "Your brother's in trouble. I have to help him—"

"No." Molly reached out her small, delicate fingers and wrapped them around my hand. She tugged. "Come with me. You have to. Tom says."

"I can't."

"Tom says." She pulled as hard as she could, which didn't budge me an inch. "Tom says. No. Noooo!" Molly started to cry as I took a step toward Lord Ashcombe. "I promised! Tom says!"

In the distance, Lord Ashcombe let go of Tom's hair. It looked like Tom might faint. His mother seemed to be thanking the King's Warden over and over again. Lord Ashcombe ignored her. He said something to Tom, and Tom nodded like mad. The King's Men had already begun to talk to the neighbors, some of whom pointed in the same direction Tom's father had, the way I'd left his house. It appeared Tom had convinced Lord Ashcombe that he really didn't know where to find me.

The little girl yanking at my fingers seemed to tell a different story. "Come *on*," Molly said. "Tom *says*."

I waited a moment more, to see that Lord Ashcombe wouldn't change his mind and haul Tom away after all. When he finally stalked off down the road, I sighed. "All right."

• • •

As soon as I agreed to go, Molly's mood changed instantly, as is the way with young children. Hot tears flipped to a gentle smile, which she kept as she wandered in front of me through London's back alleys. She hummed to herself, occasionally skipping for a few paces, playing some unknown game.

"What were you doing in the alley?" I asked her.

"Finding you." She looked up at me proudly. "Tom sent us to find you, when he seen the scary man come. But *I* did it."

I put my arm around her shoulders and gave her a little hug. "You're the best." She beamed at me for a moment, head resting against my hip. Then she spotted a butterfly and chased it, jumping to try to catch it as it fluttered up into the air.

When I'd started following Molly, I'd assumed she was leading me around the long way to the back of Tom's house— though God help me if either of his parents saw me now. But we just seemed to move aimlessly from alley to alley. Our trip was taking forever, we weren't getting any closer to Tom's place, and my back had had more than enough.

"Do you know where we're going?" I said.

"Uh-huh." Molly scanned the sky, hoping the butterfly would return. "Tom says take you to the Black House."

"The Black House?" I didn't recognize the name. "Who are the Blacks?"

Molly giggled. "Not *Black*, silly. *Black*."

"I see," I said, though it had been a long time since I'd understood four-year-old logic.

It didn't take much longer to become clear. In the last of the uncountable alleys, we came upon . . . I didn't know what to call it. It wasn't a house anymore.

What had stood here had once been the largest home on the street. Last summer, a fire had gutted it. The top floor was completely gone. The second floor was halfway to ash, too, just bare, blackened walls and charred timbers piercing upward like giant toothpicks. In one corner, the bottom of the house had collapsed, leaving nothing but rubble and splintered oak.

The black house.

Cecily was in the alley. She paced, hands tugging at the front of her lavender dress. When she spotted me and Molly, she glanced over at the back door of the house. It hung loosely from a single wobbling hinge, swaying back and forth behind the man waiting for us.

Dr. Parrett smiled. "Welcome," he said.

CHAPTER
27

THE INSIDE OF THE HOUSE WAS
just as scarred. Soot streaked across fire-licked beams
that somehow still supported the upper story. Dried mud
tracked over every floor, so thick it was like we were still in
the streets. Above the fireplace, a ruined painting of some
long-forgotten landscape hung from a broken frame, oils
melted, canvas crumpled.

Dr. Parrett. Poor, mad Dr. Parrett, whose family had
died in the blaze last summer, still living here with the ghost
of his son, James.

Molly didn't seem bothered by the house at all. She
stared in fascination at the ruins around her, too young to

understand what it really meant. Cecily wasn't so calm. She wrapped her arm around mine and pressed against me. I pressed back, chilled to the bone, wondering if James's spirit was really still here.

"My son is sleeping," Dr. Parrett whispered, "and he has to work on his studies tomorrow. So don't you lot stay up all night." He wagged his finger at me good naturedly.

"We won't," I said. It was all I could do not to make the sign of the cross.

"You can stay with James, in his room. It's in the back."

He lifted a lantern from the mantel and led us around the rear to a small room without a door. A bed with a straw mattress was tucked into a corner. The straw was fresh, and unlike the rest of the house, there was no mud in here. Everything else was badly burnt. Scraps of shriveled damask peeled away from the pitted wall. The bed's headboard was charred and broken. One leg was gone, the corner propped up by a pair of bricks. A soot-stained pillow rested at the head, and beside it, a worn woolen knight doll with a missing button eye.

"Let me know if you need anything," Dr. Parrett said.

He smiled and left. Molly immediately went for the doll. She plunked herself down on the floorboards, and soon she and the knitted knight were having a conversation about where his horse had gone.

"How did you all know where to find me?" I asked Cecily.

"We didn't." She huddled against me, glancing at the blackened walls. "When Tom saw the King's Men coming, he was worried you might go back to the house. So he sent my sisters out to look for you. He asked me to arrange a place for you with Dr. Parrett."

My battered body overcame the chill at being in James's room, haunted or not. Slowly, I lowered myself to the straw. My back howled, then cooled to a low moan, the weight finally off it. Cecily helped me down, looking concerned.

I took stock of what was left of me. My cheek was tender and swollen where Martin had hit me. The skin on my shoulder, where my shirt had torn on the cobbles of the street, was scabbed and stinging. My finger, cut by the vial I broke in Oswyn's office, throbbed mercilessly, though the bleeding had stopped, at least.

The cut on my finger wasn't the most painful of my wounds—my back won that prize easily—but it was the most dangerous. Already the joint grew red and puffy, tender to the touch. If untreated, it could turn the humors of my body sour and poisonous. Fortunately, I still had my master's sash. I tried to lift my shirt to get at it. My back didn't like that.

"What can I do?" Cecily said.

I tugged at my shirt. "Help me pull this off."

She did, sliding it over my head gently as I gritted my teeth. I packed the wound on my finger with spiderweb from one of the vials from the sash, and smeared aloe from another one as well. A strip torn from the bottom of my shirt made a bandage, which Cecily tied on tight. She did the same for the scrape on my shoulder. Then she sat behind me on the straw and examined my back, where the corner of the desk had rammed into me.

"It's really red," she said.

"Can you press on it? I need to check if anything's broken."

"Won't that hurt?"

"Yes." I sighed. "Yes, it will."

It did. But apart from an angry red triangle the width of a melon over my spine, it didn't appear that I'd broken anything. I was definitely in for an unpleasant few days, though. I wanted desperately to drink a bucket of poppy tea, but with the Cult of the Archangel and Lord Ashcombe both hunting me now, I was afraid to dull my mind. I pulled out the vial of willow bark and swallowed half of it instead. The bitter powder made me grimace. Beyond that, all I could do was lie down on the straw and take the pain.

Tom came at sunset, carrying a small burlap sack and a leather pouch in the same hand. He had a purple splotch on his face, the bruise already forming where his father had hit him. Molly leaped from the floor, still clutching the knight doll, and ran to her brother. "I found him!" she said proudly, pointing at me as I sat up.

"You did very well," Tom said. He pushed his sister's curls away from her eyes and patted her cheek.

Cecily sat next to me on the straw, her arms wrapped around her knees. "Any problems?" Tom asked her.

She shook her head. "Dr. Parrett's very nice."

"Can you take Molly home?"

She stood. "Of course."

Molly handed me the knight, then threw her arms around me. It set my back to moaning again. I didn't mind.

"Thanks for helping me," I said to her. I waved my bandaged finger at Cecily. "And thank you, too."

She gave me a shy smile, then put her arm around her sister and left. When they were gone, I turned to Tom. "I'm sorry," I said. "Are you all right?"

Tom shrugged. "Father's given me worse."

I was more worried about Lord Ashcombe. "Will he come back for you? I saw he found my puzzle cube—"

"Lord Ashcombe doesn't care about your puzzle cube. Here."

Tom handed me the sack he was carrying. Inside were a pair of sticky buns. Just seeing them made me feel human again.

Tom watched me wince as I leaned against the ruined headboard. "What happened to you?" he said.

Mumbling over mouthfuls of sticky bun, I told him about the Hall, about being trapped by Martin and Wat and the Elephant while they lured Sir Edward and Oswyn away. I thought he'd be shocked, but my story barely seemed to register. I also told him about my discovery.

"Isaac has the key to the mural in the crypt," I said.

"Oh?" Tom didn't seem interested. He waved his hand at James's charred bedroom. "Sorry about this. It's the only place I could think of. I didn't figure anyone would look for you here."

I sat James's woolen knight next to me on the bed. "I'm grateful to have it. Thank you."

"The King's Men are bound to be watching the gates

out of London. Maybe, once I figure out what the patrols are like, you can sneak down to the docks and get out." Tom handed me the leather purse.

It jingled when I took it. I pulled the drawstring open. Silver glinted in the light of the flame. I counted three shillings, and at least a dozen pennies.

I was stunned. "Where did you get these?"

"My father's strongbox, in the bakery," he said.

"Are you mad? Your father will kill you. I can't take this."

I held the purse out. Tom put his hands behind his back and stepped away. "Passage will cost a shilling at least," he said. "More, if they think you're desperate. One of our regular customers runs a barge. I think he could be bribed. I'll ask him if he'll take you."

"Take me where?"

"I told you. Out of the city. You can't stay here." Tom looked into my eyes. "You do realize that, don't you?"

"But . . . listen, I think I've figured it out. One of the Apothecaries' Guild Council members, Valentine Grey, was at the Hall today. I don't think the rest of the Council knew he was there. Then I saw him speaking to the Elephant. I think maybe he and Martin were Valentine's apprentices. If that's true, then Valentine's in the Cult, too. If I tell Lord Ashcombe—"

"You can't go to Lord Ashcombe."

"I know I still don't have any witnesses, but if I explain, I mean, Lord Ashcombe was there yesterday; he knows why I wanted my puzzle cube—"

"Oh, God's truth, Christopher," Tom huffed. "You don't *listen* sometimes. Lord Ashcombe doesn't care about your bloody puzzle cube. He thinks you're to blame for Master Benedict's death."

My jaw dropped. "*Me?* But . . . *why?*"

"You were away from the shop exactly when the Cult struck. Lord Ashcombe thought that was suspicious. When he went back to look at the shop this morning, he saw the ledger page was missing. He knows you lied about what Master Benedict wrote. He's sure there's something incriminating on it, and you took it so no one else would see it."

A pit grew in my stomach. "That still doesn't explain why I would kill him."

"He's not sure. He thinks you might be working with the Cult of the Archangel."

I stared at Tom. "That's . . . that's crazy."

"He also suggested that maybe you just made Master

Benedict's death *look* like one of the Cult's murders, so everyone would blame them instead of you. He thinks maybe you just wanted revenge for Master Benedict beating you."

I stiffened. "He never laid a hand on me!" Then I realized: He *had* hit me. Once, only once. "Lady Brent," I said.

Tom nodded. "Lord Ashcombe questioned her. She claimed Master Benedict beat you regularly. She said he was cruel to you, and you resented it. That's why he went back to look at the shop, at the ledger page. I told him it wasn't true, but he just thinks I'm lying to protect you."

Master Benedict had hit me, cursed me, to keep me from Wat and the rest of the Cult. He'd played the part of cruel master well enough to save me, at least temporarily. But Wat hadn't been the only audience. Lady Brent's word would be enough for any court to convict me. I felt sick.

"Master Hugh," I said suddenly. "He knows the truth. And he's a master in the Guild. They'll have to believe him. If we can find him, he'll vouch for me."

Tom stared at the floor. "Master Hugh is dead," he said quietly.

I sat there, not moving. It was a moment before I could speak. "Wh . . . what?"

"Lord Ashcombe told me. The body buried in the garden, the one we saw on Oak Apple Day. It was Hugh's."

I thought the news would hit me harder. I just felt numb. Maybe it was because I couldn't imagine anything more crushing than to be blamed for my master's murder. Or maybe it was because deep down, some part of me already knew Hugh hadn't left the city. That, like me, he couldn't leave Master Benedict behind. "Then . . . the Cult *did* attack them Thursday night."

"Actually," Tom said, puzzled, "Lord Ashcombe isn't sure it was the Cult. Hugh wasn't cut open like the others. Also, it was a Christian grave. He was buried on hallowed ground."

I frowned. Why would Hugh's killers give him a Christian burial? None of this was making any sense. "I suppose he blames me for Hugh's death, too," I said bitterly.

"He didn't say. He does blame you for Stubb, though."

"What does that mean?"

Tom looked surprised. "You haven't heard? Stubb is dead, too."

My jaw dropped. "What?" I blinked. "He . . . he can't be."

"They found him in his home this afternoon. He and his apprentices were murdered, just like the rest of the Cult's victims. The news is all over the streets. I thought you knew."

My mind whirled.

Stubb . . . was dead?

I didn't understand. Master Benedict. Hugh. Now Stubb?

Why would the Cult of the Archangel kill Stubb? He was *in* the Cult.

I thought of Wat. Martin and the Elephant had been waiting at Apothecaries' Hall this afternoon. Wat had come from outside.

Did Wat kill Stubb? Was that where he'd been?

The murders certainly sounded like Wat's handiwork, and the boy clearly hated the man. Was he out of control, then? Did he kill Stubb out of malice?

Or was he acting on higher orders?

I didn't *understand*.

"Christopher."

I looked up. I hadn't even realized Tom was still speaking.

"You must see now, don't you?" Tom said. "You have to leave London. The Cult is getting rid of everyone. The one man who can stop them thinks you're part of it. You can't fight them, and you can't go to Lord Ashcombe for protection."

"Where am I supposed to go?" I said.

"I don't know. Find a new city. Get a new job. Any master would be lucky to have you as an apprentice."

"A new apprenticeship would cost *pounds*," I said. "And there's no work for someone like me. You know what happens to children on the streets." I shuddered, thinking of what would happen to Sally if she didn't find a job, remembering the older children who'd aged out of Cripplegate. The lucky ones were still out there, begging, or cutting purses—or doing things even worse. Most just disappeared, never to be seen again.

The truth was, I had nowhere to go. Tom was just wishing. For a moment, so did I. I closed my eyes and ran away, somewhere safe, where Master Benedict was still alive. No more pain, no more death.

But that was just a wish.

"What are you going to do?" Tom said quietly.

What else could I do? "Go see Isaac. Get the key to the mural." And trust that Master Benedict would help me find a way out.

"But . . . you can't even walk the streets anymore. Lord Ashcombe is putting out a reward for your capture. A big one, too, five or ten pounds. Everyone in London will be looking for you."

I ran my fingers over the vials in the sash. "I have an idea about that. You just go return these coins before your father puts *you* in a grave." I handed him the purse. "And don't come here again."

"I'm going with you," Tom said, surprised.

"No, you're not," I said. "It's too dangerous."

Now he looked annoyed. "You're not my master. Don't tell me what to do."

"You have to work tomorrow," I reminded him.

"My father sends me to buy flour from the market on Monday. I'm away for hours. I'll come by after the cry of six."

"Tom—"

He threw his arms to the heavens. "Oh, would you just stop *talking* for once."

I did.

"They're not going to take you," Tom said. "The Cult, Lord Ashcombe . . . whoever. They're not going to take you, too."

Tom turned to go. He stopped at the door. "Good night, Christopher," he said. Then he left.

MONDAY, JUNE 1, 1665

The Feast of Saint Justin, Martyr

CHAPTER
28

I BARELY SLEPT. THOUGH I WAS exhausted, my back ached with every shift and shiver, jerking me awake if I moved so much as an inch. The jolt that pulled me out of bed for good came at six. It was the crier, calling my name.

"Oyez, oyez, oyez! Be on watch, good citizens! Christopher Rowe, murderer of Benedict Blackthorn, is at large! Grown rebellious against his master's cruelty, young Rowe has thrown his lot in with the Cult of the Archangel! His Majesty offers a reward of twenty pounds for the boy's capture."

The crier's voice carried easily through Dr. Parrett's ruined house. I still wasn't sure I'd heard him right. *Twenty pounds?*

"Good morning," Dr. Parrett said.

I nearly fell out of bed. Dr. Parrett stood in the doorway, holding a bucket.

"My apologies," he said. "I didn't mean to startle you. I brought you some water." He placed the bucket at the foot of the bed, water sloshing up the side. "Are you not feeling well? James says your sleep was troubled."

I stared at Dr. Parrett, saw his worn and tattered clothes, his body underneath, emaciated from begging for scraps. He had to have heard the crier. *Twenty pounds.*

I pulled the blanket to my chest. "Dr. Parrett . . . what they're saying . . . I didn't—"

"Don't listen to them," Dr. Parrett said fiercely. "They're liars! They—" He choked on his words. For a moment, reality seemed to punch through his madness, to the sorrow living behind his eyes. Then the knowledge was gone, and the man stood there, blinking away the truth. "You have a home here, with us, for as long as you need it. I have some bread for breakfast, when you're ready. Can I get you anything else?"

I asked for one more thing. He nodded and left. I downed the last of the willow bark, for whatever little good it would do. Then I dragged the bucket over and got to work.

• • •

When Tom saw me, he nearly bolted. His eyes darted around James's room, as if someone else could be hiding in this burnt-out tomb. Then his jaw dropped. "Christopher?"

I turned, arms spread. "What do you think?"

For a moment, only his mouth worked. "What happened to you?"

My hair was now jet black, stained with squid ink from my master's sash. I'd discarded Tom's old clothes, too, borrowing new ones from Dr. Parrett. I wore a pair of the man's tattered breeches, too big, and one of his son's linen shirts, too small. For that additional touch of street urchin, I'd used vermilion from crushed snail shells mixed with the remaining squid ink to mark angry maroon dots on my face. The swelling on my cheek where Martin had punched me added to the costume, though it was hardly worth the pain.

"It looks like you just got over the pox." Tom crinkled his nose. "And you smell like you didn't."

For the first time in days, I felt a bit of hope. If my disguise could confuse Tom, even for a second, it just might do its job. "You were wrong about the reward," I said. "I'm worth *twenty* pounds."

He made a face. "Keep that in mind, before you make my life any harder."

. . .

The disguise worked almost too well. On the streets, more than one shopkeeper raised a club and cursed at me if I got too close, protecting his goods from being easy pickings for a nimble-fingered thief. All the while, Tom trundled along with the traffic some distance back, dragging his empty flour cart behind.

The King's Men were out in force. Three times I passed a pair of footmen close enough to touch them, their hands on their broadswords and pistols, scanning the Monday morning crowd. Their eyes passed over me without recognition, but each time I had to turn the corner before I could breathe again. At least their presence made it unlikely Wat and the others would attack me in open daylight, even if they spotted me. Still, I hurried. The longer I stayed anywhere, the more attention I'd attract.

Isaac's bookshop was tucked away on Saint Bennet's Hill, a narrow street near the river, uncomfortably close to Apothecaries' Hall. It had no storefront, and no windows. The entrance was set in the center of an old stone building with shipping warehouses on either side. The door was thick, heavy oak, banded with iron. Nailed to it was a wooden plate.

RARE TOMES

PROPRIETOR, ISAAC CHANDLER

ALL WHO SEEK KNOWLEDGE ARE WELCOME

Another phrase, in Latin, was carved into the stone above the door.

FIAT LUX

Let there be light.

Inside, Isaac's looked more like a library than a shop. The room was small, no more than fifteen feet square. Shelves covered the walls, except where a fire burned in the stone hearth, filling the room with warmth to fight the morning's chill. Books weighed down the shelves, so heavy in places that the cedar planks sagged in the middle. In one corner, more books lay stacked in tall columns that reached nearly to the ceiling, a maze of paper and leather blocking a narrow staircase that led to the upper floors. It made me think so much of my master that my eyes stung.

Tom and I were not alone. Directly opposite the door was a short wooden counter. Behind it, an old man with wispy white hair and a sharp chin sat peacefully on a stool, eyes closed. Proprietor, Isaac Chandler.

His voice was soft, like a whisper. "May I help you?"

"I'm looking for some information," I said.

He waved his bone-thin hands over the hundreds of tomes. I guess I needed to be more specific.

"I need to know what some symbols mean," I said.

He opened his eyes. "Come closer, please. My sight is failing."

I went to the counter, Tom trailing behind. As we got close, I saw what he meant. Isaac's eyes were starting to cloud over, like the morning's fog had slipped inside them. "A curse, for a lover of books," he said. "I'd rather lose my heart. But God never seems to ask." He sighed. "Who are you?"

Tom tensed. The question caught me off guard, too. The crier had made my real name unusable. "I'm . . . James Parrett," I said, feeling my face grow hot. "I'm apprenticed to . . . Andrew Church, at Apothecaries' Hall. My master sent me to inquire about some symbols he's uncovered in an old text."

"You've forgotten your apron."

I looked down at my street urchin's kit, no blue apron to be found. "I . . . uh . . . destroyed it in the lab. I . . . got oil of vitriol on it."

"A dangerous substance," Isaac said. "But useful, in the right circumstances." He nodded. "Very well. What are these symbols?"

I'd kind of hoped that I'd just say, *I'm looking for a book on symbols*, and he'd point and say, *Of course, here's exactly the thing you need*. Master Benedict had sent me to Isaac for the key, but he'd also said to tell no one. I couldn't be sure if he'd meant to include the bookseller in that warning. I decided to give Isaac the partial truth.

"There are a number of glyphs," I said. "A sword, pointed down. A triangle, pointed up. Another triangle, with a line across it, like a snowcapped mountain. Things like that."

For a moment, I wasn't sure if he was thinking or if he hadn't heard me. Then he said, "Symbols can mean almost anything. The context is important." He seemed to be waiting for something.

"These symbols are for ingredients," I said.

"Ingredients."

"Yes." I waited. When he didn't respond, I said, "A key."

He said nothing for a moment. Then he shifted in his chair. "I don't think I can help you."

My heart sank. "But . . . my master said you were the only one who could."

"You're training as an apothecary," he said.

"I am."

"So you can read Latin."

"Yes."

He pointed upward. "What does that say?"

Behind him, on the top beam of the bookshelf, an inscription was burned into the wood. I read it. "*Et cognoscetis veritatem, et veritas liberabit vos.*"

"What does it mean?"

"It's a quote from the Bible. The Gospel of John. 'And you shall know the truth, and the truth shall set you free.'"

He nodded. "And there is your answer, young . . . I'm sorry, my ears aren't what they used to be, either. What did you say your name was?"

I stared at him. "I said it was James Parrett." He waited. "But that wasn't true," I said.

Tom grabbed my arm. "Don't."

I shook him off. "My real name is Christopher Rowe."

Isaac's clouded eyes held mine. "I knew your master."

"Yes."

"Benedict was my friend. He often mentioned his apprentice. Even if he hadn't, I would still know your name, from this morning's cry. Christopher Rowe, murderer, rebel against his master's cruelty."

"I never hurt Master Benedict," I said. "I couldn't."

"And how would I know that? You come here, with a strange name, not yours, and, I think, a strange face, also not yours. You tell me stories, then you ask me to take your word. Why should I believe you, Christopher Rowe?"

I thought of reasons, more stories to tell. Excuses. Lies. I was desperate. I needed something to convince him, or the trail ended here.

I looked inside my heart. All I could see was my master's face. In that, I found my answer.

"I was an orphan," I said. "The masters who took me in fed me, taught me, gave me shelter. I'll always be grateful to them for that. But the orphanage was not a kind place. The masters were strict, and they had quick hands, always ready to punish. And the other boys, well, some of them were even meaner. We may have all lived together, but the truth is, every one of us grew up alone.

"When Master Benedict took me in, he changed my world. He cared about me." My voice faltered. "He showed me something different, something I never knew existed. He was strange. He was human. But he was never anything but kind. He was my father, my true father, in the only ways that mattered. And I loved him."

I wiped my eyes on my sleeve. Smudges of violet smeared away. "You have no reason to trust me," I said. "You don't have to. If you really were Benedict Blackthorn's friend, then you know I could never, ever have killed him. Because he could never, ever, not for a single moment, be cruel."

Isaac blinked slowly, regarding me. Tom stayed as still as a statue.

Then Isaac stood, pushing himself up from his creaking stool. From under his robe, on a string around his neck, he drew a silver key. He handed it to Tom. "Lock the front door."

Tom glanced nervously at me, but he obeyed. Isaac turned to the bookshelf behind him with the inscription on the top and pulled three books on three different shelves forward. When he pulled the last one, the bookshelf gave a resounding *clack*. Then it swung open. Chilled air blew from the darkness behind.

Isaac took his key from Tom and grabbed a lantern from the counter. He lit it, then stepped through the secret door. In the dim light of the flame, I could see the top of a staircase, going down.

Isaac turned. "Well?" he said. "Are you coming or not?"

CHAPTER
29

I COUNTED A HUNDRED STEPS BEFORE
I gave up. The stairs spiraled downward, with nothing to
mark our place. The curved stone walls had no images
and no brackets for torches, only countless cracks in the
mortar. The only thing that changed—other than the
ache in my back—was the air, which grew cooler with
every step.

We finally reached the bottom. The stairs ended in a
small chamber that widened to fit a set of double doors so
big, they made the doors to Apothecaries' Hall look like
toothpicks. Carved into the oak in each panel was a cross,
four arms of equal length, with flared ends. Flecks of paint

still remained, white on the surface, red in the cross, gold all the way around.

Isaac touched one of the polished brass handles. "If I may borrow your youth, Thomas?"

Tom stepped forward obligingly and put a shoulder to the door. Then, eyes wide, he froze. "How did you know my name?"

"Benedict once mentioned his apprentice had a friend so loyal that no matter what ludicrous scheme the boy concocted, Thomas Bailey would be there, right beside him. Christopher is wanted for murder. His head is worth twenty pounds. And the King's Men are not the only predators hunting it. Yet here you are. So who else could you be?"

I flushed. Tom turned to me, triumphant. "I *told* you they were schemes."

The giant door creaked open, swinging on inch-thick hinges. What lay beyond nearly made me drop to my knees.

We were in a cavern. It stretched so far that the light from our lantern couldn't reach the end. Everywhere there were shelves, scores of them, rows upon rows, built to fit the titans of ancient Greece. They went all the way to the ceiling, fifty feet above, so far you'd need ladders as high as a house to reach them. And the ladders were there, sturdy beams with wheels at the bottom, set in rails on the floor.

I'd never seen so many books. The shelves groaned with them, threatening to split and bring a hail of paper from the heavens. There was much more than just the tomes, too. Scrolls lay stacked in pyramids on one shelf, yellowed and brittle with age. Stone slabs leaned on another shelf, strange glyphs carved into their surfaces. In one row, dusky red tablets were marked with arcane lines and arrows, hardened into the clay thousands of years ago.

Tom backed toward me until his arm pressed into my shoulder. "Where are we?"

"Deep under the city, in a vault built by the Knights Templar," Isaac said. "Here they stored their plundered treasures, until Pope Clement disbanded their order and burned them all at the stake. The vault was bequeathed, in secret, to the Mortimer family, three hundred and fifty years ago. Before you ask, I don't know what happened to the Templars' gold. It doesn't matter. We've filled it with something much more valuable.

"What you see is the full collection of works that I and my brothers before me have acquired. It is centuries of knowledge, from every civilization, from every corner of the world. It is available to all who seek genuine truth. Sadly, of those, there are precious few."

"You keep saying 'we,'" I said. "Was Master Benedict one of you?"

"He was. There were seven of us. All are dead, or fled the city, except me."

"But who are you?"

"We are alchemists," Isaac said.

"The people who turn lead into gold?"

"I thought they were all frauds," Tom blurted, before realizing that insulting a man when you were deep in his secret underground vault was not a good idea.

But Isaac wasn't offended. "Most are. And yes, Christopher, the transmutation of lead into gold is one of the secrets alchemists seek. But centuries of deceit have obscured why."

Isaac walked forward. We followed him, the clicks of our heels on the stone echoing throughout the cavern. When we reached the ladder beside a shelf eight rows down, Isaac pushed it, sliding it across the floor on squeaking wheels.

"The purification of base metals—turning lead into gold—is but a means to an end," he said. "What we really search for is the blessed knowledge of God Himself. We seek to discover the Prima Materia, the First Matter, the raw energy from which Our Lord created the universe. In this way, we hope to truly understand our mortal world."

The ladder rattled to a stop a third of the way down the shelf. Isaac traced his fingers along the spines of the books in the second row from the bottom, searching more from feel than from sight. He pulled out a volume bound in dark leather and held it out to me.

The cover was engraved with an image of a serpent swallowing its own tail. Tom and I glanced at each other. The drawing was identical to the snake that ringed the mural in the crypt.

"This is the *ouroboros*," Isaac said. "It is the symbol of the Prima Materia. As it circles upon itself, so do we understand that the Prima Materia is the heart of the whole universe. All things, all life, stems from the First Matter. If you could access that Matter, then you, too, could direct it. This is the true goal of the alchemist.

"Apothecaries have already discovered many of God's lesser powers. Silver heals. Aloe soothes. Oil of vitriol dissolves. Yet all of these are only shadows of the Prima Materia. Imagine the remedies you could create if you knew its secrets. Perhaps you could even prevent death itself."

"This is what Master Benedict was looking for," I said.

"Yes. You, too, I think."

That surprised me. "I don't know anything about it."

"Not yet. But if Benedict sent you here, then he wished for you to understand."

"He showed us how to find the door under the—" I began, but Isaac held up his hand.

"Stop," he said. "It's not for me to know where Benedict worked. I am no apothecary; I only keep the library. There are secrets we don't share, even among ourselves. In this way, we protect the brotherhood from those who would misuse our discoveries."

I thought of the Cult's victims. They'd been tortured for information. But if each man only knew a piece of the puzzle, all the killers would be able to get from them were scraps that led obscurely to the next man in the line. It hadn't stopped the killers, but it had delayed them for months, until they'd finally reached my master. He'd poisoned himself precisely so he couldn't be forced to tell Wat what the boy wanted to know. He'd kept his final secret for me alone.

"Aren't you worried they'll find out about you?" I said.

"This library is my purpose in life. I cannot leave it." Isaac shrugged. "As always, the future is in God's hands. If they come for me, then that's what will be."

Not if I could help it. "We found a sealed door. Master Benedict said you had the key."

Isaac returned to pushing the ladder, moving farther down the aisle. "The symbols you described earlier are alchemical. They represent instructions, written in code to keep secrets from prying eyes. Except the first symbol you mentioned, the downturned sword. That is not an instruction. It is the emblem of Michael, the Archangel."

Tom shivered. So did I. "Is this . . . are alchemists the Cult of the Archangel?" Tom said.

"There is no Cult of the Archangel," Isaac said.

I looked at Tom, who seemed just as confused as I was. "But . . . how can that be? These murders—"

"Are the acts of evil men. Yet their purpose has nothing to do with any cult. At least not in the sense people above use the word." Isaac waved a hand at the books surrounding us. "Keeping our discoveries hidden isn't the only reason we work in secret. Alchemists have, in the past, been accused of terrible crimes: treason, heresy, witchcraft. But we who search for God's gifts to His servants are not murderers. It is the killers themselves who steal that name, spreading fear and lies, wrapping holy work in something sinister. In this way, they obscure their true motives."

I thought of what Oswyn had said to me. "You said that alchemists are searching for knowledge to make the world better. I was told the Cult—the killers—wanted power."

"So they do." Isaac stopped pushing the ladder and looked up. "There. Third shelf from the top. The tome with the blue spine. Go ahead."

I climbed the ladder and pulled the book he'd indicated from the shelf, bringing it back down.

"Open it," Isaac said.

Tucked inside the back cover was a piece of parchment. On it was a chart, written in Master Benedict's hand. Symbols, rows of them, were scrawled down the paper, a label beside each one.

"That's the key you seek," Isaac said. "Take it. It is Benedict's gift to you."

This was it. I'd finally found the last of Master Benedict's message. I stared at it, awed, proud . . . and scared.

Isaac's hand on my shoulder nearly made me jump. "Be careful, Christopher. What you're doing is dangerous."

He hardly needed to remind me how many people wanted me dead. But that wasn't what he meant. "With this legacy comes a choice you will have to make," he said. "Knowledge can bring us great wonders, but it can also bring great suffering. What to do with such knowledge is a choice Benedict has always struggled with. In the end, perhaps he could only win that struggle by passing his choice on to you."

I blinked. "I . . . I don't understand."

Isaac sighed. "The person who told you that the killers seek power was correct. The Archangel Michael is God's general. He leads the armies of heaven in the never-ending struggle against the forces of hell."

Isaac opened the book with the *ouroboros* on the cover and showed us an image inside. It was an angel, with flowing hair and spread wings, driving a sword into a dragon.

"To exalt him," Isaac said, "the Lord gifted Michael with unique power."

He turned the page to a different illustration. Here, the Archangel stood over twisted, crippled, hellish figures. He held his hand high, and it glowed with holy fire. The demons below burned in God's light, screaming.

"Just as apothecaries' healing remedies take many forms, so, too, can the First Matter take many forms. The Archangel's Fire is the raw essence of the Prima Materia. It is God's power unchecked."

Isaac turned to me. "I told you before there was no true

cult, just killers who hide behind its name. This aspect of the Prima Materia, the Archangel's Fire, is what they seek. As bad as their crimes have been, if they find it, things will be much, much worse."

"Why?" Tom said nervously. "What are they going to do?"

"The battlefields of England used to be covered with knights." Isaac spread his hands, as if drawing the scene. "Sheathed in plate, they were impenetrable, the lords of the land, the pinnacle of five thousand years of war. Tell me: When was the last time you saw an armored knight?" He leaned against the shelf. "Firearms removed knights from the battlefield. Their armor, the seat of their strength, was useless against simple men armed with black powder.

"Now imagine going into battle with Michael at your side. Gunpowder would be no more sophisticated, hold no more power, than a stone from a sling. The man who discovers the Fire could change the world. And if the wrong people get ahold of it . . ."

He stared into the distance. "An army that walks with the Archangel will be invincible."

CHAPTER
30

WE RETURNED TO THE CRYPT UNDER the mausoleum in the Mortimer garden. Tom held the torch. I carried the parchment, my master's key.

After what Isaac had shown us, Tom and I stared at the mural in a new light. We saw the *ouroboros*, the First Matter, the serpent swallowing its own tail. We knew the figures inside, too. God's general, the Archangel Michael, driving his sword into Satan, the dragon, as the Devil's minions writhed below, swallowing darkness.

Armed with Master Benedict's key, we finally knew the poison to feed them.

VOCABULARIUM ALCHEMIAE

THE THREE PRINCIPLES

⊖ salt
the contractive force — crystallization, contraction

⍨ sulphur
the expansive force — dissolution, evaporation

☿ mercury
the integrative force — balancing salt and sulphur

THE FOUR ELEMENTS

▽ earth — cold and dry — melancholic

▽ water — cold and wet — phlegmatic

△ air — hot and wet — sanguine

△ fire — hot and dry — choleric

PLANETARY METALS

☉ gold / Sun

☽ silver / Moon

♂ iron / Mars

☿ mercury / Mercury

♃ tin / Jupiter

♀ lead / Venus

♄ copper / Saturn

TERRESTRIAL MINERALS

saltpeter

quicklime

✳ ☉ sal ammoniac

litharge

realgar

cinnabar

tartar

marchasite

CORROSIVES

▽ aqua fortis

⍅ aqua regia

✝ vinegar

distilled vinegar

⊕ oil of vitriol

WEIGHTS & MINERALS

M℥ one pound

Ʒ℥ one ounce

Ʒ℥ one dram

Ӡ℥ one scruple

P℥ one pinch

O℥ one pint

ANA equal amounts

INSTRUCTIONS / PROCESSES

calcination

congestion

fixation

solution

digestion

precipitation

purify

digest

sublimation

separation

ceration

fermentation

multiplication

caput mortuum

oil

filter

sugar

spirit

essence

still

take

alcohol

retort

night

day

honey

wax

powder

distill

mix

compose

receiver

boil

"We already know this is mercury," I said, pointing to the hole on the left. "The one at the top is . . ."

". . . air?" I said, puzzled.

Tom reached up and poked his finger in the hole. "Isn't there air in here already?"

"Maybe that's the trick." I turned to the workbenches with the ingredients. "Nothing's supposed to go in there. But if you don't have the key, you'd put different things in to try to crack it. So the lock won't work." *Pretty clever*, I thought.

"All right," Tom said. "Then what's the last one?"

There were three symbols to match.

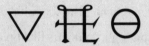

A triangle, pointed down. *Water.*

A curious ladder with a strange zigzag drawn at the bottom. *Mix.*

A circle, a horizontal line cutting through its center. *Salt.*

Water, mix, salt.

"Does that mean . . . salt water?" Tom said.

"That's what I'd guess," I said. Air on top, mercury on the left, salt water on the right.

We got ourselves ready. I poured water up to the notch in one beaker. I dumped a heaping scoop of salt into it with the spoon on the other table. I stirred it, leaving a cloudy white liquid. A second beaker, filled with mercury, went to Tom.

We stood in front of the dragons. I gave Tom a nod.

Slowly, he poured the mercury in. We heard the faint *thunk* from behind the plate.

I tipped the salt water. It splashed down inside.

Nothing.

"Did we—"

Clack.

The wall unsealed. A seam appeared, ringed around the inside of the *ouroboros*. The torch flickered as air rushed through it, whispering in our ears like breath.

The center of the mural swung open. The Archangel Michael beckoned.

I stepped inside.

A new, wide corridor was behind the seal. Here there were no nooks carved in the walls, no more ancient bones, just solid stone. The passage went another twenty feet. It ended in a wooden door.

"Look," Tom said.

He was staring at the back of the mural. It was glass, so we could see the mechanism behind it, like the design inside my puzzle box. On the right, the mercury held down a lever attached to the lock at the side. On the top, where we'd left nothing but air, was another lever. If anything had been poured inside, it would have slammed down a counterweight, forcing the lock to stay closed.

But the most amazing thing lay opposite the mercury. The salt water I'd poured had gone into a ceramic jar. At its top, between two metal prongs, sparks crackled, brighter than those from a tinderbox. They looked like tiny lightning strikes. With each one came snaps, like baby thunder.

Tom crossed himself. "What in God's holy name is that?"

We stared at it in wonder, but the light lasted only a few seconds more. The salt water leaked out through tiny holes in the bottom of the ceramic jar, and ran down the glass through a copper tube into a flat pan behind the door. The sparks stopped, and the lock clacked shut. The mercury drained through a second tube into a glass jar beside the pan. When there was no longer enough weight to keep the lever down, it reset. I worried we might get trapped behind the mural until I saw there was a handle on this side. We wouldn't need the ingredients to get out.

We went down the corridor to the final entrance. There was no puzzle here, and no key, just a plain iron latch on a plain wooden door. I pushed it open. The light from our torch filled the workshop beyond, and my heart swelled.

I felt like I was home again.

An oven exactly like ours was in the corner: iron curved like a flattened onion, enormous stacks of wood and coal beside it, the flue piercing the stone ceiling. Opposite it was a still, a giant beaker collecting drips below. The benches were covered with half-finished experiments. The shelves on the walls were laden with books, papers, and scrolls that spilled down to the floor. An ice vault was set into the flagstones beside the still, and next to that, a pendulum clock ticked on top of a stool. I hugged my arms to my chest and felt my master's presence.

Not everything was the same. There were additional chambers, one on each of the three other walls. Judging from the jars inside, the ones to the right and the left were stores for ingredients. From where I was standing, I couldn't see into the room opposite the door.

"What are these?" Tom said.

Behind us, wood planks were fixed to the stone, with

rows of nails hammered into them. From the spikes hung several pages, scrawled with words, diagrams, and symbols. A thick black slash was inked over most of them.

"Failures," I said. "These are recipes. The slash means they didn't work."

Most of the papers were Master Benedict's, but not all of them. Some of the work showed Hugh's handwriting, thick and loopy. There were other authors I didn't recognize: at least three more, judging by the different hands.

"This was their secret lab," I said. "This is where Master Benedict went all those nights."

More papers rested beneath the nailed board, stacks of them. There had to be thousands of pages here. In the first stack, as on the board, most of the papers were in Master Benedict's handwriting. As I went through the others, the handwriting changed, the parchment growing increasingly brittle. I counted at least a score of different authors before I stopped. This was years of work, decades. Maybe centuries.

"Christopher."

Tom stared at the chamber opposite the entrance. In front of it, on the floor, dark brown streaks smudged across the stone. Beside them was a bucket filled with rags, each one stained the same.

It was blood. Dried blood. A lot of it.

The door to the chamber was open. The walls around it were charred. Inside the chamber was the same sooty black, and there were scars, too, chunks of stone carved away. A dented iron table rested in the center of the room. On top of it was a heavy beaker, glass, its wide mouth stopped with cork. It was filled to the three-quarter mark with a yellowish liquid.

I picked it up. The liquid inside sloshed around, kind of goopy.

"What is it?" Tom said.

I shook my head. "I don't know."

He peered at the liquid as I turned the beaker over, watching it drip down the sides. "Looks like oil."

I popped open the cork and dipped a finger in. It felt like oil, too. The smell of it was vaguely fruity, and exotic, like those bananas imported from tropical islands. I touched my finger to the tip of my tongue.

"It's sweet," I said, surprised. It made my tongue tingle, like a syrup of hot pepper. I'd never tasted anything quite like it before.

I put the cork stopper back in and gave the beaker to Tom, who studied the liquid more closely. I returned to the workbench. Papers were scattered everywhere, covered in my master's handwriting. Beside them was a long loop of cannon fuse. Below the bench, two more coils of fuse were stacked, more than I'd ever seen in our shop. I looked at the chamber we'd taken the beaker out of, at the charring that covered the walls.

Had Master Benedict been burning gunpowder?

On the opposite side of the bench rested a short cylinder, maybe three inches high, and one inch in diameter. It was wrapped around with a thin skin of greased parchment. A wick of cannon fuse nearly two feet long was stuck into the top. It looked like some kind of strange, oiled candle. Beside it, on the floor, was a bucket of sawdust.

I remembered Oak Apple Day. Tom and I, returning home, after Lord Ashcombe had found Hugh's body. I'd used sawdust to soak up the boar's blood. Master Benedict had stared at it, fascinated.

And now here it was.

The parchment around the cylinder was pinched in at the top. I pulled it open. The tube was filled with sawdust, wet and sticky. It was soaked with the same oily goop as in the beaker.

I searched through the papers on the desk. That's where I found it, written in Master Benedict's smooth hand. There were scratches and corrections, all across the pages. But when you put the uncrossed-out lines together, it was a recipe.

The Archangel's Fire

Fill beaker with fuming aqua fortis. Immerse beaker in ice bath. Add fuming oil of vitriol with the greatest caution. Add more ice to bath until near freezing. Add, in small drops only, the sweet syrup of olive oil and litharge. Stir with the utmost care for one quarter hour. Transfer to water, and mixture will settle at the bottom. Take mixture and, in small drops only, add to natron. Repeat three times. The final liquid will have the look and feel of olive oil.

He'd done it. Master Benedict had discovered the raw essence of the Prima Materia.

I looked over at Tom. He still had the beaker in his hand. My heart was pounding.

Tom took a step back. "What's the matter?"

"That's it." I pointed at the beaker. "That's the Archangel's Fire."

He stared at it. "How . . . how does it work? Do you drink it?"

"I'm not sure." I'd tasted it. My tongue still burned.

And now I was starting to get a headache, a low pounding, throbbing in my temples. Did I do something to myself? Was this feeling because of the Fire?

I opened my hand, like I'd seen the Archangel Michael do in the image Isaac had shown us. No beams of light came out.

"Maybe you'd better put it back," I said.

As relieved as Tom was to get rid of it, he looked disappointed, too. I understood. It wasn't every day that you held the power of God in your hand.

I rifled through more of the papers. They were mostly raw notes from my master's experiments. I did find a separate recipe for how to make the "sweet syrup of olive oil and litharge." Hugh had made a note on the page, suggesting the syrup might be good for medicinal candies.

I spotted something more when I turned the papers over. On the back of one of them were more notes from my master. One familiar word dragged my eye to the last note at the bottom.

Sawdust is the key. Once it is blended into the Archangel's Fire, the volatility of the mixture is tempered by the sawdust's soft nature, and the Archangel's Fire becomes stable. Thence, only fire releases it. Take care, for only in this way may man safely touch the power of God.

I frowned, confused. Master Benedict was saying the Archangel's Fire needed sawdust to be handled safely. But sawdust wasn't part of the original recipe. It wasn't mixed with the liquid in the beaker, either. Puzzled, I started from the top and read what came above it.

It was a warning, scrawled by my master's shaking hand.

The power is too great. The Archangel's Fire was never meant for mortal men. The slightest tremor brings the wrath of God upon the bearer. What have I done?

I stood, trembling, the paper in my hand. Next to the message were faint brown smears, the same dried blood that stained the floor near the chamber where we'd found the vial, the room where Tom now stood.

A testing chamber. That's what that room was.

My head pounded, my headache growing by the second. I looked at the scarring on the stone, the charring on the door, the bucket, the blood.

I pushed back from the workbench. The stool tipped over, clattering on the floor.

"Tom." My voice shook. I ran to the testing chamber. "Tom!"

He'd placed the beaker on the dented iron table. He was still hunched over, peering at it. He jumped when I called to him, startled.

"What's wrong?" he said, and his leg bumped the table.

The beaker slid toward one of the dents. It teetered for a moment, then toppled on the slope. It rolled toward the edge, speeding up.

I thought of the blood on the floor. I thought of my master's shoulder, burnt. And I thought of Hugh's body, found in a Christian burial in a garden on Oak Apple Day, charred, blackened, and torn apart.

I grabbed Tom by his collar. I pulled, hard. He fell backward with me, outside the testing chamber, and we sprawled together on the ground.

The beaker rolled off the table.

I tried to kick the door shut.

Then came the power of God.

CHAPTER
31

I FELT STONE, ON MY FACE. IT WAS cold.

I'm on the floor, I thought.

I tried to remember how I got there.

Papers. I'd been reading something. Something bad.

My right arm was twisted under me. It felt numb, more like I was lying on a club than an arm. I shifted, slid it out. Life came back to it, pinpricks jabbing my skin.

I sat up and coughed. I sucked in acrid smoke, worse than what I'd hacked out. My head had a dwarf inside, his hammer ringing on the anvil. I put my hand to my temple. It came away red, warm and wet.

There was another boy lying beside me. He huddled in a ball, whimpering. Seemed like kind of a big kid to be whimpering.

Wait. Tom. It was Tom. I'd pulled him down with me, just before the explosion.

A fire glowed in the corner. A lantern had fallen and shattered, setting the oil alight.

I staggered to my feet. I fell to my knees.

Try again, I thought. It worked this time.

I reached for the handle on the door to the testing chamber, but the handle wasn't there. Actually, the whole door was gone. It lay beside Tom. A sliver of it remained in the doorway, still swinging from the upper hinge.

My ears were ringing.

I had to put out that fire. There was a bucket of sand in the corner. I dumped it on the burning oil, which seemed smaller than it had when I'd been on the ground. The fire disappeared. Smoke still filled the air.

"Tom," I said. He'd stopped whimpering. "Are you all right?"

He rolled over. His voice warbled. "Your head is bleeding."

"I'm fine." I sat at the bench, pushed the papers aside, and laid my cheek on the wood.

● ● ●

Gunpowder. Oil of vitriol. Madapple.

I'd always said being an apothecary was dangerous. But what Master Benedict had unlocked had, as Oswyn predicted, put our earthly works to shame. The Archangel's Fire had carved new scars in the walls, tearing off stone chunks as big as my fist. The stain on the floor, the blood; I knew whose it was now. It was Hugh's. He hadn't been murdered. He'd fallen to the power of God's general, torn apart by the same kind of accident that had nearly killed me and Tom.

I thought of my master's sad, scrawled confession. *The Archangel's Fire was never meant for mortal men. . . . What have I done?* I thought, too, about him burying his friend the best he could, in the hallowed ground below the stone angel. My master, working all alone in the dark, able to tell no one what had happened. My heart ached for him.

Even still, my master's obsession with how the Prima Materia might be shaped to help humanity made him come back. He'd kept going, even after what had happened to Hugh, to find some way to purify the Archangel's Fire, to see if it could be turned from a weapon of destruction into an agent of healing, like an alchemist turned lead into gold, or an apothecary turned the poison of madapple into a remedy for asthma. And, at least in part, he'd succeeded. The sawdust—*my* sawdust—had changed the nature of the Archangel's Fire and tempered God's wrath. The cylinder with the cannon fuse had been knocked off the workbench by the blast, but it hadn't exploded when it hit the ground. Master Benedict was right. When mixed with sawdust, the weapon would need fire to release its power.

Power. Was that word enough to describe God's terrible gift? *Tell no one*, my master had warned. I understood those words now. I remembered him asking me if I'd wanted the life he'd given me, when he'd offered me the chance to walk away. I wondered for a moment what he would have done if I'd taken it, but that was time wasted. I'd never have chosen anything else, never would have abandoned him. Even now, as shaken as I was, I was so proud that he'd trusted me.

With this legacy comes a choice you will have to make, Isaac had said. I understood that now, too. In sending me here, Master Benedict had placed the final decision about the Archangel's Fire in my hands. What would I do with his discovery? Work with it, like my master had, to try to change its nature further and unlock God's healing power? Hide it, and let no one know it had been discovered? Or should I destroy it, and keep it out of human hands forever?

Master Benedict had searched for the raw power of the universe, to be shaped for the betterment of man, and instead had found an unearthly weapon. His friend Hugh had died because of it, and ten others had been murdered in the hunt. The very first lesson Master Benedict had ever taught me was that our recipes were only tools, directed by the hearts and hands of the men who used them. The killers had already shown us their hearts. And if this tool got into their hands, so many more people would fall.

An army that walks with the Archangel will be invincible. And the mortal general who led it could do anything he wanted. Who could stop him? Who could stand against the Almighty? A man could overthrow His Majesty, Charles, and proclaim himself the new king. *Kill the king, force Parliament to fall in line, and England will be theirs*, Oswyn had said. And then what? The rest of the world?

Another war awaited us. With the Archangel's Fire, this one would be a slaughter.

The blast had rattled my head. But it also shook the cobwebs away. I remembered Wat, in his apprentice's blue apron; Wat, with Stubb, calling him Master; Wat, at Apothecaries' Hall, conspiring with Martin and the Elephant. And I knew.

I knew the truth about the murderers, the truth about the Cult of the Archangel.

And now I had a plan.

Tom stood over my shoulder as I finished writing the second letter, his hands clasped to his cheeks. "You've gone mad," he said. "The Fire's scrambled your brain."

I folded both letters and dripped wax on the edges to seal them. "You don't think it'll work?"

"If by 'work,' you mean 'get yourself killed,' then sure, it'll work."

"If everything goes right," I said, "I won't even come back to the lab. No one has to know."

"Of course. Because all your plans are *so* successful."

I wrote the names on the letters I'd sealed. "Just deliver these," I said. "And whatever you do, don't come back."

"What? No. I told you before I wasn't going to leave you to—"

"Not this time. I mean it, Tom. You hear me? You've already done so much more than I could ever have asked. I'm so grateful. But now you have to stay away, all right?" He made as if to protest. I cut him off. "Please, Tom. Stay away. Promise me."

He scuffed his shoes on the stone, head bowed. "I promise."

I handed him the letters and pointed at the pendulum clock. The Archangel's Fire had cracked its face. "Remember, tomorrow morning—"

"Deliver the first letter at nine, the second at eleven. I remember."

He turned to go. Then he turned back. He hugged me, holding me too tight to breathe.

The ingredients I needed were in the storerooms. Master Benedict had already made a large batch of the sweet syrup, which rested in a five-gallon jug on the opposite workbench, so all that was left for me to do was follow the recipe. It was the hardest thing I'd ever done. I had to concentrate to stop my hands from shaking, scared beyond measure the whole time.

The clock seemed to spin. By the time I'd finished with the formula, it was past midnight. By the time I'd prepared the room, it was almost seven. Now everything was ready.

A few more hours. That was all. Just a few more hours and it would be over, one way or another.

I left the lab and went up to the surface, to the sunlight dawning in the Mortimer family garden. There I sat on the grass, like a spring lamb, and waited for the wolves to come.

TUESDAY, JUNE 2, 1665

The Feast of St. Erasmus, Protector

CHAPTER
32

I CLOSED MY EYES.

The grass, overgrown, ruffled against my neck, its broad blades tickling my skin. The noonday sun shone warm on my face. I heard cooing, and propped myself up to see a band of pigeons perched on the fence at the end of the garden. I looked for Bridget, but she wasn't there. I hadn't seen her for two days now. I wondered what had happened to her, and worried.

Nothing to do about it now. I sighed and squinted into the sky. For the past half hour, I'd heard the sounds coming from the manor behind me. They'd set my heart to pounding, but I couldn't do anything about that, either. Just wait, and wonder, and worry.

From the alleyway, then, came another sound, the flapping wings of fleeing birds.

Time's up.

The man stepped out of the maze. He came through the gate, past the lions, up the path. At the front of the mausoleum, he stopped, leaning a shoulder against the stone.

"The entire city is looking for you," he said.

"I guess it's lucky no one lives here anymore," I said.

"More of a shame, really. Mortimer House is quite beautiful."

My heart thumped faster. "You know it?"

Oswyn gave a slight smile. "I've been here before. Never in the garden, though." He tilted his head. "Someone broke the lock on my office yesterday afternoon. Was that you?"

"I'm sorry, Master Colthurst. I got locked in."

"How did you get out?"

"Prayer," I said.

Oswyn's smile widened. "Benedict made a good choice in you."

I didn't answer that.

"I received your message." Oswyn held up the letter I'd sent him. "It says you have nothing to do with the Cult of the Archangel, and you're innocent of the murders with which Richard Ashcombe has charged you."

"I am," I said.

"It also says you've discovered something important, and you need my help. I was surprised, to say the least. With all that's going on, I thought you'd have fled London by now."

"I had something to take care of first."

"I'm sure." He straightened. "So? What did you want of me?"

My breath shuddered in my chest. I had to will myself to keep still.

"I found the Fire," I said.

"Oh?"

"That's what Stubb and Wat were looking for in my master's shop."

"I remember."

"Master Benedict hid the recipe in that puzzle cube he gave me."

"Did he." Oswyn scratched his cheek. "And?"

"I . . . I thought you'd want to see it."

"Why would I want that?"

"Well . . . this is what Stubb killed my master for. This is what the Cult wants."

"What does that have to do with me?"

I blinked, and floundered for something to say.

Oswyn laughed. "You were hoping I'd jump for that recipe."

"No, I—"

"And then what? You'd trick me into revealing it was I who wanted the Archangel's Fire all along? I suppose you'd like me to confess to Benedict's murder while I'm at it."

I felt my face grow hot.

"Christopher." Oswyn shook his head. "You're trying to play the game, but you don't even know how to move the pieces."

"I—I didn't—" I began.

"If you want to win, you need to think several steps ahead. Here, let me show you." Oswyn raised his voice, so it echoed from the walls. "Yes, I killed your master."

I couldn't move.

"I killed Nathaniel Stubb, too," he said. "And his apprentices, and Henry Mortimer, and Oliver Pembroke, and many, many others. Not by my own hand. But I sent the agents who did it." His voice went back to normal. "Will that do?"

My breath caught in my throat. *No*, I thought. *It won't.*

The door to the mansion banged open behind me. Lord Ashcombe burst out, flintlock pistol in hand. Four footmen clomped after him, spears at the ready, two of them the same King's Men who were always by his side.

"Hello, Richard," Oswyn said. He smiled. "What a surprise."

"Oswyn Colthurst, you are under arrest," Lord Ashcombe said.

Oswyn took a step backward. "I can see that."

That was too easy. I looked past Oswyn, past the gate, to the brick wall of the maze beyond. "Lord Ashcombe—" I said.

"There's nowhere to run, Puritan," Lord Ashcombe said.

Oswyn took another step back. "Why is that, Richard? If I flee into the maze, I'll . . . what? Meet the guards you hid in there to cut off my escape?"

Lord Ashcombe's eyes narrowed.

"My lord, wait—" I began, but Oswyn cut me off.

"Several steps ahead, Christopher," he said. Then he ducked behind the mausoleum.

And from the maze poured Oswyn's army.

CHAPTER
33

THERE WERE SEVEN OF THEM ON
Oswyn's side. Each held a pistol. Other, more wicked
weapons hung from their belts. The Elephant was there,
his neck red, skin peeling. Martin was there, too, with torn
cheek and missing teeth. Wat led them, his face peppered
with scabs, a flintlock in each hand.

Lord Ashcombe reacted like lightning. He fired his pistol on the quick, a sharp crack and a puff of smoke. One of
Oswyn's men fell back, his throat ripped open.

Oswyn's troops responded. Six bangs, like firecrackers,
and lead shot flew from a dark gray cloud. A musket ball tore at
my hair as it punched into the window frame behind me, send-

ing out a shower of splinters. Three more shots whistled past, one shattering the glass, the others chipping stone. Two found their mark. One soldier's knee blew backward, toppling him to the ground. A second man's eye became a mash of red pulp.

I dived to the grass and covered my head, as if my hands could stop screaming lead. Lord Ashcombe ducked as well, but too late. Wat fired his second pistol. The King's Warden jerked back with a grunt. He dropped his flintlock and grabbed his right arm, just above the elbow. Blood oozed through his fingers.

Oswyn's men threw their pistols away, ammunition spent. Then they rushed in. I scrambled out of the way, but they weren't charging at me.

With two of Lord Ashcombe's troops down, the King's Men were badly outnumbered. One of them caught one of Oswyn's thugs in the chest with his spear before falling under a hail of swords. The other soldier was immediately overwhelmed, never managing a strike before taking a club to the skull. He swayed. A second blow to the crown felled him for good.

Even wounded, Lord Ashcombe was a lion. Left-handed, he threw a knife from his belt that caught one of Oswyn's men in the neck. He picked up a spear from the ground and hurled it, piercing another man through the chest. Martin advanced on him, sword high. Lord Ashcombe grabbed a second spear from one of his fallen men-at-arms, and with a feint and a thrust, he drove the weapon home. Martin collapsed, eyes wide, the spearhead deep in his gut.

The boy's fall twisted the spear from Lord Ashcombe's hands. Lord Ashcombe grasped at the sword in his belt, but his fingers, slick with his own blood, slipped on the hilt.

And then Wat was on him.

Wat's ax swung. The first blow, low and diagonal, was at Lord Ashcombe's sword hand. Two of his fingers fell to the ground with the cracked hilt. The second blow hacked downward. It took Lord Ashcombe in the cheek. The King's Warden crumpled to the grass, his hand pressed against his face.

Wat straddled him, grinning. With both hands, he lifted his ax.

"Hold!"

Oswyn ran from behind the mausoleum, toward us. Wat's grin faltered.

"Hold, curse you!" Oswyn said. "Don't kill him!" Oswyn pulled Wat away. "Not yet."

Wat shook his arm free from Oswyn's grasp. The soldier who'd lost his knee to a musket ball was crawling toward the back door of the manor, a smear of blood glistening in the grass behind him. Wat stormed over and smashed the ax into the man's back. The soldier stopped moving.

It was over in seconds. I sat there, on the grass, motionless. A fallen sword lay two feet away from me, glinting in the sunlight.

Oswyn walked over, his eyes on me. Casually, he slipped his foot under the blade and kicked it away. It tumbled end over end, landing in an overgrown bush, far enough away to be useless. "Don't want you getting any ideas," he said.

Lord Ashcombe's breath rattled in his throat. His left eye was gone. His scarred cheek had been slashed open enough to see his teeth underneath, stained crimson. Still, he remained a lion. "Traitor," he spat.

"Me?" Oswyn laughed humorlessly. "That wretch you call a king drinks away the days on his throne, and *I'm* the traitor? The people of England fall into lechery and corruption, and *I'm* the traitor? *You* are the traitor, Richard. You, and every other man who follows him. And you will be judged for your transgressions."

"Then send me to God. I'll wait for you, tell you what He says."

Oswyn leaned over. "Oh, I intend to, Richard. But not

before you see the death of your king. And me enshrined as the new Lord Protector."

"I'll never kneel before you," Lord Ashcombe said.

"You will." Oswyn smoothed the front of his waistcoat. "Even if I have to cut off your feet to make you do it."

The Elephant knelt beside Martin. The boy had pulled out the spear. Now he held his hands against his stomach, trying to keep his guts in. He was crying. "Help me. Please help me."

Oswyn looked to the Elephant, who pulled Martin's hands back to inspect the wound. The Elephant shook his head. Oswyn nodded, and the giant slipped his knife behind Martin's ear. The apprentice stiffened, then became silent, tears tracking from sightless eyes.

Then Oswyn nodded toward me.

The Elephant stood.

I scrambled backward, fingers clawing at the grass. My head banged against the wall of the manor.

"Calm yourself," Oswyn said. "He's only going to search you."

The Elephant threw his knife so its point stuck in the dirt, quivering. Then he bent over and pawed at me. I was too scared to even try to resist.

"What did you do with Ashcombe's soldiers hiding in the maze?" Oswyn asked Wat.

Wat wiped the blade of his ax on a King's Man's tabard. "Killed them."

"And the bodies?"

"Still in the maze. No one saw us."

The Elephant's hands found my master's sash underneath my shirt. He tore it from my waist and threw it to Oswyn. "Just this."

Oswyn examined it, curious. "You have practically the whole pharmacopoeia in here." Suddenly, he looked down at me, surprised. "Oil of vitriol. On the lock. That's how you escaped my office."

Escape was exactly what I was thinking about, but there was nowhere left to crawl. "How did you know about Lord Ashcombe?" My voice was shaking. "How did you know he'd be waiting for you?"

"Oh, I've had a spy in his employ for months," Oswyn said. "Not everyone who wears the king's colors serves the man. Some support a higher ideal. Although a great deal of gold has its charms, too."

Oswyn turned to Lord Ashcombe for a response, but the King's Warden said nothing. Oswyn shrugged.

"As Richard here left the Tower with his men," Oswyn said, "my spy sent a runner to tell me you'd delivered a letter to Lord Ashcombe, suggesting a plan to trap the leader of the Cult of the Archangel. By the time I received your message at the Hall, I already knew why you wanted me to come here, and I knew Lord Ashcombe's men would be hiding in the maze. It was easy enough to set a counter to your trap, and turn the tables on you both.

"In fact, you've rather helped me. I've wanted to get rid of the King's Warden for some time. You've given me the perfect opportunity to do it. Two birds with one stone, as they say." Oswyn smiled. "You see what I mean, Christopher? Several steps ahead."

Oswyn traced his fingers over the vials in the sash. "A better question is, how did *you* know? When you fled the Hall on Sunday morning, after I'd told you to wait, I thought you'd found me out. But you returned that afternoon, so you obviously didn't realize I was behind the murders until some time after that. What gave me away?"

"Wat did," I said. Oswyn looked sharply at the brutish boy, who spread his hands as if trying to deflect blame. "You told me you'd tested every apprentice in the Guild. You said you'd never heard of Wat. But then he showed up at the Hall."

Inside, I kicked myself. I'd figured it out a day too late. "When I arrived that morning," I said, "the doorman wasn't going to let me in, even when he found out I was an apprentice. He would never have let Wat in on a Sunday, either, unless he had a right to be there. So Wat *had* to be part of the Guild. But you'd claimed he wasn't. There was only one reason to lie about it.

"He wasn't Stubb's apprentice," I said. "He was *yours*."

I thought Oswyn would be angry. Instead, he looked delighted. "I'd planned to have you killed that morning," he said to me, "just like I'd decided to get rid of Stubb. The man was working for me, as you've no doubt guessed by now, but he'd become too much of a liability. Stubb's gold was useful to our cause—it paid off our spy, among other things—but he was starting to get too pushy with his demands, and him letting you overhear him in your master's shop was unforgivable. He had to be eliminated.

"As for you," Oswyn said, "when you ran away from the Hall, I was furious. Now I'm pleased."

And although I'd known this moment was coming, although I'd tried to prepare for it, I started to shake. "Why?"

"Because, Christopher, I rather like you. More important, you have something I need." He crouched beside me. "And this time, I intend to get it."

CHAPTER
34

"I DON'T HAVE ANYTHING," I STAM-
mered. "I just said I did to get you to come here."

Oswyn looked disappointed. "I won't insult you by pre-
tending you're stupid. Please extend me the same courtesy.
Give me the recipe for the Archangel's Fire."

"Master Benedict never told me anything about it."

"That, I believe. He wouldn't have put you in danger
unless it was absolutely necessary."

"There was never any recipe in the puzzle cube." I tried
to stop my voice from shaking. "I just said that to get you
to confess."

"Oh, I know that."

"Then you know I don't really have—"

Oswyn interrupted me. "You left the Hall. On Sunday, after I'd warned you not to speak to anyone, after I'd warned you Stubb might come, after I'd *ordered* you to wait for me, still you left. If you weren't running from me, only one other thing could have made you go. Benedict must have given you something before he died. If not the recipe for the Fire itself, then some trail to follow to find it. A letter. A message. A map.

"Now you bring me to Mortimer House. When we captured Henry Mortimer three months ago, he claimed he didn't know anything. After he died, my men searched this place from attic to basement. We looked for days. We found nothing. Yet here you are. You expect me to believe this is a coincidence?"

I had no good answer for that. "What do you want the Fire for, anyway?" I said.

"I tried to tell you, back at the Hall. I want to make the world a better place."

I stared at him. I would have laughed if I wasn't scared enough to wet my breeches.

Oswyn frowned. "You're still young, Christopher, so you think King Charles is charming. The 'Merry Monarch,' you call him, you and the rest of his dogs, slurping your master's scraps. Why do you bow before these rats? What do you owe them—you, of all people, who grew up with nothing? Do you not see them for the parasites they really are? They are corrupt, wicked to the core. Yet they presume to place themselves above decent, honest men, all the while as our king"—he spat the word like poison—"drowns himself in decadence. And where that wretch goes, the people follow."

Lord Ashcombe shifted, propping himself against the wall of the manor. He'd been bleeding so badly, I hadn't even been sure he was still alive.

"I knew you were with Cromwell's traitors," Lord Ashcombe said, his words slurred through his wound. "I should never have listened to your Grand Master. I should have had you hanged the day His Majesty returned."

"A mistake you will never fix." Oswyn turned back to me. "These vermin may have their titles, Christopher, but they have no right to rule. That belongs to proper Englishmen, men like you and me. Cromwell started the revolution, but he never had the chance to see it through. We will. We'll create something better, and it will be the Archangel's gift that saves us all. England shall transform according to *our* will. Or the Fire will burn them from their homes."

"You're mad," I said.

"Christopher."

"No," I spat. "You think you're so noble. You pretend to care about the people while you murder everyone who gets in your way. My master taught me better. For all your talk about decent, honest men, all you *really* care about is power. You're just another tyrant."

Oswyn shook his head. "You're angry with me. I understand. I regret Benedict's death; truly, I do. But I had no choice. He would never have given me the Fire. Don't make the same mistake, Christopher. There's still a place for you in our future."

"I told you. I don't know anything." My voice trembled.

Wat's fingernail traced the edge of his knife. "Let me get it from him, Master."

Oswyn whirled, angry. "Be silent. If it wasn't for your incompetence, we'd already have what we need." He pointed to Lord Ashcombe, propped against the wall. "Bind him. I'll deal with the boy."

"I don't know anything," I said again.

Oswyn examined my master's sash. "Remove your shirt."

I still wore the ridiculous clothes Dr. Parrett had given me. I clung to them more tightly than anything I'd ever had.

Wat and the Elephant stripped the dead men-at-arms of their belts and used them to tie up Lord Ashcombe. When they'd finished, Oswyn motioned them toward me.

I tried to scramble away. The Elephant held me down. Wat drew his knife, the one that had murdered my master. He sliced through my shirt and pulled it apart.

Oswyn searched the sash until he found the vial he wanted. The stopper was newer than the others, resealed. I'd refilled it in the lab, underground.

"I know you're familiar with this," he said.

He popped the cork, breaking the red wax seal, pulling away the twine.

"Please," I said.

Oswyn held the open vial over my chest. I could smell its sour stink.

"*Please*," I said.

"Tell me where the recipe is, Christopher."

I didn't.

The vial tipped, and one, two, three drops fell onto my chest, spattering just above my heart.

At first, it was nothing. It felt like water, cool drops on my skin in the springtime sun.

Then I burned.

. . .

Forever. It felt like forever before the oil of vitriol finally stopped tearing apart my flesh.

I didn't look down. I didn't want to know.

"End this, Christopher," Oswyn said. "Tell me where you hid the recipe."

"No," I said.

Oswyn shook his head. "You cannot see."

He brought the vial up. His hand blocked out the sun.

"And if you will not see," he said, "then what good are your eyes?"

He tilted the vial again, slowly, directly above my face. The oil of vitriol slid toward the edge of the glass.

I couldn't. I just couldn't.

I told him.

CHAPTER
35

THE SARCOPHAGUS IN THE MAUSO-
leum slid away. Oswyn stared into the darkness below. He motioned to the trussed Lord Ashcombe, slung over the Elephant's shoulder. "Take him down first."

"Just drop him," Wat said.

Oswyn looked annoyed. "If I wanted him dead, would he not already be dead?"

The Elephant climbed down the ladder, Lord Ashcombe dripping blood across the back of the giant's vest. Wat, sullen, took the torch from the wall bracket and followed them down the hole. I waited at the edge, holding the ripped ends of my shirt together. Underneath, my scarred chest still burned. Oswyn guided me toward the ladder, his hand on my back surprisingly gentle.

"I wish I'd chosen you instead," he said.

Oswyn was amazed by the metal door behind the mural. He was even more amazed when I showed him how it opened. He stared at its glass back, peppering me with questions about its mechanism. For a while, it seemed like he'd forgotten what he'd really come here for. Soon enough, he pushed us forward, into the lab.

Wat led the way. The wooden door, shoved inward, thumped against the vinegar barrel I'd stacked to the right, partially blocking the entrance. The Elephant laid the half-conscious Lord Ashcombe down in the only place there was room, against the wall on the left, near the giant oven. I stepped sideways and stood next to him.

Oswyn stared at the equipment, the workbenches, the notes covering them all. He saw the parchment hanging from the nails on the board, the stacks of paper below them.

"All these years . . . ," he whispered.

I inched closer to the oven.

Oswyn turned toward me. "Where is it?"

I froze. "It's . . . on the workbench. Among the papers."

He made as if to go. Then he stopped. He tapped his thumb against his chin.

"Go check," he said to Wat.

Wat moved to the center of the lab, stubby fingers pushing aside glass beakers.

Oswyn kept his eyes on me. "Is it there?"

Wat shrugged. "There are a lot of notes here. I can barely make them out." He scanned the papers, flipped them over, tossed them aside. "I don't see it."

I took another step back. My shoulder touched the oven.

Oswyn's eyes narrowed. "What are you doing? Don't move."

His voice brought the Elephant's attention my way. Quickly, I bent into the mouth of the oven and grabbed the cylinder I'd hidden inside.

I wasn't quick enough. Before I could do anything else, the Elephant drove his fist into my gut. Pain spread from my stomach, a new fire hotter than the burn on my chest. Every muscle in my body seized. I heaved, but I couldn't breathe.

Wat rushed over and grabbed my wrist. He slammed it against the iron, once, twice. My fingers went numb. The cylinder slipped out and fell to the floor. It rolled away, wick bobbing around like a whip, a streak of grease trailing behind it on the stone.

Oswyn scooped it up and held it like a baby. Wat grabbed me by the hair and drew back his fist.

"No," Oswyn said. "I'm not finished with him yet."

Wat flung me to the ground, next to Lord Ashcombe. My lungs finally started to work again. I sucked in air, gasping. Wat kicked me in the side for good measure. I curled away from him, cradling my battered wrist.

The Elephant searched the oven for more traps. "Nothing else here."

Oswyn stared at the cylinder, breath quickening. He pulled open the parchment that held the cylinder together and stuck his finger inside. It came out wet. He rubbed the oily substance over his fingers. He sniffed it, then the wick.

"Cannon fuse." Oswyn waved his apprentices forward. "Clear that corner. Bring me the lantern."

The Elephant moved to obey him.

"Don't," I said.

They looked at me.

"Don't light it," I pleaded. "We'll die."

"It's just a big firecracker," Wat scoffed.

"It's not."

Oswyn's eyes narrowed again, but he looked around the lab. He saw the test chamber on the other side, its scarred, blackened walls, the broken door.

"You don't understand," I said. "It's beyond anything you've ever imagined. We're just men, mortal men. The Archangel's Fire was never meant for us."

Oswyn looked at me.

"Please, Master Colthurst," I said. "If you set that off, you'll destroy us all."

Oswyn stayed still, thinking. For a moment, I thought he might actually listen.

Then he held the cylinder out to Wat. He motioned to the test chamber. "Light it in there."

Wat grabbed the stick like it was nothing more than a candle. He took it to the test chamber and placed it on the dented iron table. With the flame from the lantern, he lit the wick.

The fuse crackled and sparked, dancing toward the grease.

Slowly, I slid backward on the stone. I gripped the front of Lord Ashcombe's tabard. Underneath, I could feel the beating of his heart.

Wat stepped backward out of the test chamber, watching the stick. Oswyn and the Elephant moved closer.

I pulled on Lord Ashcombe's vest. He looked at me.

"Get up," I whispered.

The King's Warden blinked, twice. Then he slid his legs beneath him and struggled to his feet. I helped him as he stood.

The fuse fell below the paper. For a second, there was nothing.

"Told you," Wat said.

And then the world was flame.

The blast seemed to shatter the earth. The walls shook. A chunk of the test chamber blew outward, stones bouncing from the ceiling. The barrel of lamp oil—the one I'd dragged to the corner of the test chamber before I'd gone up to the garden—blew apart, sending blazing fuel screaming outward like hell's wraiths released.

A burning torrent of air flung Wat into the workbench, scattering paper like fiery snow. The Elephant toppled backward to the floor. The press of hot air squeezed me against Lord Ashcombe, whose eyes went wide as he held his breath.

Oswyn remained in the center of the room. The iron table, ripped apart, sent a jagged shard of metal shrieking past his face. He barely flinched. He just stood there, like a statue, and stared into the face of God.

The air seemed to rumble forever, flames swirling on the ceiling in twisters. Then they vanished, and all that was left was hissing, like a chorus of snakes.

Wat scrambled backward, beating frantically against the flames that had ignited his sleeve. The Elephant stayed on the ground, mouth open.

Oswyn stepped forward, his eyes alight. "Magnificent," he croaked. "Magnificent."

Smoke burned my throat. I tugged on Lord Ashcombe's tabard again. His eyes flicked toward me.

Oswyn spoke to the others, his voice shaking. "Search the room. Look everywhere. Find the recipe." Then he turned to me, huddled against the oven with Lord Ashcombe. "Thank you," he said. He actually seemed to mean it.

His apprentices stayed where they were. Wat panted in the corner, finally having put out the flames on his shirt. The Elephant stared in terror at the broken test room.

"Move," Oswyn said to them.

Still the air buzzed. I tugged at Lord Ashcombe's tabard again, then moved my eyes deliberately toward the open mouth of the oven. Lord Ashcombe followed my gaze, then looked back at me. I nodded, slightly. I couldn't tell if he understood.

The Elephant frowned. "Master?"

"What is it?" Oswyn said, still shaking.

"The ceiling's on fire."

The Elephant pointed. Stuck to the stone overhead, a fuse raced, hissing, toward a cylinder, camouflaged gray with ash, glued to the ceiling with dried egg and flour.

Oswyn looked around the room. At four more places on the ceiling, cannon fuse crackled, ignited by the flames from the Archangel's Fire. At the end of each, waiting, was another stick, glued fast.

Oswyn's eyes went wide.

I grabbed Lord Ashcombe and pulled. With the last of his strength, he dived into the mouth of the oven. I clambered in beside him, pressed my head against his, and covered our ears.

The burning fuses reached the sticks.

"Dear God," Oswyn said.

This time, God spoke back.

CHAPTER
36

A BAD DREAM.

My eyelids fluttered.

That's all, I thought. *Just a bad dream. Go back to sleep.*

No, a familiar voice said. *Wake up, Christopher.*

Master? I said. My head was killing me. *Is that you?*

Yes, he said. *I need you to wake up now.*

Please, Master. Just a few more minutes. I'll get the shop ready soon.

No, Christopher. He poked me in the back. Pain. *You have to get up. Now. Hurry.*

I groaned.

My head was *killing* me.

I opened my eyes. At least, I think I did. It was dark.

Was I awake?

Was I alive?

It hurt everywhere. I didn't think that was supposed to happen when you were dead. My ears rang like I'd spent the night in the belfry at Saint Paul's. Every bone in my body felt like an elephant had stomped on it. A real one.

I rolled over. I half crawled, half fell from the mouth of the oven to the stone below. My body whumped against the floor, sending new bolts of agony everywhere. I lay there for a moment, unable to move.

My eyes stung. My nose was stuffed with smoke and copper. Something jabbed into my back like a dagger where my master had poked me. I twisted my arm behind me, fingers grasping. It was a piece of stone, stuck in my flesh like an arrow.

I pulled it out. My howl was the first sound I made.

There was light now, if that's what you'd call it. The air was thick with a dust cloud of stone. Everything was a haze of gray. I looked around what was left of the lab.

The ceiling had collapsed, crushing the broken workbenches below. Paper was everywhere, floating, flaming, dotted with shattered glass fragments that glinted like diamond powder. In one corner, a pile of parchment burned lazily.

I looked at the oven, our sanctuary against the five sticks of Archangel's Fire that I'd glued to the ceiling. Lord Ashcombe lay inside, his chest slowly rising and falling. The iron furnace was gray with ash. One side was bent inward, as if shot by a giant cannon.

That was where my head had been. I touched my hair. It sent a wave of pain over my skull. I curled up on the floor, gasping, until the throbbing subsided.

I tried to stand. My legs wouldn't obey. Drops of red splattered on the stone beneath my face. It was a minute before I realized they were coming from me. My ears were bleeding.

The blood made me remember we weren't alone. Or maybe we were, now. The dust thinned slightly, but I couldn't see the others. Where Oswyn and the Elephant had stood, there was nothing but rubble.

There was something else, I thought. Some*one* else. Some reason my master had woken me.

Wat.

Wat, who'd crawled into the corner before the explosion, had escaped the collapse of the ceiling, though not unscathed. He lay slumped against a heap of stone. His left arm hung lifeless from his shoulder. The left side of his face was blackened and warped. A lick of flame still quivered on the charred linen of his sleeve. His right eye—the only one that remained—stared straight back at me. Then it blinked.

All right, Christopher, I told myself. Get up.

But Wat was the one who moved. He pushed his bulk from the wreckage. He wobbled, then fell to his knees. He huffed, and spat on the stone. All the while, he stared.

Christopher. Get *up*.

Wat staggered to his feet. He took a step. Then another. His blackened fingers gripped his knife. How did he still have his knife?

My mind screamed. I couldn't move. Lord Ashcombe stirred, dragging himself from the mouth of the oven, but he was in no shape to stop the boy, either. I clawed at cracked stone, trying to get away.

Useless. A foot pressed against my hip, turned me on my back. Wat straddled me. His head bobbed, like he couldn't focus.

He could see enough. He raised the blade.

Then it came. From the side of my eye swooped a rolling pin.

I am dreaming, I thought.

The rolling pin, a rich cherry red, was as long as an arm and as thick as a tree. It bonked Wat on the blind side of his skull. His good eye glassed over.

A second blow came, a deep, solid *thwock* on the top of his head. Wat crumpled to the ground. I stared dumbly at his unconscious body.

Tom leaned over. He put his hand on my chest, his face lined with worry.

"Rrrr ooo aaa iii?" he said.

He sounded like he was underwater. I shook my head to clear the bells inside. Bad idea. I turned over and retched. Bile, sour, mixed with stone ash, bitter. I retched again.

Tom held me. This time, through the ringing in my ears, I understood.

"Are you all right?" he said.

"You came back," I croaked.

"Of course I did. The promise you made me make was stupid."

"Sorry." I slumped against him. "Was that really a rolling pin?" I said.

Tom looked embarrassed. "It's the only weapon I know how to use."

• • •

Tom told me later that I crawled up the ladder on my own. I don't remember doing that. I do remember that he carried Lord Ashcombe over his shoulder, and got us to the street, where we were nearly run over by a four-horse carriage.

The driver hauled on the reins, skidding the carriage to a stop. An irritated horse bumped his nose against my head, blowing spit in my ear.

The driver cursed us up and down. The sweating noble inside leaned out of the window to let us have it, too. Then he saw the blood, and the man Tom carried.

Lord Ashcombe opened his remaining eye. "The Tower," he growled.

The noble blanched. Drips of sweat turned to buckets. He scrambled out of the carriage and tripped on the footstep, sprawling on the cobbles.

Tom loaded us inside. The driver took us where Lord Ashcombe had commanded, whipping the horses at reckless speed through the streets.

The guard at the Tower gate watched curiously as Tom pulled the King's Warden out. When he saw whom the boy was carrying, he dropped his spear. A dozen of the King's Men rushed out to help him.

Half-conscious, Lord Ashcombe pointed at me. "Bring that one," he said, just before he passed out.

Rough arms grabbed me from every direction. I didn't resist. I couldn't, either way.

The King's Men hauled me into an empty parlor. Two of the soldiers pressed me into a hard-backed chair and stood beside me while I waited. I wasn't sure how long it was—it felt like more than an hour—before an official came. Dressed in fine white linen, he looked me up and down from beneath his wig. "Come with me," he said.

I tried to stand. The guards had to help me up the stairs. It was so far, my legs so weak, that by the time we reached the top, the King's Men were carrying me. The linen man led us through a banded wooden door to one of the Tower's bedrooms, where the king's soldiers put me down.

The sun streamed through the window, giving off a warm glow. Two chairs rested in front of the empty fireplace, plumped with plush blue cushions that matched the silks on the four-poster bed. Splayed on the bedsheets was an emerald-green shirt, also silk, and dark blue cotton breeches, with soft doeskin boots beneath. A sturdy oak table held a crystal bowl. It overflowed with fruit: apples, oranges, pomegranates, grapes.

"Lord Ashcombe has ordered that you remain in the Tower, to keep you safe," the linen man said. "I hope these quarters will be adequate." He pointed to the door on the left. "There's a bath in the parlor, already prepared."

The scent of rose water wafted from behind the door. It mixed with the coppery smell of blood on my skin.

"The king's physicians will tend to your wounds as soon as they're finished with Lord Ashcombe," the linen man said. "In the meantime, is there anything else you require?"

My voice came out like sand. "Where's Tom?"

"Who?"

"My friend. Is he here? Is he all right?"

The linen man shrugged. "You were the only person Lord Ashcombe requested."

The rug was warm, the weave soft against my feet. I looked down. Somewhere along the way, I'd lost my boots.

I stared at the bowl of fruit. "May I please have one of those?"

"Of course," he said. "You must be starving. I'll bring a proper meal at once."

True to his word, twenty minutes later he returned with

four servants. They placed a set of silver dishes on the table. There was roasted goose, braised beef and gravy, seasoned fish, spiced vegetables in white sauce, and half a strawberry cake. I smelled the sweet oil on the goose, still steaming.

It wasn't until they left that I started to cry.

JUNE 3 TO JUNE 21, 1665

Spring's End

CHAPTER
37

THREE DAYS AFTER THEY'D CON-
fined me to the Tower, they took me to see Lord Ashcombe.
He lay on the bed in a room like mine, the king's physicians
buzzing around him. A thick white bandage was wrapped
around his head, covering the left side of his face. A scarlet
slash soaked through it at the cheek. Another bandage was
wrapped around his right hand, crimson stains crusting
where Wat's ax had removed his fingers.

Lord Ashcombe shooed the doctors away as if they were
flies. He beckoned me closer and mumbled into his bandages.

"I . . . I don't understand," I said.

Lord Ashcombe looked annoyed, although whether

with me or the dressing on his face, I couldn't tell. He tried again, more slowly, slurring through the cotton. "You set. A trap."

I bowed my head. "I'm sorry, my lord. I never meant to get you hurt. I wanted Master Colthurst to confess so you'd realize he was the killer. I didn't know he'd bring so many men."

He waved my apology away. "No. In the. Underground lab. The Archangel's Fire."

"Yes, my lord. I couldn't take the chance that Oswyn might find it and escape."

"Your trap. You knew. You could get him. If he. Went down."

"I hoped so."

"Yet you. Let him torture you. With that liquid. First."

My fingers traced over my chest. Before the king's physicians had dressed my wounds, I'd seen the melted flesh. My own map of hell, forever burned into my skin. "I did."

"Why?"

Several steps ahead, Oswyn had said. But I'd already been taught that, by a man so much greater than Oswyn could have ever hoped to be. Secrets under secrets. Codes inside codes.

Traps within traps.

"Oswyn knew I loved my master," I said. "He knew, after Master Benedict had tried so hard to keep the Archangel's Fire safe, for me to turn it over to him—to anyone—would betray everything my master had given me.

"If I'd just told him about the lab, Oswyn might have suspected another trap. I couldn't take that chance. He needed to think he'd beaten me. He needed to believe he'd won."

Lord Ashcombe tilted his head. "You used. His nature. Against him."

I nodded.

Lord Ashcombe regarded me for a moment. Then he laid his head back and closed his eye.

They took me back to my room.

They kept me in the Tower for two more weeks, as a slowly healing Lord Ashcombe directed from his recovery bed the hunt for anyone connected with Oswyn's plot to overthrow the king. He discovered several more men involved with Oswyn's scheme, including two more apothecaries, a trio of landsmen, and a duke, eleventh in line for the throne. There was also the traitorous King's Man, whose interrogation had led to the capture of the others. The linen man told me that all of them—except the King's Man, who had died during questioning—would be receiving justice in the public square north of the Tower. They'd take me to watch if I wanted. I didn't. That day, I could hear the crowd all the way from the square, howling for blood, and cheering every time they got it. Closing the window didn't help. I lay on my bed and covered my ears, trying to block out the sound.

Other than that day, I didn't mind staying at the Tower. It's not like I had anywhere else to go. The linen man told me the crier had announced my innocence to the city, but I doubted that had changed Tom's father's mind about me. I did wish Tom were there. I asked if I could see him, but the guard just grunted, "No visitors." I kept my window open, in the hope that Bridget might find me, but I never saw her, either.

In the meantime, they kept me fed, and told me news of outside. Some was good—after a recent declaration of war on the Dutch, the English fleet had fought more than a hundred enemy ships near Lowestoft, and defeated them soundly—but I was worried to hear of the growing reports of plague in London's western parishes. So far, no one inside the city walls had the disease, but the casualties in the outskirts now totaled forty dead and were rising every week. I feared, with the growing heat of June, things might get a lot worse.

Still, there wasn't anything to do but wait. When they finally did release me, the King's Men marched me to a carriage outside the portcullis. The driver said he had orders to take me straight to Apothecaries' Hall, where the Guild Council had arranged a hearing to decide what they were going to do with me.

"But it's Sunday," I said.

The driver shrugged. "I do what I'm told."

Impatiently, he motioned me into the back. I braced myself for a bumpy ride.

The hearing was in the Great Hall. The last time I'd been here, Oswyn had sat at the grand table, piercing me with questions as other apothecaries, seated in rows to the side, looked on. This time, Grand Master Sir Edward Thorpe sat at the center, worn and weary. Guild Secretary Valentine Grey sat at his right, looking even more fussed than the last time I'd seen him. The seat to their left remained empty.

Sir Edward didn't waste any time. "We've discussed your case," he said. "The membership agrees that you have been ill treated. As compensation, we are awarding you ten pounds. Additionally, we shall cover, up to another ten pounds, the fee to be paid to a different guild for a new apprenticeship."

But . . . "What happened to my old apprenticeship?"

Sir Edward cleared his throat. "The members felt, given the circumstances, it would be best if you were no longer to train to be an apothecary."

My stomach churned. I'd feared the worst. It appeared that I was getting it. "Please . . . Grand Master . . . being an apothecary is all I want. Please let me stay."

"Your commitment reflects well upon you," he said, "but we cannot have the recent . . . incidents . . . attached any further to our Guild."

"That wasn't *my* fault," I said. "I didn't do anything!"

"Nonetheless, we believe this action is best for everyone. And, frankly, Mr. Rowe, we have nowhere to place you. No master is currently in need of a new apprentice. You understand."

I looked around the room. A few of the apothecaries at the sides were watching me curiously. Most avoided my eyes.

The churning in my guts sank like a pit. I *did* understand. They were afraid. Anyone who took me in would look like they wanted whatever I knew about the Archangel's Fire. Oswyn's plot—and Lord Ashcombe's purge—had made me untouchable.

"Then . . . what's going to happen to Blackthorn?" I said.

"The shop will revert to Guild ownership," Sir Edward said.

"What about Master Benedict's will?"

"We can't find his will."

"That's because Oswyn stole it," I said, my voice rising.

"We have no evidence of that," Valentine said. "The compensation we're giving you is more than enough to—"

"I don't want your money!" I shouted. "I want my life back!"

Valentine turned red. He was about to say something more when the heavy door behind me creaked open. He looked past me in annoyance. "What?"

"Forgive me, Masters," the clerk at the door said, wiping his brow. "There are two petitioners who wish to address the Council." He glanced behind him anxiously. "One of them is Lord Ashcombe."

Sir Edward glanced over at Valentine, who sat up in his chair, still bright red. "Very well."

In strode the King's Warden. His bandages were gone. Over his missing eye, he wore a plain black patch. His cheek was still stitched together, loops of thread tracking an angry red line from underneath the patch to the corner of his mouth, twisting it sideways. His ruined hand was covered by a glove.

Behind him came an even bigger surprise. Isaac the bookseller walked carefully to stand before the Council, his wispy white hair waving as he moved. In his hand he carried a scroll of parchment. His cloudy eyes barely glanced at me as he took his place beside the King's Warden.

Sir Edward nodded. "Richard. And . . . Isaac, isn't it? Welcome. What can we do for you?"

"For me?" Lord Ashcombe said. "Nothing." The slash on his cheek seemed to make his voice grate even more roughly than before. "I'm here on behalf of His Majesty, Charles the Second, by the Grace of God, King of England, Scotland, France, and Ireland, Defender of the Faith."

The room had been quiet before. Now I couldn't hear even a whisper of breath.

"I see," Sir Edward said. "How may we be of service to His Majesty?"

"The king wants it known that Christopher Rowe,

apprentice to the Apothecaries' Guild, is a true friend to the Crown. Further, His Majesty understands that Oswyn Colthurst's actions were not sanctioned by the Guild, and he reaffirms his close bond with you, who loyally supported him against Puritan traitors when he returned from France."

Sir Edward nodded slowly. "We're grateful for His Majesty's trust."

"The king also hopes that Christopher's new master will be as kind and as skilled in managing Christopher's property as the honorable Benedict Blackthorn."

Valentine blinked. "Property?"

Isaac raised the scroll he carried. "If I may, Sir Edward?" He hobbled forward and handed the parchment to the Grand Master. "Over the past few months, Benedict became concerned for his safety. I know he registered a new will with the Apothecaries' Guild. He also left a copy with me." Isaac smiled. "Just in case."

Sir Edward read it aloud. "I do hereby leave all worldly possessions to my apprentice, Christopher Rowe of Blackthorn, to be administered by Hugh Coggshall until the day Christopher becomes a freeman of the city."

My jaw dropped.

Valentine couldn't believe it either. "Let me see that." He

snatched the scroll from Sir Edward's hands and scanned it. "How do we know this is legitimate?"

"It's properly witnessed." Isaac pointed to the signatures at the bottom of the page.

"By Hugh Coggshall and Lord Henry Mortimer. Both of whom are dead."

"His Majesty will affirm the will," Lord Ashcombe said. "If that's necessary."

Sir Edward shifted in his chair. "I'm certain we may accept this document as valid. Nevertheless, a problem remains. As Valentine has pointed out, Hugh is dead. His widow, who would legally become the new guardian, is not a Guild member and may not run an apothecary. And Christopher"—here he paused—"is still an apprentice."

My heart leaped.

"His Majesty has considered that," Lord Ashcombe said. "He offers to act as ward of the shop, holding the profits secure, until Christopher is of age. In the meantime, he agrees to pay a generous stipend to cover the wages of Christopher's new master."

"And who will that be?" Sir Edward said.

Lord Ashcombe shrugged. "That's up to you. His Majesty would never interfere in Guild affairs."

I didn't think Valentine could turn any redder. Sir Edward gave a wry smile.

"No," he said. "Of course he wouldn't."

I tilted my head back, closed my eyes, and let the sunshine warm my face.

"Christopher!"

Tom, beaming, ran through the traffic outside Apothecaries' Hall. He weaved around the mob of pigs that clogged the street and wrapped me in a bear hug.

"Ooof," I said. He put me down. "How did you know I was here?"

"Isaac sent word to come," he said. "What happened?"

I told him. He couldn't believe it either. "Your own shop?"

"Well, it's not mine yet, exactly. I'm still just an apprentice. I won't really get to own it for years."

"You're getting a new master, then? Who is it?"

"I don't know." Thinking about it made me nervous. I wondered if someone like Valentine—or worse, someone like Nathaniel Stubb—might take the position out of spite.

"Well, well." Isaac stepped from the Hall's great doors,

his hand supported by Lord Ashcombe's arm. "The twin pillars of trouble."

The King's Warden reached into his belt and pulled out something silver. "I believe this is yours," he said to me. "Officially, now."

He handed me my puzzle cube. I held it to my chest. "Thank you," I said. "Thank you both." I looked up at Lord Ashcombe. "I'm so grateful for what you did."

He grunted. "You shouldn't be. I didn't win you any friends in there."

"But . . . His Majesty said—"

"Oh, no one will act against you, not openly. Some will cozy up to you, try to win His Majesty's favor. Others will resent you and work to bring you down. It's also possible there are still some remaining in the Guild who sided with Oswyn. You'll have to be very careful about who you call a friend."

I looked at Tom, who was trying to avoid the drove of squealing pigs, then at Isaac, who nodded. "Always sound advice, sadly," Isaac said. He turned to Lord Ashcombe. "Do you mind if I speak to Christopher a moment, my lord?"

When Lord Ashcombe shook his head, Isaac put his hand on my shoulder and led me a few paces away. "We had to bury Benedict while you were in the Tower," he said quietly. "But I think it would be nice to have a private memorial. Just for those of us who loved him."

I nodded, grateful. "I'd really like that."

"Come see me tomorrow, then, and we'll arrange it." Isaac smiled. "I have some stories I think you'll want to hear."

He said farewell to all three of us, and began walking home. Thinking about my master's memorial made me wonder again about who my new master was going to be. After what the King's Warden had just told me, I had even more reason to be worried.

"Do you really think any of Oswyn's men are still out there, my lord?" I said.

"Men like that are always out there," Lord Ashcombe said. "No matter who they follow. And you know Wat's still at large."

I *didn't* know that. The news sent a chill down my spine. "But . . . your men went to get him while he was unconscious in the lab."

"They did. But when they returned, Wat wasn't there."

My eyes darted down the street. "Do you think he'll come back?" *For revenge*, I didn't say.

Lord Ashcombe shrugged. "More likely he's fled the city. It's not easy to stay hidden, missing half a face." The King's Warden traced his fingers along his own brutal scar. "Which reminds me. Wat wasn't the only thing we returned to the lab for. Some of the papers survived the blast. His Majesty's apothecaries are going through them now."

I swallowed. "Yes, my lord?"

"They can't seem to find the recipe for the Archangel's Fire."

My face grew hot. "It was on the workbench," I said. "Right by where Oswyn was standing. It . . . it might have been destroyed in the explosion."

Lord Ashcombe studied me. "I seem to recall Wat saying it *wasn't* there."

"Wat wasn't very smart."

"No," Lord Ashcombe said, his one eye narrowed. "I suppose he wasn't."

Beside me, Tom shuffled from foot to foot.

"I'm sure you'll let me know if anything comes up," Lord Ashcombe said.

I nodded. I didn't trust myself to speak.

"As for you, boy," the King's Warden said to Tom, "you swing a mighty rolling pin."

Now Tom turned red. "Th-thank you, my lord," he stammered, not sure whether to be proud or embarrassed.

"Stop by the Tower if you'd like to learn a real weapon."

Tom's eyes bulged. "Are you—you mean—a soldier? Me?"

"If you can pass the training."

Tom stared at the pair of King's Men waiting for Lord Ashcombe. They looked back at him bemusedly. "Me?" Tom said again, flushed with pleasure.

"You'd be great at it," I said. I turned to Lord Ashcombe. "You should see him fight a shop bear."

Lord Ashcombe shook his head as he walked away. "I don't even want to know what that means."

The sign still hung over the front door. BLACKTHORN, it said: RELIEFS FOR ALL MANNER OF MALIGNANT HUMORS. The wood needed a new coat of paint. I'd have to redo the unicorn horn, too, faded from years of London weather. Other than that, I wouldn't change a thing. I'd never change a thing.

The shop did need a good cleaning, though, and I didn't need to wait for my new master to know whose job *that* was. Tom helped get me started as soon as we got inside, sweeping straw that had spilled from the shredded stuffed animals. "Christopher?" he said.

"Yes?"

"That wasn't true, was it? What you said before. To Lord Ashcombe." He stopped sweeping and leaned on the end of the broom. "The recipe for the Archangel's Fire wasn't really on the workbench."

I shook my head. "I didn't want to leave it out for Oswyn to see."

"What did you do with it, then?"

"I put it behind the ice vault. Before I went up to the garden, I greased it in a leather sheath and hid it in the back, under the bricks."

His eyes widened. "So it's still there?"

"I don't know," I said. "The ice will have melted by now. If water got through the grease, the ink will have run." I looked out the window. "I honestly don't know."

The Archangel's Fire. I'd been trying not to think about it. I'd been trying not to think about anything that happened that day. All I really wanted was my old life back. Days working next to Master Benedict, hearing the sound of his voice. Nights reading by the fire. This shop. Our home.

I looked around me. The shop was almost the same as when we'd fled from Stubb and Wat that terrible night. There was a patch of black where I'd started the fire, and a few more footsteps through the scattered ingredients. I didn't even want to see the mess in the workshop. But the place was still standing. Maybe some of the ingredients, the equipment, could be salvaged. I could buy more goods to replace what was wrecked, too. Then everything could be back the way it was.

No, I thought. *Not everything.*

I looked behind the empty counter, where I'd hung my master's sash. My eyes stung.

I still miss you, I said in my heart. *But I kept your secret. And I stopped your killers. Did I do all right? Are you proud of me?*

Something tapped on the window.

I turned. Outside, on the sill, a plump salt-and-pepper-speckled pigeon paced back and forth. She bobbed her head, pecking her beak against the glass.

I ran to the front door and opened it. Bridget hopped down from the windowsill with a grand flapping of wings and marched inside.

She cooed at me. I scooped her up and held her against my cheek. I felt the softness of her feathers, the beating of her tiny heart. I turned so we could see our home, and called to him one last time.

Thank you, Master.

A FEW MATTERS OF HISTORICAL NOTE

In Christopher's time, English spelling wasn't standardized. So, for example, it would be common to see "Clerkenwell Green" spelled "Clarkenwell Greene," or "Clerkenwelle Grene," or any other variation the writer might have thought correct. In this book, English names, titles, and places are spelled according to modern rules. (Many of the locations in this book still exist, by the way, so if you ever find yourself on the (no longer cobbled) streets of London, why not go discover some of Christopher's old stomping grounds?)

A further change has been made to the calendar. In 1665, England was still using the old Julian calendar (introduced in 46 BC by Roman general and statesman Julius Caesar) while much of the rest of Europe had switched to the newer Gregorian calendar (introduced in AD 1582 by Pope Gregory XIII, and the calendar we still use today). Though nearly identical, there were two significant differences. First, in England, the Julian calendar year started on March 25, not January 1. Second, the way the Julian calendar added leap days meant that, since its inception, it had fallen behind the Gregorian calendar by ten days (e.g., the summer solstice on June 21 would have been on June 11, according to the Julian calendar).

Needless to say, these differences could lead to quite a bit of confusion. For example, a traveler could take a four-day sea voyage from Rotterdam to London, departing the Netherlands on (Gregorian) March 28, 1665, and arriving in England on (Julian) March 22, 1664—more than a year before he left! To avoid any such confusion, and to match our current calendar, all dates in this book are reported according to the modern Gregorian system.

ACKNOWLEDGMENTS

A lot of magic happens behind the curtain. I'd like to say thank you to the following wizards:

To my agent, Dan "The Lion" Lazar, and to Cecilia de la Campa and Torie Doherty-Munro.

To my editor at Aladdin, Liesa "Batgirl" Abrams, and to Mara Anastas, Mary Marotta, Jon Anderson, Katherine Devendorf, Karin Paprocki, Julie Doebler, Emma Sector, Jodie Hockensmith, Michael Selleck, Gary Urda, Christina Pecorale and the entire champion sales team, Lucille Rettino, Carolyn Swerdloff, Michelle Leo, and Stephanie Voros.

To my editor at Puffin UK, Ben "Temple Raider" Horslen, and to Francesca Dow, Wendy Shakespeare,

Jacqui McDonough, Hannah Maloco, Carolyn McGlone, and all of Puffin's fine purveyors of adventure.

To my compatriots at Simon & Schuster Canada, on the job and off: Kevin Hanson, Shara Alexa, Michelle Blackwell, Amy Cormier, Amy Jacobson, Lorraine Kelly, Brendan May, David Millar, Nancy Purcell, Felicia Quon, Andrea Seto, Martha Sharpe, and Rita Silva.

To all the publishers around the world who have embraced *The Blackthorn Key*.

To the friendly folks at the Latin Discussion Forum, especially Pacis puella; and to Terry Bailey and to Alma for their help in further translation. Any errors remaining are my own.

And finally, most of all, to you, dear reader, for whom this story was told. Thank you for giving Christopher a home.